GINGERBREAD
HUSBANDS

Barbara Else

PAN BOOKS

First published 1997 in New Zealand by Godwit Publishing Limited

This edition published 1999 by Pan Books
an imprint of Macmillan Publishers Ltd
25 Eccleston Place, London SW1W 9NF
and Basingstoke

Associated companies throughout the world

ISBN 0 330 37029 4

GINGERBREAD HUSBANDS

Barbara Else runs a small literary agency with her husband in Wellington, New Zealand. She has published short stories and plays for adults and children, and is active in the New Zealand Society of Authors. Her first novel, *The Warrior Queen*, was published by Pan Books in 1998. She has two daughters.

CONTENTS

For Dorothy, with love

With thanks to Chris Else for his insight and encouragement.

This novel was written with the support of
Creative New Zealand Toi Aotearoa.

GINGERBREAD:

n: a sweet bread, flavoured with ginger.

GINGERBREAD:

adj: showy but worthless; sham, counterfeit. The allusion is to the gilt gingerbread toys sold at fairs.

GINGERBREAD HUSBANDS:

gingerbread cakes fashioned like men and decorated with gilt, commonly sold at fairs up to the middle of the nineteenth century.

HUSBAND:

n: a married man who has vowed to forsake all others and cleave only to his wife.
Alt: one who manages his affairs (i.e. the business kind) with prudence.

TO GET THE GILT OFF THE GINGERBREAD:

to appropriate all the fun and profit, leaving behind that which has no value; to destroy the illusion.

ref: *Brewer's Dictionary of Phrase and Fable* (Avenel 1978), *Chambers Twentieth Century Dictionary* (1947 reprint).

GINGERBREAD:

n: a sweet bread, flavoured with ginger.

GINGERBREAD:

adj: showy but worthless; sham, counterfeit. The allusion is to the gilt gingerbread toys sold at fairs.

GINGERBREAD HUSBANDS:

gingerbread cakes fashioned like men and decorated with gilt, commonly sold at fairs up to the middle of the nineteenth century.

HUSBAND:

n: a married man who has vowed to forsake all others and cleave only to his wife.
Alt: one who manages his affairs (i.e. the business kind) with prudence.

TO GET THE GILT OFF THE GINGERBREAD:

to appropriate all the fun and profit, leaving behind that which has no value; to destroy the illusion.

ref: *Brewer's Dictionary of Phrase and Fable* (Avenel 1978), *Chambers Twentieth Century Dictionary* (1947 reprint).

Part One

WHOOSH!

SMUDGE HAS A FIRST BEST DAY

Dad stirred the paint. He crouched in the bouncy man way with the tin of paint out between his knees, bouncy man knees.

Next door's chooks *pucker-pooked* like they always did on sunny afternoons. It was a lazy noise, you could lean on it and be comfortable. *Pucker pook* meant it was the weekend and Dad was home and Uncle Todd would come round, and Mum would stay in the house and leave the men to it.

Pucker pook, oook. The paint smelled sharp in Sophie's nose. She watched the flat wooden stick go round and round, up and scooping down.

'It's not white,' she said.

'Wait till I stop stirring,' Dad said. Loops of yellow mixed up in the paint and down again. The smell still prickled in her nose. 'Keep back, Smudge. Get paint on that dress, there'll be trouble.'

'Mum didn't make it,' said Sophie. 'Mum hates sewing.'

'She'll have to clean it, though.'

Sometimes Mum went hissy when she had to clean things. Sophie pressed her hands on her skirt to keep it away from the tin and leaned her chin out to sniff. 'I like the horrid smell,' she said.

'Too much'll make you dizzy.' The loops of yellow got little and thinner and soon there were none. 'Here we go, Smudge.' Dad's knees bounced him up. Sophie jumped back because she didn't want a splash. Her dress had butterfly stand-ups on the shoulders and it was her favourite and she wanted to wear it for ever.

He carried the tin and a brush and the paint rag down the side of the house, and Sophie followed, playing *keep in his shadow*. Dad never knew she played it. She nearly bumped into his bottom when he stopped.

'Going to watch?' Dad rubbed the paintbrush back and forth over his hand, *flick flick*, before he dipped it in the paint first time. Sophie backed away and sat on a pile of bricks under the tree tomato tree. She nearly asked why he was painting the shed, but a feeling in her tummy like a worm meant she didn't want to hear what he might say. Even though she knew he wouldn't say, because no one ever said. Sometimes they yelled a lot, but no one ever *said*.

Mr Angus next door began to mow his lawns, *whirr-chkk-chkk*, like the mower was purring and clucking at the same time. She loved the smell of the grass when it had just been cut. By tomorrow it would be stinky.

Dad's arm moved up and down, slow and smooth. When Sophie was little, she used to paint beside him but it was only water in her tin so she soon got sick of that. The shed turned white all along to the window

Then she heard what she knew would come. Uncle Todd's car out in the street. It had a special creak when he pulled the brake on. She lay on her side in the weeds to look up at Dad's face. There was the grin, the first grin, best grin, that made the wee scar on his chin wriggle, the scar that Mum said was from The War but he said was from seeing a man about a dog that had no sense of humour.

She scrambled up. 'I'll go and say a man would like a cup of tea.'

Dad laughed. 'Good on you.'

Sophie walked up the side of the house, swinging her arms and legs in a man walk. Past the kitchen window, in the back door, and she was Sophie again. The kitchen smelled rosy warm like strawberry. She hopped on the stool beside the bench and put her finger into the jam pan. It was just hot enough to hurt nicely. And it was strawberry. Best.

Mum wasn't hissy about making jam today; she looked pink and pretty with her book open near the tea caddy. She rapped Sophie on the arm with the wooden spoon, but not hard.

'Cheeky.'

Uncle Todd's face was red. He grinned at Sophie. 'I suppose a man would like a cup of tea?'

'A woman might too,' Sophie said.

Mum looked at her and smiled. 'She certainly would. You're getting smart for your age.' She put a butter knife on her library book, and closed it for a book mark.

'It could be a picnic, if Uncle Todd carried a tray.'

Mum and Uncle Todd both laughed. First best day. First best. Sophie leaned on their laughs because it was comfy. She wanted to say that a picnic should have scones with fresh hot jam and cream but, in case that was leaning on the laughs too heavy, she only crossed her fingers and hid them in her skirt.

First best day, all right, because Todd opened a tin he'd brought with him, and scones were there, steamy from the oven, with their smell of hot crunch outside and soft white in.

'They'll go nicely with fresh jam,' Mum said.

'You're a bobby dazzler, Kath.'

Todd winked at Sophie. Mum gave a pink-cheek smile all soft at Uncle Todd. Sophie opened her eyes wide and Mum nodded, and Sophie found some cream in the fridge, and the beater. Mum spread the jam and Todd whipped the cream fast and noisy. He let Sophie dollop it on the jam like bird plops, but they didn't let Mum hear them say it.

The tray was all ready now, the big wooden one with handles. Sophie knew a man would be waiting for his cup of tea so she ran to her bedroom window, opened it and called down to let him know a surprise was coming.

'Good-oh, Smudge,' the man called back. The shed was shining wet along past the door now.

Sophie bounced back to the kitchen.

'We'll have a procession,' said Uncle Todd. 'Sophie first.'

She marched out, Mum behind her carrying the outside rug, and Todd with the heavy tray. They reached the side of the house where they could see Dad painting.

Mr Angus's mower whirred, then screeched against his oil drums. Sophie started. A long whining screech came again, so hard it hurt her ears. Then he bashed the drums, *bang*! where he kept his chicken food, *bang*! *Whang*!

Sophie stopped marching. Mum and Uncle Todd stopped as well. Their eyes were strange, but they weren't looking at Sophie, or at Mr Angus's place. They were looking at Dad.

He was still painting like he hadn't heard, but he had, because his arm wasn't painting the shed any more, it was waving in the air, painting the air, all wobbly, jerky, faster, faster, and he started to make that scary moaning. It was a really quiet moaning, like he was trying not to, but you heard it.

Todd shoved the tray at Mum and ran to Dad, but the tray tangled with the rug and tipped and the picnic went all over the garden. Sophie tried to catch it, and she sprawled on the gravel with a grazed knee. She had to make her teeth sit tight and straight so she wouldn't cry, because Mum would soon be doing that. She closed her eyes tight too, so she wouldn't see Mum's face, and Mum's hands shaking, Mum trying to pick up the teapot and the plates and tray.

Mr Angus jumped over his fence. 'Bloody hell, sorry, Kathleen, I never thought,' he said, then he took off down to Dad too.

Dad was crouched and crumpled. But the grown-ups made him stand up and they got the rug around him and helped him inside. There wasn't much a Smudge could do except sit and pick the little black stones out of her knee.

When the moans had stopped, and Mum was in the bathroom, crying all right, and Todd was knocking on the door and saying *Kathleen, Katie-Kate*, Sophie found one scone left under a cabbage. So she ate it.

Then she went and put the lid on the paint tin. There were tiny flies stuck in it where they'd tried to swim, but she didn't care about them. You had to find the hammer and bash the lid round the edge to make it stick down tight. You put the paint rag on the lid first though, so the bashing wasn't loud: Sophie'd seen Dad and Todd do that, so she knew.

And then what a Smudge had to do was sit and wait, and hope that the worm in her tummy would go away.

When it was nearly dark, Mrs Angus came over and gave her a cold sausage and a tomato sandwich. Mrs Angus was nice. She always put sprinkles of parsley in her tomato sandwiches and Sophie couldn't figure out how she got the green so tiny.

Mrs Angus could probably hear Mum still crying in the bathroom, and Todd saying things to Dad to calm him down. The worm wouldn't go away till both the men started saying, *Yep. Right. Yep.*

Mrs Angus gave a sigh and put her cardigan around Sophie's shoulders, though it wasn't cold, just getting dark with a scratch of moon out. The cardy smelled of chook food and talcum power, a fat dusty smell. 'D'you want to come in with us, dear?'

Sophie held the tomato sandwich to her nose and shook her head. The moans had been really scary, more than she remembered.

But all a Smudge could do was sit and wait.

It's a mistake. The thought flitted through her mind like a streaker on a chilly day. Astonishing thought, absurd. How could it be a mistake? The house, at the end of the long metal driveway, was exactly right, everything Russell had promised. *You'll love it, Soph. Magnificent, the best we've ever owned. Or it will be. And I'll call. As soon as I get the equipment going, I'll call. God, Sophie, you're delicious.* She stopped the car and climbed out. The kids scrambled out too and gathered round her, staring at the house.

It was fifty or sixty years old, and needed attention. But the size of it, the possibilities! Three storeys with grand old sash windows, a row of gables and a red-tiled roof. Wide stone steps and ornamental balustrades swept up to the big front porch. At the foot of the steps, on each side, was a concrete griffon, one with broken wings.

The southerly whipped up a wintry cloud behind the pine plantation and the native bush at the back.

Rory gave a grunt, or perhaps it was a quiet *fu-uck*!

'Cool!' breathed Hugh. 'The Hammer House of Horror!' He ducked under Sophie's arm and launched himself at the steps.

'Wait!' she called. 'The keys are in my . . . ' But he'd hurtled across the porch, banged the door open and disappeared, ululating like the Hound of the Baskervilles.

'Does he have to act his age?' sighed Lisa.

Odd: the house hadn't even been locked.

Lisa shoved her wind-blown hair out of her mouth. 'God, Mum, it hasn't been painted for years, it's the colour of dishwater. The guttering's like old men's eyebrows.'

Hugh's face squirmed against a second-floor window: a living gargoyle.

'It's only clumps of grass,' Sophie said. 'We'll clean it out, we'll get the chimneys straightened.'

'I will never be able to let my friends come here. If I ever have friends again. This is a disaster for my social life, you realise.'

Sophie pointed. 'There's the stained-glass window. It'll be fantastic when it's cleaned.' *Wait till you see the window in the stairwell, Soph, the way the light glows through. You'll love it, little fox. The potential in the place is huge. A mansion, love, a palace, you and me!*

Lisa had begun to weep, chin up like a Rossetti heroine.

'Fu-uck,' said Rory clearly. His Adam's apple jerked a couple of times before he lugged his pack up the lichen-covered steps, across the porch and into the darkness of the hallway.

'I'll see what's round the back.' Sophie huddled the neck of her jacket closed and ran down an asphalt side path past a separate double garage and an overgrown hedge. This wing must be the flat that Russell said was full of stuff from the previous tenants. She peered through the windows but found them boarded up from the inside. When she tried the door handle, it turned only a fraction.

A large back yard, though, and a long verandah, ripe for restoration. Wind whished through the pines and tugged her jacket. She shivered, tucked her hands inside the sleeves, and hurried round to the front again. Lisa was still in the driveway, sulking.

The removals truck backed through the gate. The young moving man heaved the truck doors open while the old one with fan-shaped wrinkles round his eyes hopped out and flexed his shoulders. 'Cheer up, missy,' he said.

Lisa scrubbed her nose with the back of a hand, tossed her strawberry-blonde hair and gave the man a filthy look. 'It's *Ms*, thank you.' She stalked up the steps.

The man grabbed a load of boxes. The small one on top was marked *Sophie Redlove. Personal.* 'Where d'you want these?'

'The study, I suppose.' Sophie remembered the floor plan Russell had drawn for her. 'Ground floor, second right.'

The man had already swung after Lisa, two steps at a time, his middle-aged hips doing that nifty male swagger. Sophie followed in a tingle of anticipation, across the threshold and into the front hall.

The strip of carpet was so threadbare it looked like sacking. Dark man-high panelling covered the walls below an upper strip of exhausted wallpaper: 1950s roses, overblown. Doors led off to either side. Beyond the staircase, the hall narrowed to a closed door at the far end. And yes! The stained-glass window, colours of ruby, purple, rose and tangerine. The pattern curved like flames, a nest of fire. The gentle lumination bathed the stairs, a palette of colour soft as down, caressing. The sun strengthened momentarily and its rays glowed through the glass in beams of light as glorious and rich as archangelic pathways in the Old Masters. Sophie let out a yip of glee.

The moving man reappeared from behind the stairs. 'There's gear in there already, love,' he said. 'Previous owners?'

'That will be Russell's,' she said. It was too difficult to explain further: none of the man's business anyway.

'Bit musty.' He sniffed. 'Been shut up for a while?'

There was the faintest odour, familiar, on that strange border between pleasant and foul. Mould? Boys' socks? Jockey shorts?

'The house used to be a boarding annexe for a school,' said Sophie. Though surely any smell should have gone by now. Besides, there had been owners after that who'd begun some renovations, so Russell said.

The man tried the door at the end. 'Painted shut?' He shook the handle. 'Nah. Bolted.'

'It's a flat. It's locked till the tenants move their stuff out.'

She stepped around the man, wriggled her jeans to be

comfortable, and looked in the study. Yes, Russell's gear was piled around the walls. Tripods, rolled-up screens, the Kapro II, his first personal computer which had to be antique by now. Stack upon stack of file boxes, drafts of his papers. Heavy cartons labelled *vid. equip.* She'd learned to operate the first camera, though sometimes she'd wished she could drop the thing and let it smash.

Her own small box was sitting by itself. She pushed it against the others with her foot. Tears prickled behind her nose: she was still churned up from the delirium of the last two weeks and queasy from the ferry crossing. She wished Russell were here, his dazzling green eyes and brilliant smile. Thick sandy hair, wide shoulders. Big, warm, energetic Russell. Feathery kisses growing into gentle bites, and the hot smell of him, broad shoulders, sinew, curves of muscle. The most encompassing lover, the sense of tumbling into something soft and strong where you'd be safe for ever.

The house creaked and whispered. The southerly clattered a rash of rain against the windows. Tendrils of spider web floated in the air currents. From the second floor, right above her head, she heard Lisa scream. Sophie sprang into the corridor.

'This place stinks of boys!' shrieked Lisa from the top of the stairs. 'I loathe the male sex and I completely refuse to sleep in a room that stinks of stale ones!'

The brave young moving man (wearing a crop-top singlet even in mid-winter) stopped on the threshold clasping a tea chest and gazed, open-mouthed, at Lisa, blue-eyed and blonde. She continued to scream her hatred of males, lit by a nimbus of sunlight through the filthy flame-coloured window.

Sophie prodded his shoulder. Although the wind outside was icy, his flesh was warm, rock-hard (and slightly damp). 'That's for the kitchen,' she ordered.

Navigating with one eye still on Lisa, he heaved the chest off through the door of the dining room. The kitchen was beyond it.

'Choose another room, Lisa,' Sophie called. 'Dad said it's just the flat we're not to get into yet, and the attic. Don't on any account try the attic. It's not safe till he's checked it. There's a skylight, and possums might get in.'

'All the rooms are horrible. He's put our names on the doors. What a wank! I'm not four years old any more. If he'd ever stayed home long enough he'd know that! Bloody hell!'

Sophie shooed the other moving man into the dining room as well.

'Darling, I have to tell them where to put the furniture. Open some windows and air the place out.'

'Why did you let him push you into coming to this Gothic pest-hole?' Lisa crumbled on to the top step in another rush of furious tears and Sophie climbed up to comfort her. They sat together, Lisa's head buried on Sophie's shoulder.

'It's all Dad's fault.' Angry smothered noises followed, along the lines that Russell was ignorant of Lisa's needs, totally uncaring that Lisa had lost all her friends by moving here, selfishly preoccupied with getting back with Mum, even more selfish to drag Mum away from Mary Jane and the art gallery, patriarchal not to ask Rory, Hugh or Lisa what they thought about the whole business, bloody stupid to organise the move for the first day of another of his egocentric expeditions and only two days after he and Mum got married again, and even more ridiculously wanky to insist on calling it a wedding when they'd never got properly divorced and how totally obscene it was to expect anyone else to find middle-aged sex and romance the least bit appealing when it was all one disgusting egocentric wank on the part of that grinning dipstick of a figurehead who called himself Lisa's father.

Suddenly Lisa shoved her hair out of her eyes, gave a hiss like an exploding kettle and pressed a hot cheek against Sophie's. 'You'll put things right, though, won't you, Mum? You always do.'

Sophie tried to speak firmly. 'Darling, you mustn't talk about your dad like that.'

Lisa stood up with a twitch of denims and a toss of hair. 'In fact, I spoke much more nicely than I wanted to and I found it very difficult. Fourteen's a problem age, you know.' She flounced down the corridor and banged a door behind her: the stale room, Sophie gathered, which stank so badly of boys. Sophie couldn't smell a thing now. Anyway, boy smell was not so bad: nascent testosterone, aimless, a defenceless odour, puppyish.

She blinked at both the men who stood holding boxes in the downstairs hallway, staring up at her. Neither of them budged until she rose and pointed to the dining room, like the Cherubim with the flaming sword placed at the east of Eden to give Adam and Eve the boot. *Out, go on, clear off.* Another beam shone through the stained glass right on cue, and the windows rattled in a gust of wind.

Thanks: a pint-sized woman like herself could use a few special effects.

Sophie hadn't seen the boys since they arrived. She hadn't looked downstairs properly either, or at the bedrooms, the bathroom, and God alone knew what the third floor would be like. The boys first. Hugh's excitement might have turned to tears by now, and though Rory was sixteen he wasn't finding this easy. That Adam's apple was a dead give-away and made her ache with tenderness; how awful the chrysalis years could be for boys.

She called them, heard no answer and hurried down.

Through the front door, she saw them near the car. When had they gone out? Perhaps they'd found the back door. Was that unlocked too? Anyway, there they were, short and weedy Hugh and his tall brother, holding hands, stepping solemnly past the stationwagon in a delicate gavotte, as graceful as if they floated above the pine needles littering the driveway.

The moving men, focused on their muscle power as only men can be, and taking no notice of the boys, continued to haul furniture out of the van and into the house. It was dazzling how fast they worked. The dining table was going inside now. The older man held Great Grandma Violet's chamber pot in one hand like a ceremonial vessel. Why it would have come unpacked she didn't know, but he seemed to sense it was an heirloom.

When she looked at Rory and Hugh again, they were waltzing. 'Suitcases,' she called. 'And the ice chest?'

They stepped apart and bowed to each other; Rory punched Hugh and Hugh kicked Rory's ankle.

Rory sprang the boot of the wagon. He hoisted the cane picnic hamper under his arm and grabbed the handle of the ice chest, while Hugh heaved a little case in both hands. They bumped up the steps and indoors.

They were being very understanding. She'd been shaky for so long — still was, though now it was because the miracle had happened.

Whoosh! Russell was back in town.

Whoosh! The magic was still there.

Whoosh! He'd organised a venue, a huge party.

Whoosh! He found a celebrant who thought it charming rather than bizarre that they wanted to have another ceremony. Russell even found the words for them to say.

He had also gone to see Matthew and settle the account. *All that legal work for nothing, eh? Chuckle chuckle. Thanks for trying to sort things out.*

Matthew had been badly disconcerted. Sophie didn't blame him. But he had been most discreet. Mind you, you would expect him to be discreet, especially about what he'd been doing with his client's toes on certain mid-week afternoons.

And what else could one do but be discreet, when — whoosh?

Still reeling, she'd let Russell whisk her off to a luxury suite at Noahs for an astonishing night-long romp in the king-size bed: the memory of it even two days later lurched back to make her melt all over again.

And . . . whoosh! *Oh yes, sorry Sophie. Chance of a lifetime, love. There are only two months of the year when a boat can land on the* (what were they?) *Islands, but I've got the latest radio equipment, I'll definitely keep in touch. It's crucial that I go, this is vital to* (what project? Last time it was the fungal invasion of the pancreas of the

Stinking Lemur or some other marginal animal). *Darling. Mmm, thank God you haven't changed your perfume. I know I promised, love, but this is the last time now I've got the job at the university . . . ooh, that's good . . . mmmph, you taste more scrumptious as the years go by. That little bit just under your left ear, God, Soph. Do that thing with — yes, lower — grrowrr! Ouch, no it's okay, your hair got tangled round — that's better. It won't be so bad my going away so soon, you'll be busy sorting out the new — grrowrrrr! God! I've arranged everything, it should be easy for you . . . Oh, Soph. Sophie! Ooh. Aah, wait, I . . . wait, I . . . You're . . . Sopheeee!*

Sophie leaned against the Honda to steady herself..

So she didn't know when he was coming back. Nor did she know where the What's-it Islands were, or whether he was off somewhere else after that before he finally settled down. This was exactly why she'd chucked him out in the first place. Chucked his things out, rather: Russell was too large to be physically moved himself. But he was so eager about his work, so successful. And now he was going to be Associate Professor. Sophie burned with pride.

Oh, Russell. Whoosh.

But this would not organise the furniture. She grabbed some bits and pieces from the car and began to run up the steps. A study. A room of her own: she only had to decide what she wanted to do. Art consultancy? Freelance articles? Her thesis again? Sophie laughed. Why not? All things were possible from now on. She did her own small waltz steps round the porch, shrouds of cobweb in the corners, drifts of dead leaves, the corpse of one small sparrow. On top of a hill, whipped by all winds, no neighbouring homes in sight. A house so good you could eat it.

So at the moment it resembled Nightmare Abbey? Just wait.

Oh, Sophie. Whoosh!

The dining room with the adzed rimu table, eight matching chairs and twelve-foot dresser that she'd thought was overdoing it but Russell had insisted on, looked impressively baronial. The murk and old stained carpet only added to the atmosphere. He'd love hosting dinner parties here, and so would she. Mind you, the room would be used mostly as a thoroughfare from the front door to the kitchen which, if you ignored some ghostly white curtains, already seemed the most comfortable place in the entire house.

'Main bedroom, love!' shouted the old moving man. They were grappling with the bed base on the front steps. Sophie ran upstairs while the men fetched the queen-sized. She turned the handle of the room at the top of the stairs.

And, for a shimmer of a moment, she was Dorothy stepping out of black and white into the opulent Land of Oz. A fantasy. A centrefold for *House and Garden*. Interior design to perve at. This room alone was reason enough for Russell to buy the place.

The carpet was buttery-yellow as an omelette, the walls were cream with a gold and yellow frieze. Sashes as plump as the flesh in Restoration paintings tied back gold and yellow curtains edged with green, and the fireplace had a rococo carved surround. Oh Russell, yes! — naked on the rug in front of toasty flames, door safely locked, kisses marinated in chianti, please.

And the bed. The only place to put it was on a low dais. Glory be.

HOORAY! THE ANGELS SMILED!

Soph, you're together again, a marriage remade in heaven. Lo! Sophie, wreathed in satin (*off*-white), crowned with flowers against a background thick with cherubim red as jam the way Guido Ricci liked them (Italy, fifteenth century, extremely little known). And under them the bright blue seraphim, the saints, apostles, martyrs and the patriarchs arrayed like figures on a baking tray, all smiles and adoration at your nuptials.

Nearby (let's mix the styles) an angel plays a harpsichord, another strokes the cello, their glittering haloes held on high by small fat *putti*, rosebud-decked. Doves, shafts of light and rainbows fill the firmament, while Russell's arms, aglow with strength and passion, reach out to you through plumes and pink-tinged clouds, the rosy crowded air.

Below, grey imps of misery, demons of desolation, flee in panic, disappear beneath the gnarly roots of trees . . .

Mind you, that dais. And what Matthew might make of such spectacular access to her metatarsal arches . . . Sophie pressed her fists to her stomach to make herself stop it at once. Past history. Finished. Done. Though her toes didn't stop scrunching till she got rid of Matthew and pictured Russell kneeling on the dais instead.

She opened a mirrored sliding door. A double wardrobe, space enough to build an aviary. It seemed a pity to hang track suits and jeans in here. Just as well Russell brought clothes back from overseas: black dresses from Milano, palazzo pants from Amsterdam. They were usually too big, she never wore them, but they'd look wonderful in the wardrobe. And a second wardrobe, large enough for Russell's up-market leisure gear for media interviews, the Swanndris he wore on his hunts for the giant migratory lichen of Tierra del Fuego or whatever parts remote, the Italian suits for when he was after grants and funding, check shirts when he had to be one of the boys.

The moving men finally struggled in with the bed base. They thumped it down on its side, screwed the legs in, and thudded downstairs for the mattress while Sophie went into the ensuite and splashed cold water on her face.

A gust of wind whacked the kitchen windows. Sophie and the moving men jumped.

'But Russell said he'd taken care of everything.' The ragged net curtains ghosted momentarily towards her, then hung limp. 'I thought that meant he'd paid in advance. Or you'd send an account.'

The movers shrugged in the wordless language used by men. Sophie's stomach tried to fold up on itself. Her cheque account had two hundred-odd dollars in it. Setting up an antique and art gallery with a friend and pulling out before it's made a crumb of profit means you don't earn very much money. And if you do, your children eat it. She might get something back from Mary Jane eventually, but that was no help now.

She grabbed her handbag from the top of the microwave, found the envelopes Russell had given her and dug into them.

A new chequebook. It was still on the joint account he'd kept open since she bolted the door on him a year ago, and there was plenty in it, thank God. More than enough for the day's expenses. Enough for at least two weeks' housekeeping, even given Rory's hollow legs. It would easily last until the next lot of money was direct credited from Russell's trust fund, grant money — whatever he'd arranged for this particular month.

Half way through writing her signature, the pen went wobbly.

The men grabbed the cheque as soon as she tore it out, mumbled thanks and vanished.

She tipped against the table for a moment. The children were upstairs somewhere; she could hear them arguing. Good: she wouldn't have to say why she was tottery. She didn't know. The chequebook, her memories of Russell's enthusiasm and appetising randiness, Matthew nibbling her little toe — who on earth would believe that a middle-aged divorce lawyer could turn out to have a mild fetish of that nature? — and she was nearly in a shivery fit of sobs.

She picked up the phone, the only one she'd seen.

The line was dead. Damn. Hadn't Russell said it would be on?

But there was no one to call. Mother was away, it was too late in the day to arrange new schools for the children, and she couldn't get hold of Russell, even if she knew where he was. Though without the phone on, he couldn't call her either.

She swore and punched the buttons on the microwave until they stopped saying HE:LP and said 2:30.

Get cracking, kid. First best house. Roll up your sleeves and smile.

She found another locked door on the second floor, a back stairway to the out-of-bounds flat. The children's rooms were large, all begging for new paint and paper, and back downstairs the grimy hallway gave her bubbles of excitement. It would be magnificent with proper floor covering once she'd ripped up the scruffy runner.

'It's spooky, Mum,' Hugh called through the banisters. 'I might have nightmares.'

'Exciting ones, I hope.' She reached and dabbed a finger on his nose. 'What nonsense. Sort your stuff out, kids. I'll organise down here.'

In the living room Sophie placed Great Grandma Violet's blue and white Stafford jug in the centre of the mantelpiece. The embossed grey roses on the wallpaper were just like decaying funeral wreaths: how drab they were, how they deepened the meaning of dismal, and how the carpet here was like remnants of sackcloth and ashes. The room was vast enough to hold a church service. Old Violet would have liked it. She had taken to religion after Great Grandad died. Little Sophie had been so impressed with the way her scary old eyes read the teeny tiny Bible always on the arm of her big black chair.

'Ghouls. Gloom,' moaned Rory as he hauled Hugh downstairs by his legs. 'Spooks. Doom.'

'Do it again!' Hugh screamed.

'Oh, God, they're both such pains,' sighed Lisa.

Sophie would wash that chandelier as soon as she could. And with a rub of linseed, the oak mantelpiece would glow. The oil would make her hands silky-soft as well, though there was no one here to feel the benefit. At a memory flash of a springy mattress and sheets in a concertina rumple at the foot, she covered her face. Was it Matthew she remembered? Russell?

Straighten up, Soph. Fly right.

Hugh tugged her sleeve. 'I'm hungry, Mum.'

But the older kids weren't fussing about food yet, so she shooed him off to help Rory hunt for the hammer, and had another look at the study. She could use Russell's desk, get a new chair. Most of his gear would move up to the university once he started there.

Next to Russell's stuff, her own box seemed minimal. She hadn't looked in it for twenty years, only strapped fresh tape around it every time they'd moved. She wasn't even sure what was in it.

Open it, she thought. She jabbed the corner with her belt buckle to break the tape and rip it off. Deep in her belly was a coiling, shrinking feeling, like a worm.

The stuff for her PhD was on top. Her hands felt strange as they lifted it out, the fragmentary jottings, file cards, half thoughts scribbled on foolscap, address lists of museums and galleries worldwide. Angels in European Art: Iconography and Social Expectation. A working title she'd never refined further.

Underneath were her dog-eared reports from boarding school. The first was from 4A. Creepy: the different kinds of handwriting, all those teachers she couldn't remember, and their comments on her. A string of As for everything but conduct: C minus. *She has become a subversive element.* She shuddered, dumped the reports on the desk and found her Dux medal with the ribbon twisted and discoloured. The metal had gone a funny shade of green and the motto had turned black: *CASTITAS ET TEMPERANTIA* (Chastity and Temperance, oh give Soph a break). Next was her Scholarship results booklet and an Abba poster (those white and gold costumes and perfect smiles, that unity of four, that squeaky cleanliness), and underneath were three old photos.

Mother, Dad and Uncle Todd, and the frames she'd bought but never put them in. The pictures that she'd stolen and kept hidden all these years.

She lifted them out and touched the thin white edges of each one in turn. Todd's face: smile lines bracketing his mouth, the winky eyes and curly hair that even then, pre-war, poked out beneath his soldier hat. Impossible to give Todd a short back and sides, he'd always been so shaggy, irrepressible. The one of Dad, slight, eager, a secret smile above his neat uniform collar and tie. No scar then, just a smooth young handsome face. The post-war one of Mother as a deb, soft lighting, tulle, a marcasite necklace with a pearl. A faraway gaze.

Underneath the photos was a piece of paper that looked as if it had been screwed up then straightened out again and folded neatly. She eased it flat in case it ripped. FAVOURITE PEPLE 1957, said the printing in stabs of red crayon: DAD AND UNCLE TODD AND NO ONE ELSE THE END THE LAST LAST END.

Mum, how do you spell favourite? Why do you want to know, Sophie? It's a secret, I'm not going to say.

Then, tucked into a corner of the box, green with age like her medal, was the magic eye, the little copper tube with a strange old lens that Dad had made for her.

She picked it up and looked through it at the study window. *What d'you see, Smudge, eh?* One tiny glinting pane in the centre, and round about a wreath of replicas, overlapping, glistening, the colours deepening, lightening, turning as she turned the tube.

Banging noises upstairs made her jump, and told her that the boys had found the hammer. There was a yell from Rory, a plaint of misery from Hugh, a screech of laughter from Lisa. All normal, but she'd better see what was happening.

She bundled the junk from school and her university notes into the box, and tucked the tube back on top. Just as she was closing the flaps, she saw the photographs still lying on the desk. How curious: she didn't want to shut them up again. Somehow, it didn't feel fair. What an odd thought. Why fair? And such a strange word: fair is *just, impartial*, even *pleasing to the eye*. Fair, also, is *carnival and candyfloss, sideshows, fairy dolls with sparkling skirts, muscle men and shysters*.

The banging noises continued upstairs. She slid the photos into the frames, took them to an alcove in the front hall and called Hugh to bring the hammer down.

She wasn't sure where to put Mother, because the sizes didn't match. Between Dad and Todd? Quite separate? She tried Todd and Dad side by side. They looked so good, *yep, right,* that she banged two nails in and left Mother propped against the wall till later.

Later too, she realised, she'd have to deal with how Mother might react when she discovered Sophie had the photos. Mother was a logical woman, but unpredictable for all that. She might think it was funny. She might be mad as hell.

Sophie's insides did the shrinking thing again.

But Hugh mimed being speechless with starvation and pretended to die on the threadbare carpet, so she went through into the kitchen to see what she could find for dinner.

'Witch picnic, Mum, witch picnic,' he cried as he bounced along after her.

The house made strange noises. There were peculiar groans that first night when everyone was meant to be asleep. It had to be Hugh.

Sophie clambered down off the dais, grabbed her dressing gown and felt her way along the corridor. She couldn't find a light switch, but the moon skulked from behind a cloud and flickered through the stained-glass window.

It was him. A crumpled little boy who wanted comfort. She sat on his bed.

'Oh darling. I hoped this wouldn't happen.'

'I'm not a lucky boy, Mum.' Whine, grizzle. Moan.

He was dewy, not sweaty: it hadn't been a nightmare. Hayfever, caused by the dust of generations of the old dead boys Lisa swore she still smelled though Sophie couldn't, and though they'd vacuumed the bedrooms, with difficulty because of surprisingly erratic fuses.

'Go on, Mum. Tell one. Please.'

Sophie sighed. 'You didn't like the one last night in the motel. You said it sucked.'

'Make up a new one, Mum.' Groan. Whimper, meep.

'Are you worried about something?'

'New school.'

She leaned over and gave him a little hug. 'Snuggle down, love.'

Hugh dragged the bedspread up to his neck. Somewhere a

floorboard creaked. The plumbing coughed and burped.

Let him grow out of this soon, prayed Sophie; he's ten years old, he's too old now for this, though I know how he feels, poor love. She dredged some words from underneath the carpet at the bottom of her mind:

The skillet spat and sizzled on Ms Prettie Pugslie's element. The mushrooms were lined up, neatly sliced with her sharpest vege knife through their silky, tenderest middles. This time she'd only carved off half her thumb, and the blood tasted tangy like Coke.

She took two eggs. Smooth, secret and tight round the white, and yellow goodness inside their hand-sized, promising brown.

But ah, they might be rotten. Who knew what hid inside? Ms Prettie grinned with all her pointed teeth, imagining the possible flavours to come — sweet and sour, savoury, or alligator-blench.

On the side of a bright blue china bowl, she cracked the brown eggs neatly. 'So you wanted to be chickens?' Ms Prettie Pugslie snarled . . .

Was he asleep already?

And she put another victory cup on her mantelpiece under the skulls of the moose, the police dogs, and the very tasty librarian who'd become the paté for which Ms Prettie won her second Diamond Spatula Award, Sophie whispered.

As she moved back along the hallway, the shadows seemed to stir. She heard a sigh. The plumbing? Or possums in the attic. The southerly complained in the chimneys, the floorboards wheezed softly as they shifted in the frosty night air.

She found her way back to bed. A waste of such a setting: up on the dais like the Virgin Queen when she'd far rather be the naked truth in a voluptuous wallow by Tennessee Williams. Russell, darling Russell, hurry home. She toppled into sleep again where little wind-up moving men with expandable biceps kept vanishing into a corner, and the wooden lion doorknocker, bearded with lichen, insisted on singing 'Old Man River'.

'Our records show there is a telephone at that address already,' said the voice on the phone in the call box.

Sometimes, though she was just a little woman, Sophie felt gigantic with rage at the stupidity of people. 'There isn't one that works,' she said.

'Do you want another line?' asked the cheerful public relations lilt.

Sophie understood exactly how one could transform oneself into a werewolf. 'I want a phone. One I can use to call people up, so I can talk to them and ask them things. That sort of telephone, okay?'

But once that was dealt with, she managed to get the children into schools by the last day of the week. Lisa threw a full-blooded tantrum at the sight of her new uniform; Hugh became an electric quiver of nerves; and Rory's Adam's apple travelled up and down so fast it wrenched at Sophie's heart. He didn't say a word, but he bumped into the kitchen table and dropped two plates at breakfast time.

So they were all three off, and she was on her own.

There were movements in the house. A dull thud. Creaks. She phoned a builder Russell had told her about. His tone made it clear he thought her worries about the age of the place were entirely female vapours. 'Solid workmanship,' he said. 'Lasted thirty years of boys and not a structural flaw that I could find. I checked it when the Choi-Berunda bought it.'

'The what? When was that?'

'I'll be along inside three weeks,' he said as if she were retarded. 'Good as gold, love. Mind you, it could be five.'

Carry on, Soph, carry on.

It would be easy as long as she could ignore this old familiar feeling, this double hollow in her lower belly which she always thought was her ovaries longing for Russell to come home. He hadn't called yet, even though he had the latest equipment.

Being solitary was not good for the human psyche.

A blink, brief vision, *mistake*, chilled streaker, Matthew lurking round a corner . . .

So she hurried to wash some windows, got numb to her marrow because the hose connection kept bursting, but made the porch look — the word 'welcoming' scurried off like a rodent and hid behind the garage with its crumbling roof of mossy concrete tiles. The porch just looked scabby, because more paint had peeled off. But Russell would come home, and then they'd spend an evening over the colour charts.

Her eyes had blurred and her nose was like ice. A migraine waiting for a chance to land. Oh, shit!

It landed on Sunday morning. Sophie staggered round trying to organise kitchen cupboards for an hour or so. Rory hammered things in his room, and patiently fixed fuses whenever they blew. They blew often. She was sure Russell said the house had been rewired.

Hugh grizzled because they'd only found one hammer. Lisa sighed and moaned because she didn't have any friends. The phone went several times. It still wasn't Russell. All for Lisa.

Sophie gave up and collapsed into bed. Then Lisa had been out and was home again, in the living room just under Sophie's bedroom, playing videotapes of soap operas which she'd borrowed from the new best friends she'd made. In a piercingly sweet voice she sang the theme tunes. She ran upstairs (*thumpity-patter* and *thump*!) to see how Sophie was.

Hugh grizzled because Dad had promised there'd be heaps of computer stuff, and did he have to go to school on Monday? Did Mum want a disprin and a cup of tea?

Rory, an apprentice ministering angel, banged the door open a remarkable number of times to bring her plain dry toast cut into triangles. He was all six foot of shaggy head and knobbly shoulders which promised soon to split out of adolescence and grow solid like his father's. A ministering angel would need solid shoulders if he had some wings to flap.

He brought her a bucket as well, but Sophie didn't throw up. She was determined not to in the luxurious ensuite, and certainly not in a bucket on the sumptuous carpet.

She kept her head under the duvet. She liked it when the kids made a noise, when they sat on the end of the bed and grizzled, thudded round. That's what kids were for. It made her feel like the Madonna in the Ricci oil, waiting out her pregnancy while overweight angels and po-faced handmaids milled about with useless objects in their hands.

That painting had been very nearly banned. Ricci had used a young nun as his model, and she was delivered of a baby of her own. They were supposed to have done the deed on the very couch the Virgin lay on in the painting, up on a dais, just like Sophie's. But some clever Doge or other saved the picture from disgrace: he decreed it be renamed *The Birth of Prudence*.

Hugh's knitted toy All Black lay on the kitchen table, skewered on a cross made of barbecue implements. Some things it's best to ignore. Sophie put muesli, marmalade and other bits and pieces out for breakfast.

'You're better this morning.' Hugh stuck another skewer in the All Black. 'Your nose isn't blue any more. Why can't we look in the flat? This house has got spooks.'

Sophie shrugged. 'You like spooks. What is there for dinner tonight?' She looked in the fridge again. 'Give thanks, there's a chicken.'

'With honey and bacon?' He came and put an arm round her waist.

'And rice piled round like maggots,' Sophie said.

He squeezed tighter. 'Do I have to go to school, Mum?'

She twitched an eyebrow at him. 'Eat your muesli.'

'Bum.' Lower lip stuck out like a dripping pan, Hugh sat down and picked up a spoon.

Lisa skimmed in. 'What's up with fart-face?'

'No friends yet.' Sophie found the heavy Sabatier knife to joint the chicken for a marinade.

'Nor have you, and you're not bothered. You haven't even phoned your mother.'

Sophie waved at the toaster so Lisa would make her own slice. 'She'll still be in Sydney.'

'You could have left a loving message on her answerphone.' Lisa glanced at Sophie sideways. Sophie ignored her. 'Hugh hopes Grandma Kathleen will bring back presents.'

'He'll learn,' Sophie said.

'She will!' said Hugh.

'She's an old bat to go on holiday just when we arrive.' Lisa pulled hair around her face, pushed her jaw out and looked like a strawberry-blonde orangutan.

'She was asked to give a paper at a conference.'

'Well, don't ever do that to me, I'd freak out.' She puffed her hair off her face and set about getting her own breakfast, elfin, practical now she'd finally got around to it. 'Sandy hasn't written to me. She promised. We had a ritual, we threw a duck into the Avon. I knew she was a bitch. Don't you hate secret bitches? It's lucky you don't need someone to talk to. I'll have heaps of friends when I'm a mother. Just kids would drive me off the planet.'

Sophie winced at a clash of knives and the toaster popping, and sighed, which hurt down round her ovaries.

'You're not missing Dad, are you?' Lisa's disbelief jolted Sophie. So did learning that Lisa knew what sort of sigh it was: Sophie hadn't known till she was eighteen. 'Hell, Mum, we all know what he's like.'

'Logic doesn't come into it,' said Sophie. 'What do you mean, you threw a duck? How did you catch it?'

'Mum, you can always find a dead duck near the river.'

Sophie jointed the last chicken leg.

'We dismembered it first.' Lisa spread marmalade on her toast and got up to fetch more milk. 'Don't look horrified, I've watched you do it with chickens. Like now. Easy. We used that knife too.'

Duck guts. Sophie closed her eyes for a moment. There was a

clatter. Lisa had tripped over the extension cord coiled up between the fridge and back door.

'Why do you have to use this death trap arrangement for the laundry?'

'Lord knows,' said Sophie. 'The electrician's coming today. But your dad said the wiring was new.'

'Figures,' Lisa said. 'The house still stinks. You're weird if you can't smell it. I bet Grandma will say there are stinks. Oh, God, Hugh's crying.'

'Eat your muesli, Hugh,' said Sophie.

'It's real tears,' said Lisa. 'It's getting on my nerves. He's pathetic.' She grabbed her school bag and tugged at her uniform skirt. 'Pleats suck. So does this new school.' She planted a kiss behind her little brother's ear, and flounced off.

Hugh screamed. 'She kissed me with her fish-bottom face!'

Rory lumbered behind Hugh with his backpack on. 'Spoo-ooks,' he moaned, grabbed a fistful of toast and left by the back door. Hugh screamed and sobbed. His face was purple-white, all blotches.

'Yuck, dear, you're dripping.' Sophie pulled his plate to a safe distance. 'It's awful starting somewhere new. I know, love.'

'But when will I get used to it?'

'Soon, soon, before you know it. I'll take you down again this morning.'

Hugh swallowed another sob, but his thin shoulders quivered.

'Good boy.' She longed to tell him that he didn't have to go, to keep him home with her, and safe. 'Good boy. Now, how many power points does your bedroom need?'

'Dad put it on a list,' Hugh mumbled, damp and snotty.

'At least your grandma's still out of town,' Sophie sighed aloud, meaning at least Mother wasn't here to badger her about Russell.

Hugh's tears vanished. Energy surged through his skinny body as if he were being inflated: the energy of indignation. 'Don't you love your mother?'

'I do,' said Sophie. 'Of course I do.'

'You haven't put her picture up. You've left her on the floor for days. Can I put Grandma up?'

'Darling, I have to take you down to school,' said Sophie.

His tears started again. Little pest. But she sat down and pulled him against her till he quieted.

SMUDGE KNOWS ABOUT MUM AND THE MEN

'Stone the blinking crows.'

Dad hauled the hammer out of his belt and looked at all the tea chests and the boxes of Mum's books.

Todd straightened his shoulders and put his hand up like a soldier. 'Give the orders, Kathleen. We'll leap to it.'

Mum bundled Sophie's arms into her coat. 'Just be started by the time I get back.'

Dad opened up a box and picked out a book. It was thick and had gold letters on it, and there were other books in the box that matched it. Sophie liked to stroke their little ribbons, but the words were long and hard. Dad frowned like he was puzzled and looked round for a shelf.

'Leave those for me.' Mum said it with a tiny little hiss. 'I won't be long. Do your coat up, Sophie. And one of you can find out where the church is.'

'That'll be me,' Todd said. 'I'll find it for you, Kath.'

Sophie stuck her arms out and hung her head on one side and dropped her mouth open too, because she was being Jesus.

'Thanks.' Mum smiled at him, but the smile melted off when she looked at Dad. 'We can behave as if we're normal, surely, Jack. Sophie, your hair is in a tangle. Get your arms down. Get your coat done up.'

Todd crunched the claw bit of his hammer under the lid of a tea chest. 'Good heavens,' he said, 'it's full of little guinea pigs.'

'*Eugh*! *Pooey*,' shouted Sophie but it wasn't really funny. Her nose stung like she might almost cry.

'Don't tease, don't egg her on,' snapped Mum.

Sophie did a stitch-mouth face at Todd and a mouth-down face at Dad, and walked out, legs stiff like a scarecrow. Stone those crows. Mum had made the men feel bad and it wasn't fair because now Todd didn't say *Good-oh, bye, Soph* and Dad didn't say *Toodle-oo Smudge*.

Mum told a story about a girl who danced in little red shoes, but Sophie's nose prickled again while they walked along new streets. 'You'll learn about geography,' said Mum. 'And history. I've talked to your teacher. You'll find out what little Ancient Greeks and Romans learned at school. Lots of little girls weren't allowed to learn what the boys did, so you're a lucky one these days, Sophie, I hope you realise.'

Sophie didn't give a piffle for those Romans. Mum kept talking about what a good school this new one was, but Sophie didn't want to go to any school, and she hoped it wouldn't happen.

It was a long grey building, long like a stingray that will grab so it can bite you while you drown. Sophie's nose stung even worse. Cling. Swallow hard.

'For heaven's sake. Let go,' said Mum, 'the teacher's waiting.'

Big empty playground. Cling.

'Sophie, I have to get home to the men.'

But Mum didn't have to look after them, because they were big, and anyway Todd looked after Dad.

'Come along, Sophie,' said the teacher. Her name was Mrs Willie. 'I'll find Penelope, she'll be your minder while you settle in.'

The teacher and Mum unstuck Sophie's fingers from Mum's coat, and Mum gave her a kiss and a hug but then she walked off, quick, quick, and didn't look back for a wave. Sophie was like tissue paper packed with sobs. It would be awful if she tore and the sobs came out.

'How do you spell Sophie?' Penelope asked.

Sophie spelled it.

'That's stupid,' said Penelope. 'It should be a eff. You do not spell it with a puh-huh.'

The tissue paper nearly tore then, but she felt so mad that she held on. 'Your name spells funny too,' said Sophie.

'New girls are stupid,' Penelope said. 'I hate minding you.'

Mum was fibbing. She could have stayed with Sophie. Mum would be home now, making the men feel they'd done something wrong and they would be like big lumps watching her like she was going to bite. And they always gave funny smiles, like they really hoped she would bite and they'd jolly well deserve it anyhow.

It wasn't fair. Not fair was being squinched between big walls and wherever she looked was another wall and they pressed in hard to make her feel like tissue. Oh please, don't squinch. Please please, don't let it tear.

Hugh gave a weak wave over his shoulder as he crept through the school gates. He was the sum and substance of forlorn, the absolute Platonic form of it. If he didn't settle quickly, she would have a talk with his teacher, or the principal. She would visit all the schools in the next week or so, anyway, to make sure the three children were okay.

She started the car. Back to the big empty house. Though the electrician should be nearly there. He would be just a pair of passing overalls, but at least it meant another adult round the house for an hour or so.

Except he wasn't. He was two pairs of overalls (orange ones with bibs) because there were two electricians, one with an old rusty beard and the other with high youthful cheekbones. Jaws angled with determination like sleuths in a TV movie, the electricians examined the list of jobs Russell wanted done, and Sophie's list, and then the fuse box on the back verandah.

'Nah, only the flat's been rewired,' they said. 'We did it. Where's the manholes again, love?'

Sophie had to think for a moment. Manholes. Lisa would probably refer to them as person access points. She showed them the opening under the verandah. 'Yep, right,' they said. Then she directed them to the third-floor ceiling where they began to set up their ladder. She still hadn't had much more than a quick look at that floor herself. There was a skylight but it wasn't broken, only cracked at one corner. Possums would find it very hard to enter.

'Nah,' said the rusty electrician to the other. 'Did this, remember? Months back. That young chap had us sign those papers.'

'Bloody red tape,' said the younger one, and they took their ladder downstairs.

With grumbles and curses the electricians thumped the house again from below. One of them muttered something about dwangs, and they pounded the walls in all the rooms.

Though Sophie liked the rumble of their male shorthand conversation, she wished they'd hurry up. With the electricity off, it was freezing. She bashed a hook into the wall of the alcove and put Mother's picture up at last, above Dad and Todd but in the middle.

That curly brown hair, the dew of romance in her eyes. Mother was the least romantic woman Sophie had ever known.

She kept warm for a while up on the stepladder, sandpapering the paintwork at the end of the corridor and around the study door and the locked door to the flat, where Lisa swore the peculiar reek was sometimes very sour indeed. Sophie'd have liked a spirit lamp to blister paint off. Dad owned one when she was little: stinky hissing meths or kerosene that made your nose want to cry. She'd thought it might be Aladdin's genie lamp and had watched from round a corner when Dad used it, just in case.

Ouch! God stone the bloody crows! Ah! Ow!

Dad? Yes, Smudge. Is it stone the crows, or God stone the crows, or blinking crows, or bloody crows? Cough-cough: *Crows, Smudge, just crows.*

These days, you could buy plug-in heat guns. That might be fun.

The rumble of the electricians' voices stopped. She had no idea where they were. It was as cold inside as out, so she thought she'd deal with the shadowy, icy cavern along the back verandah that was the storeroom, laundry and outside toilet. Spider webs and wind-blown dirt; old soap scum.

She examined the twin tubs. Concrete, with moss growing on

the inside. Should you want a good hallucination, the various green stuff here looked strong enough to help. If Russell could find interesting fungi at home, he'd never even have to leave the house. She wrapped the thought away to tell him when he finally managed to get through on the new equipment, poured bleach over the mould and moss, and left it all to die.

The toilet bowl was brown. She sloshed more bleach, crashed the old oak lid down and worked a broom into corners of the big room, along the wide shelves, low under the tubs. How horrible, if anything should run along the broom handle and land on her. Some of the long-dead stale boys must have been nascent motor mechanics. The corner beside the toilet was piled with metal chains and a dusty block and tackle. It looked like something in a gallery that was supposed to challenge your notion of art, a readymade by Marcel Duchamp on an off day.

Sophie tried to lift the chains to clean beneath them. Too heavy. She'd leave them for Rory. She had developed a headache: not a migraine, just a normal one. It seemed to echo an ache in her chest, a diffuse kind of empty ache because Russell hadn't phoned yet, because he'd gone quick as lightning to the What's-its.

She wiped her nose, dripping because of the chill. Russell was worth some suffering: a tasty stud-muffin with a brain. Before she'd met him, she found most other men at university were boneheads. The ones she tried in bed were insufficient there as well. She recollected the Young Christian with the Cro-Magnon jaw, her first. Poor boy: her whoop of surprise and delight had shocked him so much he withdrew and ran naked down the corridor of his hall of residence. But it hadn't put her off sex. She merely sidestepped Christians for a short while.

Anyway, once Sophie'd found Russell, she never bothered with another man till Matthew. And she'd been separated then, so it wasn't an adulterous betrayal on her part.

Russell wasn't interested in other women, either, once he found his Sophie. But where was he now? It was ridiculous, not knowing.

Somewhere mid-Pacific wasn't enough. Not other women, but foreign places and the interface of species, microscopic mycelia. That was the competition.

The day had darkened and the sky was trying to squeeze out rain. The thumping in the house began again. Her headache thumped as well. Sophie felt dizzy, not in the least a centre of gladness, more like the dejected little demon in the lower left of Ricci's first *Mystic Nativity* while the seraph overhead looked very scornful. She wanted to scurry under the wash tubs despite the tight little balls of spider nests still stuck there, and have a racking, miserable, bad-tempered weep. God, it was cold.

She knelt to swish the broom under the tubs again but a scream began to swell inside her. 'Where's the joy and happiness?' she whispered. 'Oh, Sophie, damn well stop it, *stop*.'

Footsteps, lighter than the electricians' boots, sounded on the verandah near the fuse box. She straightened up too fast, and a strange scent made her dizziness increase. Not the nasty reek Lisa kept talking about: this was rich and delicate, the essence of all gardens, childhood days in the lazy sun, all moon-drenched nights, all pleasure promised in that deep soft scent. She filled her nostrils. Her eyes were clouded. A form like an angel appeared in the blur, through the dazzle of light from outside.

It was a strange kind of angel, extremely beautiful, lithe and graceful, male, white clothing, shirt and trousers, a glitter like a watch face on its wrist, its halo an aureole of golden hair above its beautiful astonished face, before it vanished.

Her eyes hurt. A watch? A man's watch?

She crouched on the dirty grey floorboards as giddy as if she'd drunk a pint of woeful gin. The day had turned dark, rain about to burst down any second, but silver specks floated in front of her eyes. It might have been angel dust. But she had only caught a glimpse of it. Him. She must have imagined him. The angel. It certainly was not an electrician.

Sophie had sung about angels when she was scarcely big enough to see over the back of the pew in front. Mum pinched her when she tried to put in sound effects:

Casting down their golden crowns around the glassy sea
Crash! cried Smudge. *Smash crash*!

Those angels would have got in awful trouble if their crowns broke.

Lo! the fainting spell, she thought as it began to descend, and wondered if the angel — was he real? — had come to tell her something. She doubted that he'd come to call her blessed among women. They only said that to the Virgin, and Sophie hadn't been a virgin since long before Russell.

And lo again! The blessed dark came down.

SMUDGE AND TODD
MAKE A BLESSED BLINKING MESS

It's dark inside the oven till you turn the knob on. Then it gets hot and red like devils might live in there, and the witch tried to push Gretel in the oven but Gretel shoved the witch instead. So there, got her.

Todd remembered the recipe in his head. 'Blend a quarter cup of butter with a half a cup of sugar.'

'How?'

'Make the butter squishy, little dodo.'

'How?'

'We could leave it in the sun, eh, Soph, or we could heat it over a pot of water.'

'Got to be quick in case Mum comes.'

'No worries, kid. She's gadding.'

Beat the melty butter with some drippy golden syrup. Sift cups of sneezy flour with soda, and cloves to prickle your nose, and cinnamon, ginger and salt. Add the siftings to the butter-mix with water. Roll the dough out, *bash*, roll, sticky, *bash*, roll again, *bash*, *bash*.

'Gingerbread man!'

'But we mustn't squabble over the cutters. There's a gingerbread lady, a star, and . . . I might like the man best, too. We have to share, Soph. Share, I said. Put them on a greased oven tray and bake till what, Soph?'

'*Golden brown*,' in a whisper. She could smell how good it would be already, the ginger and the spices in the mixture. But taste ginger on your finger and it makes you have to spit.

And Dad stuck his head in the window, and pretended to dab her with his paintbrush. 'What a blinking mess. Are you two having fun?'

Yes!

'Got something for you, Smudge.' A copper tube to look in. 'What d'you see, Smudge, eh?'

She thought it would be jiggly colours shifting. But oh, much better, real magic like a dance around and round, turning, shining, changing. 'It's the kitchen and the kitchen and the kitchen! It's Dad and Dad and Dad!' She held the tube tight to her chest. 'For me?'

Dad laughed and pretended to dab her again.

We wish you a happy kitchen, we wish you a happy kitchen, we wish you a happy kitchen, and a crunch! munch! crunch! crunch!

The bed was very hard. It was icy too, and there didn't seem to be a duvet. Sophie wanted to turn on the electric blanket but her arms were too cold to move.

'Mum!' Hugh's voice said. 'What are you doing?'

'Mrs?' said a man's voice. 'We'd better have you up.'

She opened her eyes and saw a pair of scuffed tan work boots where her dressing table clock ought to be, and someone's feet were in them. The boots were on dirty floorboards. So was her head.

'What's the time?' she asked.

'Lunchtime,' said the rusty electrician. He slid an arm under Sophie's shoulder and helped her sit. He smelled of dust and sweat, and had two bandaids on one hand as well as a black blood blister that showed he was a real chap. He wasn't the angel. She peered around: of course it wasn't there.

'Mum, why are you on the floor in the laundry?' asked Hugh.

'What are you doing home?' She shuddered. The cold was inside her bones. 'Did they send you home? Are you sick? Why didn't they phone me?'

'I hate that school,' Hugh said.

'Let's make you a cuppa, love.' The electrician helped her up, but when he let go she collapsed again and had to grab his bib.

He hooked her into the crook of his arm, like a roll of carpet.

His sinews were iron beneath his overalls; she knew she wouldn't fall a second time.

'I thought you looked a bit pale when we arrived. I said to Mark, that woman's overdoing it. No wonder, the state this wiring's in. The house is a fire trap, begging to go up. Even if these things aren't in your actual consciousness, they prey on you. I did a course on ESP one time.' By now he was carting Sophie along the back porch. The rain, which she'd expected to have split the sky, was holding off, but wind slapped at them.

'Mark was one of the chief disciples.' Sophie immediately wished she hadn't said that, but her mouth opened again despite herself. 'So was Matthew.'

'Matthew's your divorce lawyer,' said Hugh.

Shut up, you little tripehound, Sophie thought.

What she meant was that it couldn't have been the handsome young electrician she saw in the laundry because she didn't think there was an angel called plain Mark. Mark was only an evangelist, though the four of them had special little seats in Heaven in all the big religious paintings. Angels filled the sky and bore extravagant names like Gabriel, Hashmal, Zephanpuyu. Uncle Todd used to tell her about angels. He reckoned that at the end of the Battle of something in Egypt, one had given him a hurry-up.

Anyway, the young electrician was in the kitchen filling the teapot. In profile, he wasn't handsome at all. He looked surprisingly like a tortoise. What a let-down. She'd seen Galapagos tortoises once in a zoo she'd visited with Russell on a scientific purpose. Something about the fungi in their shell cracks. The tortoises had been mating but the female, not a fraction entertained, kept plodding with the male attached behind: he staggered on his hind legs, uttered a desperate moo and dribbled loops of mucous.

The rusty electrician released Sophie. Like a rag doll, she tumbled on to a chair.

'Can I give your — um, your chap a call?' He turned to Hugh. 'Sonny, how about your dad's number?'

Hugh shrugged. 'He's somewhere. He loves us, and I think he sends us money. She isn't getting divorced after all, so we're forgetting about Matthew, and anyhow we never saw him.' He climbed on the kitchen stool to reach a high shelf in the pantry and pulled down a packet of cocoa.

A certain wariness showed in the older electrician's eyes. 'Your dad travels, right?' The certain wariness tinged his voice as well.

'Dad's like that man in a shirt with lots of pockets,' said Hugh. 'David Attenborough. And the French one with a funny voice. But I don't think people are that interested in Procellariformes.' He dumped two spoonfuls of cocoa into a mug and spilled another on the bench.

'Tube-nosed seabirds.' Sophie wondered if she could faint again.

'Not interested?' the rusty man asked, even more warily.

'If people were really interested in diseases of Procellariformes, they'd know about them already,' Hugh said. 'Dad's nuts.'

'Why aren't you at school?' Sophie asked more sharply than she meant to. Hugh hunched his shoulders and snivelled. Sophie folded her arms on the table and rested her head on them. 'If I let you stay home today, promise you'll go without a fuss tomorrow, Hugh.'

The snivel vanished. 'Cool.'

The phone burped on its little table next to the sofa. Hugh darted to snatch it up and handed it to Sophie.

'Darling,' said a deep rich voice like whisky.

'Pardon?' she said.

'It's me!' Matthew said, most offended.

What? He knew it was over. There was no point in thinking otherwise. Anyway she couldn't talk to him with Hugh and electricians in the room.

The receiver fell from her hand. Hugh hung it up.

It rang again.

Hugh snatched it this time too and smiled as he listened, an expectant, schoolboy smile. So it wasn't Matthew having another try. 'I hate school,' he said into the receiver. 'This is one way freaky house. Mum thinks it's brilliant. She's got men round.' That wholesome smile: it made her hopeful that some day, some year, the world could be a warmer, cleaner place. Perhaps he was talking to Russell. Sophie dived to grab the phone.

'It's Grandma Kathleen, Mum,' said Hugh. 'She's back.'

Sag. Clutching the receiver, Sophie half crawled on to the sofa. The young electrician put a mug of tea down for her. Both men thumped the walls as they left carrying their own mugs. She managed a hello.

Hugh grabbed her arm. 'Did she bring back presents?' he hissed.

'I found a book on mathematical prodigies for Rory,' Mother said.

Hugh's mouth opened and Sophie saw protests jostling on his tongue. She found the energy to pat him.

'Upstairs,' she whispered. 'Or get yourself back to school.'

Hugh left. The slump of his shoulders indicated he felt thoroughly misjudged.

'Good,' said Mother

'What?' Sophie fumbled with the phone. Her hands were still as weak as silly putty.

'You're taking a tough line with him. High time. How's Rory? Filling out yet?'

'The children are okay, I think. Early days. We'll manage.'

The young electrician walked back into the kitchen from the dining room, staring at the floor. As he crossed and exited through the back door, he counted his steps aloud. Nine.

Perhaps this whole day was a nightmare. She'd wake up and it would all have been a dream: the tortoise electrician, the angel. The angel couldn't have been real, of course. An hallucination, a trick of her cold tired senses.

'How is the new house?' Mother asked. 'I drove up there, before I went away.'

'It's exactly what we wanted.'

Sophie took the mug and held it to her cheek to warm herself.

Hang on, Soph. You'll wake up, soon this will all be over.

Down the line came the soft purr that could still make men's eyes widen, no matter how old they were: Sophie'd always known it really meant Mother was exasperated.

'It's what Russell wanted, God knows why,' Mother said. 'What's he up to?'

'Oh, you know Russell,' Sophie answered. 'How did the conference go?'

'Well enough. I also chaired a session on gender expectations in travel advertisements.' The soft purr sounded again. 'Sophie, from your clever little dodge, which I did notice, I'm guessing that Russell's off in the wide blue yonder again and left you with a millstone round your neck. How long did he hang about for this time?'

'When I was little, I thought you had eyes in the back of your head,' said Sophie. 'You've still got them. They work over the phone too.'

'You could have gone ahead with the divorce,' said Mother. 'I suppose you thought it would be a bad move, to leave a successful man without an equal means of support really solid in the wings. But you're much better off than you think, Sophie.'

Shit! Mother must know about Matthew.

'I know you don't have a job,' continued Mother, 'nor a private income. But you do have a degree, and quite a good one. I didn't even start my tertiary education till I was in my thirties.'

Upstairs, an electrician thumped and swore.

'You're putting yourself under too much pressure of the wrong kind, Sophie. Now come to me if it gets too much. At least I can advise you. Don't do something silly in a rage.'

'You've never forgotten those guinea pigs, have you?' Sophie said.

'What on earth brought that up?' Mother asked. 'You were four or five years old. I'm talking to a rational human being, I should hope.'

'I am not going to snap, Mum. I'm happy. Fizzing with it.' While

Mother was like sandpaper on some tender bits.

'Sophie, I do know men. I know the need for compromise, for give and take. I know about marriage, after all.'

'It's changed a lot since your day and you've only done it once.'

Exasperated purr. 'But compromise, apparently, is not a word in Russell's book.'

Sophie longed to say she hadn't known Mother owned a book with that word, either. It was the catchphrase for today, that's all, like a text street preachers mumble. The angel of the Lord will descend in the final days. The angel of the Lord. The final days. Descending. Petering out, exhausted, like Sophie on the laundry floor.

The best response is silence, when you have so little energy for speech.

'Compromise,' repeated Mother. 'If you're determined to stay with him and he won't give, it's time you did some taking.'

'That's not what compromise means,' Sophie said.

'Have you unpacked your dictionary?' asked Mother.

Of course. All three: the two-volume *Shorter Oxford*, an odd little *Concise Webb-Sterling* she'd picked up overseas that was politically incorrect because it said Filipino was a housemaid, and her battered *Chambers Twentieth Century* in spotted wartime paper. Sophie thought she might be about to faint again and waited, but damn it, the dizziness passed.

'He is internationally famous, Mum. The interesting cellular cryptogamia live overseas. But it's all going to change now, Mum.'

'I was born in the Depression and I went through World War Two,' Mother said. 'I saw people doing without. I did without myself, for most of the fifties.'

'You'd got to be a deb, though. That was privileged stuff. I bet you don't tell your audiences that, these days.'

An irritated *tch* came down the line. 'Then I went through the sixties and seventies. I know what it's like to do with. It paid your school fees, remember.'

School fees. Sophie didn't dare take that thought any further, not that Mother would have stopped if she'd said anything. It had been the best private boarding school in the country, though it hadn't had the effect Mother had expected. Look at what Sophie had done. Or not done.

'The eighties were pretty darn good too and now's the best time of my life. Believe me, Sophie, I've seen both sides, I know what's best, and it isn't doing without. That house, Sophie, is doing without. That husband is doing without. What I'm getting to is this: when will you take your blinkers off?'

'I love him, he's intelligent and sexy,' Sophie said.

The purr, the *tch*. 'I've got another paper to prepare so I'm too busy to see you for a while, though naturally I'd like to. Have you anything to contribute on nurturing images in modern skipping rhymes? There's a whole new rash of them.'

It was no use being mad with Mother. It only made Sophie want to throw up.

'Let's feed the little beast inside you,' said Uncle Todd. 'I know you're sick, Soph, but the little beast is hungry for mashed egg.'

He had a tray with a blue gingham cloth on it, and it matched his apron. When he wore it over his flat hard tummy, Dad sometimes laughed and called Todd *Missus* and asked Mum to show Todd how to tie a bow. Sometimes she would, but sometimes she'd only pat it. Or make her lips go puckered like a button hole. Todd would laugh and say, 'Whatever takes your fancy can't all be wind and water,' and he'd wink a big blue eye at Mum and you knew he hoped she'd smile and go all curvy. Sometimes she did, but you never counted on it.

Sophie was too tired to talk but she said anyway. 'Where's Mum?' A scratchy whisper.

'Still out,' he said. 'She's left us to it. Let's sit you up.'

He plumped three pillows behind her, one straight, two slanty, so they made a couch to rest on, and pulled the blankets warm around her chest. She raised her chin for Todd to fold the damask napkin with the scallop edge into the neck of her winceyette nightie. Todd had sewed rabbit buttons on it, to match the rabbits in the pattern of the wincey. There were plenty of rabbits having picnics with baskets full of lettuce. She could count six picnics on one sleeve but the other one had only five. Uncle Todd said it didn't matter, it was still a good nightie.

He picked up the glass with the peeled boiled egg in it, took the knife, scooped a knob of butter up and held it over the side of the glass. The butter slid, *woops*, down the side of the egg because the egg was all hot. He took a little fork and mashed the egg and butter up. She saw it squishing, golden, around the tiny cut-up bits of white. She began to want it, she did feel hungry after all.

Forget about the beast inside: this mashed egg was for Soph.

'Wee dash of salt?'

Please, she thought, and she didn't have to say, he understood. Mash mash.

'Can you eat it by yourself, or shall I feed you?' Again, she didn't have to say.

Into her hands he put the warm glass, the scent of egg all *gobble me* and cosy. She flicked the spoon down into the mashed-up egg, five, six, seven, scrape scrape, gone.

So lovely and warm with the tiny taste of salt, and never enough.

'Now cuddle down. Measles means you have to sleep in the afternoon.'

Measles meant you didn't really sleep. You stayed awake and dusty slinks of sunshine through the curtains made slices in the air. Inside your head it went all grey and you saw lines of children holding hands, smaller and smaller because the lines stretched into the distance but there wasn't any ground for them to stand on. They were like paper dolls, like lines of washing in the air, the misty air. The slinks of sunshine were still there but you couldn't see them now because of little grey children in grey lines, all waiting to come inside when everyone had stopped their rowdy yelling and the hissing and the tears. And it was silly, because you were inside, you were in bed, so how could lines of children be outside and you could see them? But they stretched on and on for ever, waiting, waiting, waiting for the voice to call *Come in*.

Mother's purr still sounded in her head but Sophie said to hell with throwing up. She phoned the school to say where Hugh was, left the electricians to it and dragged him with her into town. Rain lashed around outside by now. He sulked.

She bought plain green blinds for the kitchen, a new slip cover (blue and white stripes like men's pyjamas) for the sofa, and half a dozen artificial sunflowers to shove in an old cracked-glaze jar at the end of the kitchen bench, very Van Gogh, very bright, to indicate that summer would appear. Oh har-de-har, as Mary Jane might say. She found a heat gun, too.

Back home, still in her wet raincoat, she passed the alcove and Todd's grin. It was more than thirty years. Where might he be now? Maybe he would like to meet the kids, and to see her again. If he was still living in this city. If he was still alive. She went into the kitchen, picked up the phone book and realised she didn't know Todd's surname anyway. It might even be Todd. She tossed the book aside, ripped off her coat and wrenched down the appalling spooky net curtains.

Hugh was still pouting, but Sophie didn't care about Grandma Kathleen's micro-interest in them all. One foot on the bench, the other on the window sill, she screwed in the fittings for the blinds. 'Harridan,' she muttered. 'She-devil.' Baba Yaga, with her running house on chicken legs, had been Smudge's favourite witch when she was small. Prophetic. Oh, so pertinent. 'Vile old crone.'

Outside, rain whipped the windows, the wind had a tantrum in the pines. She curled up on the sofa in the evening with her letter-writing things. The radio hummed next to her, the dishwasher hummed along with it, the smells of dinner lingered tasty in the air. The oil heater kept the place cosy. Lisa and Hugh mumbled busily around the table as they did their homework and Rory thumped heavy books around doing his.

Sophie sat up. 'Why are you all down here?'

And why hadn't she asked them before? Instead of disappearing to their rooms to play their tape decks or sit at their own desks, Rory, Lisa and Hugh had commandeered the kitchen table.

Hugh kept colouring in a border for his project: *Ten Things I Like About Myself.* Sophie noticed he'd gone off the boil half way through Number Five: *Once I didn't scream when I thought I saw —*

Rory slammed his Sixth Form text shut and opened a fatter one with a library mark on the spine, *The Calculus with Analytic Geometry.* He fixed her with an intent stare for three seconds, and concentrated on a page with a red and green heading.

'Honestly, Mum,' Lisa said.

'Honestly what?' Sophie adjusted the cushion behind her and scrawled Mary Jane's address on an envelope.

'One,' said Lisa, 'this is the warmest room. Two: it's the nicest, apart from your bedroom which I don't actually like, it's too theatrical and hardly suits you. Three: upstairs stinks.'

'Spooks,' said Rory in his deepest voice.

Hugh pressed his hands over his ears.

'Four,' Lisa continued, 'if I can't have friends round, and they won't come all the way up here and who can blame them, I must have some human company. Though I have to say two of the people in this room are not so much human as humanoid.'

Her brothers, expressionless, glanced at her.

The wind hooted like an owl in a Greek tragedy. Upstairs, the roof seemed to lift and sink again, doors rattled, the organs of the whole house creaked.

'Have you heard any possums?' Sophie asked. 'I've never dealt with possums. I hope they won't come through the pines.'

'I heard heavy breathing but it wasn't possums.' Lisa sniffed scornfully at Rory's very sexist grunt. 'You can tell when it's possums,' she said with force. 'They do it like Darth Vader — *hheeehh, hheeehh*. If it's men, it's more like — ' She filled her lungs to demonstrate, but Hugh interrupted.

'If it's men, they pant. Their breath comes in long pants.' He laughed far more loudly than the joke deserved. Rory reached out a grubby hand and clamped his little brother's jaw shut. Hugh goggled, Rory unclamped him and he dived on to Rory's back. Rory was filling out. Those shoulders would break hearts one day. Sophie's own heart gave a pang.

'There are moans like something from the grave!' Hugh yelled. 'I know, I've read *Goosebumps*. There are stinks like grave clothes.'

'Possum farts,' said Rory. They disappeared under the table. Hugh shrieked while Rory bellowed. The heavy table lifted and thudded down.

'No wonder I don't like boys,' said Lisa. 'It's probably twisted my sexual identity. Plus never having a father around.'

'When he gets home from the Where-evers, he's going to be around. A lot of academics think he's veered towards the populist, love, but he was still offered that job here.' Associate Professor. The bliss of it washed over her: Russell home each evening, real conversation with him, dinner with the children round this big old table.

'Even if it's true, he'll last ten minutes.' Lisa kicked a brother who'd rolled against her leg. 'Then he'll be off.' She drew her feet on to her chair and piled her hair up like a candyfloss fountain. 'I cannot stand this town. And you can see what it's doing to Hugh.' Beneath the table, he had begun to cry. 'Oh, we get quite sexy books at school. That might help my maturation process. Though I doubt it.' Lisa closed one folder, hauled another from her pile of homework, sat properly again and opened her French dictionary. 'This is useless, it doesn't have the French for lesbian.'

Rory emerged from under the table. '*Lesbienne*,' he said. Hugh slithered back up too.

The phone rang. It was right at Sophie's elbow, but she took a moment to pick it up: the burst of hope that it was Russell. Her toes curled inside her slippers: a shock of under-hope it might be Matthew. But it was Mary Jane, more garbled than usual, full of half sentences, and flatteringly anxious about Sophie.

'I'm fine,' she reassured her. 'I've just written to tell you. What a waste of effort. We're all doing fine.' The children turned their heads and stared, reproach in six blue eyes. Guilt buffeted her for making them go through this for her — for her and Russell. 'Mary Jane, I miss you.'

Lisa leaned across and grabbed the phone. 'Dad's his usual absent bastard self!' she shouted. 'Mum's on her own with us again. If you were a real friend, you'd be here on the next plane. You would absolutely not believe this place.' She chucked the phone back to Sophie.

Mary Jane made expostulating yelps about Russell. 'Not this soon? That's so unfair to you. If you want me come and keep you company, of course I will.'

'It's his last trip. Couldn't be helped. But this is a fantastic house. Why don't you come and see?'

Mary Jane's yelps rose to an up-note like a question, and a firm down-note which was probably decision.

'But not if you're still filthy about me leaving,' Sophie said over Mary Jane's noises. 'What's happening with the gallery? Did that woman come and buy the John Breeze dish?'

But Mary Jane railed about Steven and how abominable he was, how depressing to be alone with him for the first time in years now the twins were off to Europe.

'If you need a break, you should come,' Sophie said. 'Mary Jane?'

After a yes, and a malevolent complaint about men and their alien psychology, Mary Jane had gone.

'She's coming to stay,' said Lisa. 'Good. She's weird.'

'*Uhn*,' said Rory, nodding.

'I hope I'm that weird when I'm as old as her,' Lisa said. 'God, Mum, she's nearly fifty. How did you find a friend that old?'

Only five years older than Sophie. But while it was possible to tell your children that your best friend used to be your English Lit. tutor, it was completely otherwise to reveal that over coffee in the student caff she'd advised you on the male sex as well. Their friendship began with the A+ Sophie got on Herbert's poetry. The religio-sexual imagery, the sexist leanings. *You must sit down, says Love, and taste my meat:* excuse me while I throw up.

'She suits me,' Sophie said.

'We're not enough for you, are we?' Hugh stuck a felt tip in his ear. 'Nor's Dad, is he? Not even when he's around. He hasn't phoned us, Mum. His latest equipment must be buggered as per usual.'

'Hugh!' said Sophie.

He looked extremely prim. Lisa pulled her fish-bottom face, Hugh screamed and pummelled her, and Rory pitched in to thump them both.

Knowing they'd ignore it, Sophie waved a hand for them to shut up and began to scribble a list of what to do before Mary Jane arrived. Mary Jane would love the house. Mary Jane admired Russell, wore colourful garments like a gypsy, and had a vivid turn of phrase. She'd stop Sophie missing Russell so very, very much, and put the lid on those annoying niggles that kept popping up about Matthew.

Sheets of rain splattered all over the windows. *Whoo-who,* wheezed the wind. *Whoo-oof,* it coughed into the chimneys.

Sophie wished she'd had carpet laid already, though last time she'd dealt with carpet layers they'd done a whole house in a day and slunk off at four-thirty in the afternoon before she discovered none of the doors would shut. Lisa and Hugh had screamed like demons about having to go to the toilet with the bathroom door ajar.

Before Mary Jane arrived, she could rip up the hall runner at least. Great fun. The heft of the crowbar, the ripping sound, clouds of dust, thousands of tiny tacks around the edges . . .

The phone rang. Spitting dust, she ran to answer. Plumber? Electrician?

Matthew.

'But it's nine-thirty in the morning!' Sophie said. The shock of it. Phone in one hand, crowbar in the other.

'Please,' the deep voice repeated. 'Darling.'

The crowbar toppled to the floor. Blood trembled in her veins, beat in her ears and thrummed in her throat muscles.

'Sweetheart. I'm desperate.' Low, the roll and timbre of it. That rumble and the texture of his chest hair underneath her cheek . . .

How dreadful that she longed for him so much, that it leapt out of the bottom drawer, full frontal. Thank God this was a toll call.

'Matthew, I've gone back to Russell. He came home again. Matthew, it is over. Do not phone me.'

'My secretary's not in today. Sophie. Darling.'

The dolly-bird assistant? The one Sophie knew had been his bit on the side before her? So? But her hand pressed to the base of her belly. And her toes were tingling, damn them.

'Matthew, he went to see you and he paid the bill.' But her fingers curled on the receiver, pulsing, gripping, curving. 'I wouldn't have blamed you if, in the circumstances, you'd upped your hourly rate.'

'So how is your new home? The one he bought without consulting you?' Matthew paused, but Sophie was paused too. 'How are things? Darling?'

Sophie's pause continued; she didn't know how to stop it. Nor how to unstick her fingers, treacherous things, and slam the phone down.

'Ah,' said Matthew. The subterranean sound, vibration in her ear. God, if he pitched that a half tone lower she might crumble.

'Matthew, just because you don't have a new love life yet or your wife is still —' That clench in her stomach muscles meant that she was jealous.

'Sophie.' The voice now liquid chocolate. 'Jenny thinks she wants to call it quits. She's going to see Petersen, unfortunately. He's as good with divorce as I am.'

Sophie couldn't help but give a yip of laughter. Her hips were swaying slowly.

'Darling,' said the rich full middle-aged voice, 'I've been on holiday. We — ah, I went to Sydney for a break. I was a wreck, still am. But I'm resolved. We have a future. Come away with me. Just give us one more chance.'

His broad chest, its thick black pelt, the wiry white hairs on his shoulders: a panda, black and white. The air whoofed out of her.

Down, put down the phone! Stand straight!

But the black and white moustache, the thinning hair that showed his satin curve of scalp. White over his tummy, the panda tummy . . .

Slam. Phone down, she'd managed. It rang again but she knocked the receiver off and fumbled till she heard the dial tone. Her heart clattered like hoof beats.

Oh, Russell. Darling Russell. You had better hurry home.

So she left the phone off the hook, finished ripping up the carpet and hurried out to buy a flokati rug for the first box room on the third floor to make it nice for Mary Jane. She chose ivory paint for the walls to make it seem bigger. There was enough room for a double bed and bedside cabinet, and she ordered a free-standing wooden clothes rack. It would all be delivered in time: curtains too.

Hey presto, Sophie.

Writing cheques seemed to bring Russell closer, for a moment.

While paint dried on the door and window sill in the guest room, she savaged a scraper at the wallpaper at the end of the downstairs corridor. The children's bedrooms would come before the living room, she decided. No wonder they wouldn't bring friends round. Poor things. Three mornings in a row now she'd driven Hugh to school and sat with him in the car till he stopped sobbing. Rory had teased him into a crying jag about spooks again last night, otherwise Rory was not even monosyllabic. Lisa? The usual bundle of contradictions. Sophie must visit the schools; by next week their teachers could have something useful to tell her.

Curious again about the locked door, she rapped on it when she climbed down from the ladder: no echo. Sound-proofed.

The house creaked, and she jumped in case she had another hallucination, saw another angel. She didn't, of course: it was a normal creak.

She left the wallpaper hanging in tatters and went back to the guest room. The walls of the little room turned ivory as she painted, along past the window, back round to the door. Pity, but she didn't have to use the heat gun. It stayed in its packet in the downstairs hallway. The smell of paint mingled with the *whoo-who* of the wind in the chimneys.

She baked a sickening chocolate cake to cheer the children up. That's what mothers were for. She also left a semi-loving message on Mother's answerphone and told her about a great new recipe she'd found for lemon chicken. But Mother didn't get in touch again: old bat.

Matthew didn't get in touch again either, and that was just as well.

But still no word from Russell.

The hot-water cylinder clicked and began its midnight growl. Shadows from outside played across her bedroom curtains. She tugged her pillow further down and tried to nestle with it.

She remembered when she was little, a daguerreotype of a distant family connection named Edith propped on top of her wardrobe. It had frightened her, especially nights when Mum was off to evening class. The almost life-size head and shoulders, pursed lips above the choking lace collar, the flare of the long-dead nostrils; but it wasn't the look of the woman that terrified her so. There was something about the slightly curved surface, the faint glow of the china on which the image was captured. As if it longed to move, but couldn't.

Uncle Todd knew. 'Can't sleep, eh?'

Shake your head.

'Why not?' Coaxing gently, and the light from the hallway behind him showing his wide shoulders.

Whispering at last, 'She's looking.'

'In the dark, eh?'

Nod. But mainly it was because the woman was stuck. Edith was angry but she never said. And she stared worse in the dark.

He reached to the top of the cupboard and lifted scary Edith down, no trouble. He put her behind his back while he leaned over Sophie. 'Off to sleep now, eh?'

She never knew what he'd done with it. And Mother never asked.

Sophie turned over and tried to arrange her legs more comfortably. The bedside clock blinked 12:05 at her. She closed her eyes. The other half of the queen-size bed felt cold. Sleeping on her own was great in hot weather, but in winter it was nice to have another source of heat beneath the duvet.

It was over a year since she'd slept with someone. The two weeks with Russell wasn't sleeping. They'd spent most of the time diving at each other (*God, Sophee!*) then sitting up with cups of tea talking about what had been wrong with the last twenty years and how wonderful the future would be over the many more than twenty still to come.

Afternoons in Matthew's river cabin, she never slept.

She tugged the duvet higher. 12:07. At the back of her throat was a faint metallic taste. Her nose needed to sniff. Blast. Migraine coming on. Just what Sophie needed, with Mary Jane due in the morning.

She tried to relax, sink further into the pillow. The peaceful dark began to wrap her round.

But. Moan. Groan. Whine. Wail. Hugh.

She shoved back the duvet and swung her legs over the side of the bed. Although she'd grown accustomed to the house's complaints, the whinges of timber, protest of windowpanes as the wind pressed in, she still didn't like this night-time trek along the corridor.

Hell, it was going to be the world's worst migraine.

Hugh was sitting up in bed, a little dark wigwam against the lesser dark of the curtains.

'I'm a worry to you, Mum.' Sniff, grizzle. 'Mum, I'm at cracking point. I bet one day I'll snap.'

Sophie sat on the bed, put her arms around him and took a breath. The specific spicy scent of human boy aged ten with dirty hair.

Her children smelled so good to her. Scientists — that is, Russell and his cohorts — went on about pheromones and how necessary they were for sex. No one pointed out how important it was for mothers that their kids had a personal smell. Good on you, Mother Nature. Otherwise, Sophie would have bawled Hugh out for this midnight rubbish years ago.

'Cuddle down now.'

Hugh flopped back as if she'd loosened all his guy ropes. 'Go on, Mum.'

Sophie sighed and wondered what on earth would come out this time. She opened her mouth and discovered.

Ms Prettie Pugslie ripped off the twistie tie. Bash! — *the frozen bread hit the chopping board. She punched it and the slices crunched apart. Ms Prettie whisked up her biggest Swedish spatula and showed her fearsome teeth.* Smack! *went on the butter.* Slap! Spank! *went on more butter.*

She walloped up one lot of sandwiches with lettuce, corn and tea leaves stewed in prune juice. She whacked up a set filled with beeslobber jelly and the spiciest, spikiest stings. And, because she was fed up to the back of her needle-sharp teeth with making sandwiches for people who never said thank you, she left the last lot of sandwiches completely and utterly blank.

It was not her best effort but Hugh fell asleep when she got to doing something vengeful to the custard squares.

She eased off the bed and into the corridor. The glow of moonlight through the stained glass was more like a glare. Her eyeballs were hot, though her nose felt cold as an ice cube.

A cup of tea might only make her sick, but she wanted the comfort of the mug between her hands. Gripping the banisters, she fumbled down the stairs, then through the darkness of the dining room. Wind called softly in the chimney as she passed the fireplace.

The thought of turning on the kitchen light made her eyes hurt, but enough moonlight wavered past the edges of the blinds for her to find the electric jug and see it had some water in.

Waiting for it to boil, she leaned her forearms on the bench. The comforting faint first seethe of water, the answering rumble in the belly of the jug. Even through the taste of metal in her throat she anticipated the soothing tea to come. She smelt the — not the tea, it wasn't made yet.

What did she smell?

It grew louder. Yes, a loud smell. A dank one. A wet socks, body odour one. A frightful reek. In North America, this smell would be a skunk: she'd smelled them when she journeyed there with Russell. In England it would have to be the ripest fox.

Did possums smell this bad? Diseased ones might. Was a diseased possum in the kitchen with her?

Sophie opened her eyes in the shifting moonlight, was aware of steam rising from the jug, heard the click as it turned itself off, and turned around. The migraine made it difficult to focus, but a shape, man high, hesitated in the middle of the kitchen. The powerful stench, now thick as mist, accompanied it. It wasn't Rory — too tall even for Rory — and its shoulders were too narrow, and it stooped. Snakes seemed to dangle round its head. It hunched and writhed as if its skin were painful to it. An anguished susurration seemed to come to her: *Oh, God, oh sorry. Sorry, sorry.*

She couldn't help but reach a hand towards it. What are you doing, she asked herself, horrified, but her hand kept reaching out to comfort. The shape stooped further, hovered, seemed to shrink and ducked away. The sorrowful mourning filtered through the midnight air again. *Oh sorry, sorry, sorry . . .*

The sound was so awful, a stronger whiff so bad, that Sophie reeled against the bench. The migraine spiked with full force and she didn't think she'd make it back to bed.

Excuse me, sorry, sorry . . .

The moan and stench grew less, she felt a waft of air, and then she knew she was alone.

The moonlight slowly faded as the migraine swamped her like a breaker. I wish it had been the angel, Sophie thought. This time it was a devil, no, a ghost. I hope it wasn't a devil. But a devil wouldn't have said sorry. So it had to be a ghost. Poor ghost. Poor sorry ghost. If she had space left to worry, she'd be worried about herself as well, but she'd do that later on. The task right now was to get across the kitchen floor, then crawl upstairs to bed.

Mary Jane's hair stood out like a sepia haystack as she wheeled her suitcase through the front door. 'You're as washed out as that Hoban watercolour we couldn't sell until we put the price up,' she said. Her little hatchback sat in the driveway. Dead leaves scurried in around her feet. She didn't look that good to Sophie, either: a little edgy, drawn.

'I expected you to fly. You said you'd get a taxi.' Sophie's lips were stiff with cold and she had a crick in her back from crawling round at midnight.

'I don't want to rely on you for transport while I'm here.' Mary Jane stared at the hallway and staircase, gave a little shake and put her arms round Sophie for a hug.

Sophie moved to shut the door. 'How are you? Is Steven over his abominable phase? He is a lovely man.' He was a dentist with very gentle fingers, but Sophie had stopped going to him: it didn't seem right to have the fingers of your best friend's husband in your mouth, especially if you had to pay for it.

'Steven. *Euff*!' Mary Jane flapped her hand as if she swatted a blowfly.

Sophie pointed the way to the kitchen, but with a familiar rattle of jewellery, Mary Jane walked into the living room, squinted at the still dirty chandelier, sat gingerly on the sofa nearest the door and spread her long aubergine-coloured skirt to cover her ankle boots.

Sophie sat beside her, a drab Little Match Girl beside a modern Mother Goose. 'How was the trip?'

'There was a yo ho male sports team on the ferry. Jollity and sexism too early in the morning. What a ghastly room, no wonder you look like death.' Mary Jane frowned and leaned back on the cushions: her colour was returning. 'So. Russell's off again.' She eyed Sophie. 'Heard from Matthew?'

When you don't want to say yes, and can't say no, silence is a definite response.

Mary Jane clasped Sophie's wrist briefly. 'You can't tell me the man will give up easily. You were always a damn sight better after therapeutic Wednesdays with Matthew. Oh Lord, it's been a complicated year.' She got up and peered at the wallpaper. She nearly touched it, but with a tremor of revulsion drew her hand back.

'Let me show you where you're sleeping,' Sophie said.

'I thought he was too old for you at first. Fifty-eight: hell, nearly ready to retire.' Mary Jane poked and peered around the room. 'But that river is a godsend to the over-stressed. All those sated lawyers, it's better for them than golf. Even bankers, I've heard, though I can't bring myself to believe it.' She shuddered again. 'Anyway, once men are well on in their fifties, developing a paunch and not as limber, they feel abjectly thankful, flattered. Exactly what you needed.' She shifted the Stafford jug to the end of the mantelpiece, then on to a side table.

A paunch? It could be comforting, you could wallow in it. If Matthew's chest slipped, it would be a tempting paunch. And he'd certainly had stiff muscles now and then. Sometimes, when his back was strained, she'd . . .

Sophie stood up. 'Come on. A cup of coffee.'

'You haven't told Russell, I hope.' Mary Jane's bracelets rattled as she moved the Stafford jug to its original place, though askew. 'But then, maybe you should.'

'Why? You've never told Steven what you get up to.'

Mary Jane wiped a hand over her eyes, sniffed, and sat on the arm of the sofa with her fists clenched.

'Is it Steven?' Sophie asked. 'What?'

'I should have stuck to older men myself. I've made a terrible mess with a younger one. Oh, bloody men, and bloody Steven too.'

Sophie had always known a smorgasbord of extras was a mistake. She and Russell had it right, no question. She imagined the smug little glance they'd share, if he were here. But an unexpected knife edge, small and sour, slid through her. She cleared her throat.

'I'm not surprised Steven's being abominable if he's found out this time.'

'Look, if he calls, I'm not here. I have to have a break.' Mary Jane ran her hands through her hair. 'And it's important to keep you company, with that miserable Russell gone.' She glanced around and shivered. 'Dream house? *Euff.*'

The sour knife twisted. No one realised what a treasure this place was. Though a dream house would have Russell in it.

'It smells odd, too. Men's underpants.' Mary Jane bounced to her feet. 'To hell with tears. I brought a bottle with me. When we have lunch, I'll pour you a gin large enough to drown in. Because I've got some news you will not be expecting. It should make your wretched Russell . . . Sophie?' she asked. 'Why are you looking like that?'

'Russell is not wretched. And it is a dream house, no matter what you think.' Without meaning to, Sophie burst into simmering sobs. 'But he hasn't phoned. I don't know where he is.'

Mary Jane hugged her again. 'Let's call it lunch time now,' she said.

Mary Jane planted the bottle on the kitchen table.

'So he thinks he's got the right to swan off again so soon to be a man and wear his oilskins. Well, har-de-har to that. He is a recidivist jerk.'

'I thought you admired him.' Sophie's sobs stopped with one last *ip.* 'You and Steven both. Steven's always going on about how he'd give his eye teeth to be like Russell. Russell is very talented. We have a deal. This is his very last time.'

'He's a bullshitting arsehole,' said Mary Jane.

'Your language has gone downhill since I last saw you.'

'Oh, bloody hell.' Mary Jane poured hefty gins and added tonic. 'Well, Soph, at least you don't have to worry about the gallery.' She tasted, then had a larger sip. 'We lost on it, but not too much. I've flogged it to a couple of physiotherapists who'd got fed up with making people scream. I'll find another outlet for my whims. Rejoice. Even as we drink there'll be a direct payment in your cheque account.'

Sophie clinked her glass on Mary Jane's. 'Great.'

'That'll show Russell,' said Mary Jane. 'You can leave him again if you like.'

What a ridiculous thought. Sophie nearly snapped at Mary Jane but let it pass. She took a sip: she'd had only a banana for breakfast so ought to go easy with the gin.

Money. She took another little sip. The gallery had been a risk, but the money for it had come from a share of their savings which, thank God, had been in her name. And the venture had shown signs it might succeed. Mind you, Russell had organised things so well, she didn't need any extra at the moment — except, maybe, a laptop of her own, a proper computer work station . . .

Mary Jane waved her glass at the kitchen ceiling. 'Nice room. But I'd bulldoze the rest of this place. How do you spell mausoleum? God, he deserves to be set upon by a rabid she-wolf for this.'

'Stop irritating me about Russell or go back home, okay?' Sophie pushed her chair back, snatched a bowl from the bench top and stirred it. The mixture had been steeping all morning: tomatoes chopped into rabbit-sized bites, olive oil and a handful of fresh basil, fat cloves of garlic cut in half, salt and pepper. She shoved the bowl and spoon across the table. 'I'm doing bruschetta. Fish the garlic out.'

Mary Jane made a face that meant apology. Sophie ignored it, found a big platter and two small matching plates, put cheese and olives on the table, hacked a fresh loaf of peasant bread into slices and jammed them in the toaster. She'd make plenty for when the kids came home. Cooking soothed her, usually. Not necessarily when Mary Jane was being a pain. She grabbed her gin, sipped till the toast sprang up, rubbed the garlic on to it and dolloped tomato mixture on top.

'You're a woman made by angels. I am starved.' Mary Jane grabbed a piece of bruschetta in both hands and bit into it. 'Poetry for taste buds. None of that wanky modern fluff, either, this is a good solid love poem by Petrarch.'

Sophie tasted her own bruschetta. More garlic next time. But it went quite well with gin, and her cricked back felt easier now.

'So. Tell me,' said Mary Jane in English tutor mode. 'What happened just after we met up again? When we decided to take accountancy classes?'

'Hugh was a baby. Um. Russell and I bought the house on the western hills?'

'It had to be thoroughly gutted, you had no spare time for months. Russell was off somewhere. I did the classes on my own. I had the devil of a job with my reconciliations, but in the end I got them beat.'

'That place had splendid walls of bookshelves. Steven coveted them like crazy. You nearly bought them from us, but Steven decided just to have them copied.'

'Stick to the point,' said Mary Jane. 'I'm trying to make you see it. What happened when I suggested you come into partnership in the pottery shop?'

'Mother thought it was disgusting that I wouldn't use my brain. It made her look bad.' Sophie spluttered in her glass. 'We bought the house near the golf course and Russell did his Arctic trip. I wrote five articles on home decorating and sold them to glossy magazines. Mary Jane, we made big profits on the houses, they were in both our names, we were really busy doing things together, he and I, sort of —' Had she missed something, somewhere, besides breakfast?

'Your pottery shop ran at a loss.' She spluttered again.

'Then the house nearer town.' Mary Jane's voice had become mighty as a Pugslie knife. 'And my paper recycling shop turned out a minor triumph. You were Jill of all trades and Russell rocketed overseas again. You stayed home.'

'I left him, actually. I thought it would bring him back fast.' This gin was terribly good. It helped you not remember the awful year of the mistake. Which wasn't a mistake in the end though. How satisfying gin could be at lunch time.

Mary Jane laughed. 'You left him? He didn't seem to notice.'

'You told me he came and sobbed on your shoulder one night.'

'Bugger.' Mary Jane wiped her hand over a splash of gin on the table top. 'Let me correct myself.' Her cheeks were red as plums now; her voice thumped like a meat tenderiser. 'He may have noticed, because you had papers delivered to him. Matthew sent couriers all over the globe, for crying out loud. But you didn't leave him, you had the locks changed. You packed up his gear and sent it into storage. You finally got organised to start a life. We were going to have a ball, once you'd stopped crying.'

'He didn't come back fast,' said Sophie, 'but he came back slow. I did stop crying. Like, reader, I married him, whoosh!' A foolish smile lit upon her like a butterfly. Butterflies would come in summer, too, and sit on sunflowers — oops, no, that was bees. And it was lovely having Mary Jane around, they'd done so much together. Or they hadn't done them. Well, who cared: she had a larger gulp of tangy gin.

'He's done it again, Soph.'

'Whoosh.' Sophie pulled a second piece off her bruschetta, sat it on the rim of her plate beside the first and picked up the bits of dropped tomato.

'Another gin.' Mary Jane banged the bottle down near Sophie, who hadn't realised she'd finished one. Two, in fact. She'd been keeping up with Mary Jane.

Something made a burping noise. It wouldn't stop.

'The phone,' said Mary Jane.

One of Sophie's feet tried to trip the other as she crossed to pick it up. She staggered again as she said hello.

'Darling. Please.' A delicious deep voice sent a liquid slide right through her.

'Wrong number! Try the SPCA, it's only one different digit.' She dropped the phone. Her face had gone all tight and tingly. Had that been Matthew or not? It can't have been. It was.

'You keep taking care of people, don't you, even wrong numbers on the telephone.' Mary Jane reached out to push the handpiece on to the cradle. 'When Russell came back and was hang-dog, you had to cosset him.'

'He just ignored everything I said and he was so sexy and insistent. He purrs like a tiger when he's cosseted.' Sophie blinked: hang-dog tiger? Didn't fit. 'You know, he is really contagious.'

Mary Jane groaned and buried her head in her arms.

Sophie seemed to be standing in the middle of the kitchen with both hands round the gin bottle. There was plenty of bruschetta left, but first she'd pour another glass, just pour, she didn't have to drink it. Hang-dog tiger. God, it wasn't a mixed metaphor, it did fit. Tall, russet-haired, rangy, bent towards her, pleading, wide paws running up her sides, hot breath of him, and whiskers. Her hips did a dance of their own.

Mary Jane eyed her. 'Mating dance. Christ, Russell's studied the effects on that of fungi in penguins, butterflies, carnivorous plants all over the world. Of course he's good at it. You fell for it, too.' She began to cry. 'Don't we all? I mean. Christ. It's terrible what happens when we're nearly forty-nine.'

'You are forty-nine; I'm only forty-five, nearly. So is Russell. You're going to go through menopause first and tell me all about it.' Sophie patted her friend's shoulder under all that tickly yellow-brown hair. 'Never mind. When you've calmed down, you can tell me whatever your lovely doggy-eyed Steven's being abominable about, though I suppose it's that young man. Then I'll have a turn at giving advice or else it isn't fair. Coffee. It better be latté, because of the calcium.'

'Stop taking care of people!' cried Mary Jane. 'Tell them to get stuffed!'

'Get stuffed.' Sophie was fuzzy with contentment because her friend was here and they could be as silly as they pleased and Mary Jane would soon see how stunning this house was and how lovely it would be when it had a mummy and a clever daddy home with all the little ones.

Mary Jane hiccupped. 'Not me, don't tell me to get stuffed.' Sophie patted her again. 'Soph. I thought you were so brave to leave Russell at last, I thought it was the ideal thing for both of —' She put hands over her mouth to hiccup some more.

'You're right, I didn't leave. I stayed. He left the country. Again. After he'd promised. It was like the last camel. Haystack, like your hair. Things in them.'

'Needles?' said Mary Jane, as if Sophie was entirely mad.

Damn it, friends were meant to understand you. 'Straw, straw,' muttered Sophie. The walls made a swaying motion. She clung to the table and edged to her chair. She'd spent enough time on the floor last night, thanks, crawling up the stairs. 'Anyway, Russell is back. He's got a job here.'

'But you're in exactly the same situation with another monster of a house to pull into shape, and if you don't —' Mary Jane stopped. 'I'm completely pissed. I had a great insight into the female spirit then, but it's vanished.'

Spirits. Sophie discovered her hands unscrewing the top of the gin again. She tucked them into her armpits and frowned at the bottle. 'I've seen spirits. In the laundry. Right here in the kitchen too, last night. I mean, it can't have been real. I'd better see a doctor for these migraines. Mary Jane, I might need help. I think I might be worried.'

'I need to put my feet up. I feel more seasick now than I did on the ferry,' said Mary Jane. 'What a pair, sloshed at one-thirty in the afternoon. All we need is for your mother to walk in.'

There was a bang on the door to the dining room. Sophie gasped and Mary Jane grabbed her arm. The door opened a few inches. Nothing came through.

Spirits. Sophie had summoned them. Or maybe it was the electrician.

The door bumped open a little further. Through it appeared a smallish, grimy hand holding a schoolbag, then Hugh, sideways, and finally his other hand holding a Laura Ashley cotton bag laden down with something oval-ish and heavy. He struggled to the pyjama-striped sofa and sank on to it. 'Hello, Mary Jane,' he said. 'How are you?'

'Fine, Hugh,' said Mary Jane. 'And you?'

'I've run away from school again.'

The Laura Ashley writhed. 'What's that!'

Hugh chewed his mouth a bit before he answered. 'It's a rabbit.'

'Hugh!'

'Mum'll look after it,' Hugh said. 'It's got a runny eye.'

Sophie retained enough self-regard not to look at Mary Jane. She rested her forehead on the table instead.

'Your mother isn't on this planet to play Mrs Goody Two Shoes Earth Mother to every waif and stray,' said Mary Jane. 'Are you not coping well with a new city, Hugh?'

'I don't know about coping. But you have to act or die. Are you drunk?'

'Why do you ask?' Mary Jane spoke carefully. Sophie rolled her head and watched the Laura Ashley wriggle across the floor.

'You look as if you want to cry,' said Hugh. 'Whenever you come and see Mum you usually get drunk and cry. Or cry and then get drunk. Other times, you get really excited about things you're going to do. I don't think you do them for long, though. Grandma calls you a dabbler and a dissipating influence. Mum? Where can we put the rabbit?'

Sophie eased up from her chair and lifted the cotton bag from where it had ended up against the fridge. The walls still moved slightly, so she kept looking at the bag. It had a zipper. She unzipped enough to see long grey ears and a whiffly nose with white whiskers, and to be hit with the sting of fresh ammonia.

'Anyway,' said Hugh, 'if you've come to stay with us, you're a stray and a wafer too.' He bobbed off the sofa and hugged Mary Jane.

'Waif,' she said. 'God, a boy who can spout the scientific names of foreign fungi ought to know a simple word like waif.'

'Boys don't have to be perfect.' He ducked Mary Jane's second kiss.

'What's more, Hugh, I'm hardly a waif. Waifs are small and forlorn, more like your mother.'

'She's usually reliable, though.' Hugh examined the platter on the table. 'Don't be unhappy, Mary Jane. She always sorts things out for me, she'll have a go at sorting you out too. You think you do the organising. But.' He picked up a piece of bruschetta. 'Cool. Stinky soggy food.'

'Where did the rabbit come from?' The bag squirmed in Sophie's grasp. 'Where did you find it? Hugh?'

He chewed hard, swallowed and took another bite.

The phone gave its sudden, horrid burp. The rabbit kicked. Sophie yelped, dropped the bag, and the rabbit booted out of it like an agitated tramper kicking off a sleeping bag.

'Get it!' Hugh yelled.

Mary Jane went one way, Sophie another; Hugh and the rabbit seemed to go everywhere. The rabbit had the best time because it could run into smaller places. No one got the phone, though Sophie tried to. It wasn't easy, aiming at things when the walls moved. The burping stopped

Mary Jane managed to throw herself full length and trap the creature under her chest, with both arms tightly locked.

'You've killed it!' Hugh shrieked. 'You're too fat!'

'Shut up, Hugh!' said Sophie.

'It's still wriggling.' Mary Jane raised her head off the floor and stared the rabbit in the face. 'You're right, its eye is weepy. Christ! What if it's myxomatosis!'

'Don't let it go!' Sophie and Hugh cried together but Mary Jane, with an astonishing balletic leap, was already on the back of the sofa.

The rabbit sat up and untwisted its ears.

'I need another gin,' said Mary Jane. 'I need a bath. Disinfectant. Hell, Sophie, I need to pee, where's the bathroom?'

'Wait,' Sophie ordered. 'No one move.' The obedient silence surprised her. Even the walls stayed still. 'Mary Jane, take the phone off the hook so it doesn't scare the rabbit again.' Mary Jane managed to do so without leaving the back of the sofa. 'Hugh, what's the rabbit's name?'

'It hasn't got a name,' Hugh said. 'It's cruel to leave things without a name.'

A quiver went through Sophie's spine. She found herself wriggling as if she too were a rabbit and had to avoid the dog, the gun, the trap, and other rabbits.

'Here, rabbit,' she called softly. 'Rabbit, rabbit.' She backed up until she could open the fridge, knelt, fiddled a lettuce leaf out of the crisper and laid it on her lap. In less than a minute, the rabbit was magicked into her arms, munching. It didn't seem concerned about her gin breath.

'Now you can go and pee,' she said to Mary Jane. 'There's an outside loo in the laundry along the back verandah, there's a main bathroom on the second floor, and an ensuite in my room. I mean in our room. Russell's and mine. It is the most fantastic room you've ever seen. Hugh, find me the clothes basket, the big red one.'

'Your mother can be so efficient when she tries,' said Mary Jane. 'She was my favourite student before I dissipated. She's got a marvellous way with small boys and sick rabbits.'

And drunk friends, said Hugh's expression, with a hint of admiration for his mother that Sophie found endearing, though it might have been her squinty vision from the gin.

Sophie and Mary Jane stood at the bench with large glasses of water and peered beneath the new green blind. Hugh, in the back yard, pushed lettuce leaves through the sides of the upturned laundry basket. The rabbit seemed more interested in chewing the plastic. A playful wind flipped the rabbit's ears and parted Hugh's hair in successive directions.

'I should send him back to school,' said Sophie. 'But it would only be for the last hour.'

'Send him.' Mary Jane rubbed the top of her thigh. 'Hell, that jump on to your sofa did for me. Alcohol's meant to relax you. But I'm rolling drunk and I pulled a groin muscle.'

'He won't go unless I drive him, and I've too many gins in me for that. I certainly wouldn't let you drive.'

'Well, what are you going to do about that rabbit? You're getting rid of it, I hope. Give it to the school, they'd love a rabbit.'

'It's got a weepy eye, that's all. Anyone can get a bug in their eye.'

'Buggy Bunny.' Mary Jane began to laugh but the chuckle turned into another hiccup, and that was the first in a series of gasping, tearing sobs that coincided with a banging on the front door.

Sophie took Mary Jane by the shoulders and eased her to the sofa again, neither of them very steady. It was no use asking what the matter was; all Mary Jane could do was choke and whoop and occasionally say *Steven* in a strangulated groan, though once she said *Russell*, and someone at the front door seriously wanted in. Sophie hoped it was the electricians back to finish the laundry. She put the gin and one of the dirty glasses on the phone table, told Mary Jane to have more and sit quietly, wove out of the kitchen over Hugh's school bag and a pile of Lisa's homework, and found the front door.

She opened it. A gust of wind forced the door out of her hands; it struck the wall and nearly hit her on the rebound.

The man on the doorstep wore a brown leather jacket, check shirt, blue jeans and cowboy boots. He had one hand in his pocket, the other waving loosely as if he didn't know where to put it.

'Ah,' he said. 'Mrs Redlove, you are home after all. We couldn't get through on the phone. Remember me? Nick Watson.'

So he was, the deputy principal from Hugh's school. Hugh's teacher. Come in, Nick.

Sophie ushered the deputy principal through to the kitchen. Mary Jane stopped sobbing at once. He had very slim hips and the kind of intelligent look that Sophie had always found intriguing. He was a little like a younger Russell. When Russell was in intellectual mode, his bright green deep-set eyes spoke of gazing at the far horizons of mental endeavour to see if the little dogies of scientific discovery were charging home to the corral: it made you wriggle in your blue jeans and was exciting cerebrally as well. Nick had a more ordinary air: folk wisdom, prairie philosophy, appealingly simplistic. His expression probably spoke of trying to see what the hell Billy Jeffs and Annie Wottle were doing on the far side of the playing fields.

'Cup of tea?' Sophie asked.

Mary Jane gestured to the gin.

'I can't stay long, someone's covering my class. But, since I'm here.' Nick's spare hand wandered in the air again. 'I'd like a brief word about Hugh.' Which Sophie took to mean he'd love a gin and school teachers didn't have rules about drinking on the job. Parents should, though. She decided to have no more today, if ever.

'I am sorry.' She remembered to put the phone back on the hook at last, carefully so she didn't misjudge the distance. 'I should have called the school when he got here. I should have brought him back at once. I wasn't really up to driving. He arrived here with a rabbit.'

'Um,' said Nick. 'That's partly why I came. It's — um. It belongs to the school.'

'He stole it?' asked Mary Jane. 'The little toad.'

The walls turned around and curtsied.

'Strong word, stole,' said Nick.

Mary Jane said shit.

'Let's say it was a cry for help,' Nick said, after some moments of silence. 'Hugh is a sensitive child.'

'He tells us so,' said Mary Jane.

'But he's no wimp.' Nick shoved both hands in his pockets and eased his shoulders up and down, staring at the gin bottle. Sophie remembered the rules of good hostessing and gave him a glass.

'Have another yourself, Soph,' said Mary Jane. 'If you don't keep the flow going at the right pace, you'll feel very down by dinner time. You mightn't be able to cook.'

'Hugh has this problem, though,' Nick said.

'He's never stolen a rabbit before.' How dare the man imply!

Nick pulled one of the kitchen chairs from the table and sat down, elbows on his knees, gin in both hands, leaning forward. Sophie noticed Mary Jane raise her jaw to stretch her incipient double chin away, glanced at Nick herself and forgave him for his implication. She loved it when men posed like that. They did it so unconsciously but, at the same time, awkwardly. A sort of crotchy pose. She blinked and decided she should take things in hand.

'So. Hugh.' She sat down at the table.

'It seems to centre round his father,' Nick said.

'Most things do,' said Mary Jane.

'Have you got any carrots?' Hugh yelled as he rushed in the back door. 'Oops.' He backed out.

'It's okay, Hugh,' Nick called.

Hugh's face appeared, offered a cautious grin, and disappeared a second time. The door closed with a quiet *snip*.

Nick's left cheek twitched and he laughed, showing trustworthy white teeth. Mary Jane watched him and sighed.

'You can go to your room and have that lie-down now,' suggested Sophie.

Mary Jane shook her head and curled her feet up on the sofa. Rather too big to be kittenish, but giving it a very good shot. Sophie realised she'd gone catty about her friend: that wasn't like her. Besides, Mary Jane couldn't go to her room; Sophie hadn't shown her where it was.

'Is Hugh much into fantasising?' Nick sipped his drink and his mouth stretched downwards for a moment.

Sophie raised her shoulders. 'Children do.'

'Let me explain. You see, we're puzzled. He says his father makes movies. It could be true. Then he says he writes books. Well, hey, we try. He says his father is a millionaire. It's possible.' He shrugged. 'And then he says he's on an expedition but he can't remember where. His father has also lived in Jakarta and Dubai, trekked across the Great Australian Desert, and had lunch with President Reagan for helping save the — um. I've forgotten that one.'

'Bald eagle?' Mary Jane suggested.

Nick seemed nonplussed by Mary Jane. He shifted his left leg so that the bottom of his jeans rose up and showed his cowboy boots. So ordinary, so tastily amateur night *Oh-ok!-lahoma*. He glanced at the bruschetta. 'Taken all in all, it seems . . . what? Unlikely?'

'Oh, unlikely's right, but it was some kind of eagle, and President Reagan was very chuffed about it being saved. It's true,' Sophie reassured the deputy. 'Most of it, anyway. Russell is a dilettante. In the old-fashioned sense, that is; there's nothing shonky or fly-by-night about him, he's not a dabbler.' Mary Jane bridled but Sophie ignored it. 'He is an academic, no matter what some of the others might say. He's got degrees in botany, biochemistry and engineering, and he's twined them all together to make something new which somehow gets him heaps of kudos. He's the modern Renaissance man, in fact. He is a show-off too, though it won't sound loyal of me to say so, but people love it when he does, I promise. Like Mary Jane's husband, he's absolutely fascinated by Russell's ideas and makes him go on and on about them over a bottle of whisky. Steven wanted to be a scientist himself, you see, but he had to settle for being a doctor or a dentist and the teeth won out.' Ah, change subject: Mary Jane did not look pleased and was making dismissive gestures about poor abominable Steven.

'Russell's an honorary thing in communications as well, he knows amazing things about —' Sophie's forehead contorted, she could feel it, but she couldn't recall what the next words were meant to be. 'As for millionaire, well, he made a killing on the stock market just before the Crash. His parents died about then too, just after the Crash, so he made a killing out of them, too. I didn't mean that the way it sounded. But he's not a millionaire. That part really is a fantasy. Now and then we've been very hand to mouth.'

One gin seemed to have turned Nick's early diffidence to brushstokes of bravado: an eyebrow cocked in a young Sean Connery way, he held an empty glass out to Mary Jane, who smiled and tinkered with the top of the bottle.

Sophie shoved the plate of bruschetta towards Nick. 'And I don't know where Hugh's dad is at the moment. Russell's never liked to settle down.' A prickling in her nostrils meant she'd had too much to drink and too little food, as well as far too little of Russell since the day she married him — first married him as well as the recent pseudo one. She rubbed her nose hard: the tip of it was cold again. 'I went on field trips with him in the early days. All everywhere, name it, I've been there. I held the video camera quite a lot at different times. The last field trip was when I got pregnant with Rory. We had a little weeny tent, and the stars were astonishing, like sequins on God's cummerbund. When dawn came, the earth was so red, the sky was a different-coloured glowing red, and we were so in love. I think it was Australia. Dingoes barked all night. Dingoes don't bark in fact, though they have a tuneful howl. Russell is unutterably clever. I'm talking too much.'

'Did you make this stuff?' Nick finished one slice and took the last as well. 'It's brilliant.'

The telephone rang. Mary Jane looked inquiring and Sophie nodded. Mary Jane lifted the receiver. 'Yes? Oh. Hughsh here. I mean, he is here. I am not tight.' She jerked the phone away from her ear as if it had bitten her, and put it down again, looking sick. 'Your mother. She's on her way.'

'She's your emergency relative.' Nick wiped crumbs off his blue check shirt. His spare hand wandered again; he brushed more crumbs and pushed the plate away. 'When we couldn't get hold of you, we called her. She'll be worried about Hugh.'

'Sorry,' said Mary Jane, 'I'll have that lie-down now. Where do I go?'

Mother was coming here. Mother would see Hugh wagging. She'd see Mary Jane. Sophie'd had an early morning banana and two bites of bruschetta. All she could do was hold on to the table with one hand and, with the other, point up, and up again, to show Mary Jane that she had to climb a lot of stairs before she found the guest room.

As Mary Jane scurried out Nick stood up, just like a gentleman, and gave a little bow. He turned to Sophie. 'Are you all right? You're not, are you? I'll make a cup of tea.' He led her to the sofa to lie down and, without any questions, found the electric jug and the teabags.

Outside, the wind squealed and whined around the house; inside the kitchen it was warm and calm. It would stay calm too, till Mother arrived.

'How often do you minister to drunk parents in the middle of the afternoon?'

'It's a special clause in the school charter.' Nick handed her a steaming mug. 'Sit tight till you've got that into you. I'll stay and explain to your mother, how's that?' His hands ducked back into his hip pockets.

'I have to do something about the rabbit before she gets here.'

It was difficult to hold the mug steady. She rested it on her chest and felt her heart thud crazily. Nick stood at the kitchen bench and gazed out at the looming pines in true deputy manner. He'd been very helpful, but Sophie'd had enough now, thanks. She'd like him to act the one-man posse, rescue the kidnapped critter and hot foot it into the watery mid-afternoon sun before the one-woman troop of cavalry arrived.

'What are you going to do for a cage?' Nick asked.

'Hugh stole the rabbit. You have to take it back to school where it belongs.' Sophie climbed off the sofa, still clinging to the mug of tea. 'I don't want to be rude. But take it. Take it now.'

Nick didn't move. 'Kids give you some way-out ethical problems to deal with.' Hands on hips, back to her. Standing the way only men can, one hip askew, both feet upon the ground. *I'm a-goin' to do some thinkin' then I'm going to do some lopin' and I'm goin' to go moseyin' on down.* Sophie used to practise in front of the mirror when she was little but her pelvis couldn't do it right. 'See, Hugh's act was a cry for attention,' he said. 'He also knew we were trying to get rid of the animal. No one's mother would let them take it home because of its weepy eye. His criminal act, strong term, was prompted by his inner need but also — um.' He clicked his fingers twice, hunting for the word.

'Altruism,' Sophie said, and sat down again because she'd been so meek and biddable.

'Right.' Nick shook his head and laughed. 'Kids!'

A clatter, rattle and slithering on the back verandah made Sophie startle.

'Wouldn't have thought he had the muscle,' Nick said. 'Good on the little chap. He's thinking. He's got it wrong, mind you, but he's thinking.'

Still holding her mug of tea, Sophie wavered up off the sofa to the window. Hugh had hauled the chains out of the laundry. He was staggering backwards down the steps and dragging with all his willpower. The chains clanked after him. On the lawn was the green city council recycling bin. It seemed Hugh had some concept of binding the bin and laundry basket together to make a hutch.

Sophie dropped the mug in the sink and found herself at the back door, yelling above the clatter and the gust of wind that tried to bundle her off her feet.

'Put those down! They're far too heavy! That rabbit will dig its way out of a makeshift hutch in no time. Hugh!'

Hugh kept tugging and dragging. Fiercer than the wind, she swooped and heaved them from him and, shouting how heavy the shackles were, tripped and stumbled with them back up the steps and along into the laundry. She tossed them down in the corner beside the old toilet. One loop of chain crashed into the bowl, which gurgled.

'Mum!' Hugh pulled her sweatshirt from behind. 'A dog might get the rabbit if I don't weigh the cage down.'

Sophie pushed past him on to the verandah. 'If a dog wants to get your rabbit, then get it the dog certainly will and no amount of chain will stop it. Give the poor rabbit a fair deal.'

'How?' whined Hugh.

Sophie's hands were on her own hips, Annie Oakley ready to draw. She fired a furious look through the kitchen window at Nick, who proved how practical a deputy he was by staying firmly under cover and in the warm. She wanted to hit him but there were other ways to show that she was boss in her own house.

With a splendid surge of realisation she discovered that not only could she haul large weights when she was drunk, she could also be a venging harpy, just as Mother could. How she'd screamed at Dad and Todd sometimes.

Harpies, though, were rapacious hissing filthy monsters with the wings and claws of eagles. Ministers of the Vengeance of the Gods. Bag-lady angels. As far as the nameless rabbit was concerned, Sophie was going to be a seraph, Uriel, Kemuel, even Metatron. She descended the back steps, whisked up the laundry basket and tapped the rabbit on the rump.

'Go,' she ordered. 'Scamper. Hop.'

The wind diminished, sank to its forepaws and sang gently in the pine trees. Sun filtered from the weak blue sky to sift through the branches. A drift of obliging needles floated through the glimmer. The rabbit hopped once and sat still.

'This is a very naughty thing I'm doing,' Sophie said. 'Hugh, we're going inside.'

He used his head to bunt her shoulder.

Sophie turned her back on the rabbit, took Hugh's hand, climbed the steps, crossed the verandah and glanced out the kitchen window. The expanse of ground outside was clear of all small animals. Under the pine trees, sunlight sieved down prettily.

'You're an accomplice,' Sophie said to Nick. 'Remember that. You're guilty because you stood idly by and let me do it.'

'I don't suppose you want to hear my speech on animal pests and the environment right now,' said Nick.

'I don't,' said Sophie.

'In fact, one reason we wanted to get rid of the rabbit was that no one could control it. It bit my thumb, see?'

Nice man after all. Handsome was more or less as handsome did. The best heroes all wore signs of battle but didn't risk their necks without good reason.

Mary Jane entered the kitchen wearing a green chenille dressing gown. 'What the hell was all that racket? I was asleep. Has your Mother gone?'

Sophie's hands were covered in filth from the chains and her muscles were as limp as boiled spaghetti. While she'd been lifting the rusty shackles she hadn't felt a thing. Now she seemed completely drained. She slumped at the big old table.

'I'm rather dizzy now,' she said, 'but I do want to talk to you seriously, Nick, about Hugh.'

'Not when I'm here,' Hugh said. 'I'd be embarrassed.'

A car swerved up the driveway. A slam, firm footsteps in sensible heels, and a rap on the front door. It made Sophie wish she had the strength to run and hibernate.

'Is there a back stairs?' cried Mary Jane. 'I can't let your mother see me while I'm dressed like this.'

'It's very fetching,' said Nick. He took his hands out of his pockets and tucked his shirt in tight.

'Grandma's got standards,' said Hugh. 'But Mum says, just like Great Grandma Violet's were, they're only for appearances, thank the Lord, give praise.'

The telephone burped. Hugh picked it up. His eyebrows hit his hairline and he stretched the receiver to Sophie.

'Two weeks on the Gold Coast,' rumbled Matthew's chocolate whisky voice. 'Darling. I'll be with you on the next flight. Bare feet in the sand, my love, the surf between your toes.'

Good grief, Sophie told the dizziness. The grain of the kitchen table seemed to beckon her towards it, down. She shook her head to clear it, felt Hugh take the phone from her hands and heard him tell Matthew to call again later please, Mum looked really weird right now.

More knocking, the sound of someone letting themselves in.

'My dear, this house is even worse inside than I'd thought possible,' Mother said. She paused. 'Ah. Mary Jane. And?'

'Nick.' He held his hand held out for shaking. 'Nick Watson.'

Through the daze, Sophie noticed Mother hold her shoulders back before the much-ringed wrinkled hand reached out and laid itself gently in the deputy-sized paw.

'Kathleen Briddleton,' said Mother. 'Please call me Kath.'

'I was one of your students once,' said Nick. 'You won't remember me.'

'Maybe not,' Mother said.

'Your work on the influence of birth order. It really spoke to me. I'm a last-born. I wrote a paper for you.' He tipped his head and showed those teeth again.

'What year?' Mother asked.

'Nineteen eighty-five. Stage III.'

'Ah.' Mother looked him up and down. 'A B-minus group like most of them. Dependable, but no genius. So. I presume you're going to tell me what the problem is with Hugh?'

Nick's boots moved in a hesitant side-back-side. 'Um. He and I dropped something off for a school project. Just going. All a muddle, but we've sorted it. Sorry to have bothered you by phoning, Kathleen, but you can't take risks with kids. Too complicated to explain in a hurry. A pleasure to meet you again, Dr Briddleton. Kath.' Once more he bowed just like a gentleman and Mother's nostrils flared like the faintest thought of a moth's wings: she had such a knowing twinkle in her eye. Crones are not meant to be sexy.

'Hugh,' Nick said and, with a hankering sort of glance at Mother, clicked his heels.

Head lowered, Hugh followed the deputy from the kitchen at a regulation sidekick's pace behind. Exit, upstage left.

Nick was a coward, Sophie realised. Mother had chased him off like a chicken, and Hugh was a coward as well. She gazed through her dizziness at Mother and Mary Jane who faced each other now like characters in a B-grade Western: the school marm and the whore. Both interchangeable, both woefully miscast.

Woops, I'm chicken too, she decided. I'll faint now.

And, looking at the invitation in the swirly grain of the kitchen table, she let her spaghetti muscles coil right down like the pasta when you can't find the colander to drain it properly and you use the pot lid, and the strands sneak out and slide, woops, down the sink by accident.

Goodbye.

SMUDGE HAS A ROWDY SING-ALONG

It was a really big church, and chilly. But Uncle Todd held her hand and said the buttons on her new yellow coat matched the eagle's feathers. She looked for the eagle and it was just a big brass chicken, very hissy with its wings out. The minister would stand behind it later and open up his book and talk about this and that.

'There are chickens on the window, too,' Smudge said.

'Be quiet,' said Mum.

'There are. Look at the chickens!' Smudge cried.

'It's three angels,' said Todd. 'Blow me if you're not right, Soph. They're like a row of boiling fowl.'

'Dad would like the chickens,' said Smudge.

'Be quiet,' Mum said. Dad didn't come to church because of the loud noises, that's why he stayed home, and Mum was mad with him, and he was in the dog box.

Soon everyone stood up because the noise like big rude bottoms came out of the pipes, and the minister stood in the middle with his white embroidered dress on. Everyone sang and it was a first best song that Smudge really liked because it was about all the bread you'd get in Heaven.

Feed me till I want no more, tra da da daa, went the people and the pipes, rowdy as anything. Sophie giggled because Mum had said be quiet and everyone was being noisy as they could.

The minister stood behind the angry chook and talked about

visiting and generations. There was scramble-rumbling when everyone knelt down, and mumbling-rumbling prayers, then scramble-rumbling when everyone stood up again. *Therefore with angels and archangels and all the company of Heaven* were some of the words, so they'd need plenty of bread. Jam sandwiches, she bet. Smudge closed one eye, then opened it and closed the other, and one of her curls tickled her eyeball, *eugh*, and she watched the chickens on the window and wondered what they'd done to make the brass chook mad. Todd's tummy gurgled and now Mum tried not to laugh, and Todd grinned all red at Mum over Sophie's head. Then they sang more. One man in the church sang different from everyone else, he took longer to finish each bit, and if the chickens were real, they'd squawk just like that man.

On the way home it was a sunny day but still cold, so she kept her brass buttons done up.

'How did you like that?' asked Uncle Todd. 'Makes you feel good, just the one hour on a Sunday.'

'It's not fair if it's only fathers,' Smudge said. 'Why don't they have sins of the mothers?'

Todd gave a sort of choke and looked at Mum and away again. He stuck his hands in his pockets. Todd and Mum started to walk faster. Sophie got fed up because she had to run to catch them and Mum was hissing at Todd, they both looked madder than the angry chook, like they wanted to peck and slap. They kept their hands in their own pockets, but Sophie knew their hands wanted out and to be grabbing. Even when she could only see their backs, Smudge always knew.

So they were silly and annoying, and she went to find Dad and he was being quiet in the workshop.

'Come to join me in the dog box, eh?' said Dad.

Sophie pressed her cheek against the hairy back of his hand for a rub of it, and scratched her fingernail along the wrinkles on Dad's knuckle. When she looked up, the scar on his chin wriggled.

Upstairs, there were noises and a door slammed.

Dad turned his chisels in his hands and fetched the oil and sandstone ready to sharpen them to put them in their new places. Sophie sat on an apple box and tasted the oil with sniffing it.

Her ears rested on the smoothing whispery noise of the sharpening, *slide*, *slide*, *slide*, and Dad just stood there working, being quiet with his Smudge.

'We do not have nervous breakdowns,' said Mother's voice. 'In my house we might have had a darn good blow-up now and then, but we did not give in to things.'

'This is our house,' said Lisa's voice.

'Whatever's going on, she isn't well.' That one was Mary Jane's. 'I saw it the minute I arrived.'

'I've phoned my doctor,' Mother said. 'She's coming round.'

'No she isn't, Mum's still fainted,' said Hugh's voice.

'The *doctor*, you sexist little yuck,' said Lisa's voice. 'The doctor's coming.'

Sophie. Open your eyes. But their lids were heavy as the lids to coal bins and it was black beneath them, too. Sophie tried to work out where she was. Not on or under the kitchen table, though that was more or less where she last remembered.

Thank God she'd got rid of the rabbit.

'She said something,' said Mother.

I didn't, thought Sophie.

'What rabbit?' Lisa asked.

'Why don't you children go and do some homework?' said Mary Jane.

'What rabbit?' Mother asked. 'Good grief. I told her she'd snap.'

'I'm sure you children could find something to do,' said Mary Jane.

97

'Like tidy up,' Mother said. 'A kitchen is not the place for school bags. What's that?'

'Gross. It's Laura Ashley.' Lisa's voice. 'Oh sorry, Mary Jane, it must be yours.'

'No way,' said Mary Jane.

'It's my teacher's bag.' Hugh sounded highly offended, which pleased Sophie because he was very good at it. She'd tell him so; all kids should know they're good at something. 'His wife sent us some costumes in it.'

'He's married?' Mary Jane asked.

'It might have been his mother,' said Hugh.

'Whoever it belongs to, the bag should not be in the kitchen,' said Mother. 'So you take it up to your room and . . . it's wet. It's . . . *eugh*!'

Sophie managed to heave her eyelids up in time to see Mother wrinkle her nose and drop the bag the rabbit had arrived in. Sophie found the look of revulsion very tasty. Mother pointed to the bag, and Hugh carried it off to the laundry.

'Can someone please tell me where to wash my hands?' Mother asked.

Sophie, somehow, had been placed on the kitchen sofa, head flat on the seat cushion, feet on the pyjama-striped arm. 'Mum,' she said.

Everyone crowded round and peered at her. Lisa, Mary Jane, Mother. Hugh must have just hurled the pee-soaked Laura Ashley at a washtub so he could return to the action at once, for his head pushed in between his sister and Mary Jane.

'When did Uncle Todd come to live with us?' Sophie asked. 'Was I four? Where did he go when Dad died? What was his surname?'

'Grandad died because of an emu,' said Hugh.

'That was Great Grandad,' Lisa said. 'It was ostriches, not emus.'

'They kick worse than horses,' said Hugh. 'It gashed him from stem to stern. I suppose your stern's your bum.'

'Mum?' said Sophie. 'Tell me.'

'Lie still and wait for the doctor,' Mother said. 'You don't have to bother about Todd, for goodness sake. This fainting, we can't put up with that.' She looked at her hands like Lady Macbeth in a state of disbelief at rabbit pee instead of Duncan's blood, though she probably thought it was the pee of a ten-year-old boy. 'I'll find the bathroom myself. I assume there's one upstairs.'

'Todd, Mum. I really want to know.'

'You're not well. Talking nonsense.' She disappeared from Sophie's sight line. Damn it.

Mary Jane's face wore a very tart expression; she quirked one side of her mouth at Sophie.

'I had a lovely childhood,' said Sophie. 'Truly. I thought grown-ups were weird.'

'They are,' Hugh said. 'They're cool.'

Footsteps as heavy as a giant's thudded in the dining room and Rory loomed over the horizon of her vision. 'Mum.' A word of one syllable. Good for Rory. Sophie smiled at him. 'I found this old lady at the front door.'

A complete sentence! He smiled back, his outdoor apple-cheek smile, and disappeared behind the others.

'I'm Dr Stern,' said a sensible-sounding voice. 'You all move off about your business, and I'll see what's going on with mum.'

She listened to Sophie's chest and took her blood pressure.

What was going on with mum was probably anaemia, simple iron deficiency which Dr Stern diagnosed in a plain old-fashioned way by pulling down Sophie's eyelids hound-dog style and making her stick out her tongue. She had twinkly sympathetic eyes and treated her in such a calm, professional, motherly way that Sophie felt very wobbly. Not physically wobbly but — wobbly. It made her think of living next to Mr and Mrs Angus, and of Uncle Todd again, and that was very strange because for years now she hadn't thought of him at all.

'We'll do blood tests.' Dr Stern produced a syringe from a briefcase and slid it into Sophie's arm. 'Green vegetables, plenty of sleep, and take more care of yourself. For instance, not so much alcohol in the middle of the day, *hmm*?'

'I'm not having a breakdown,' said Sophie. 'I haven't got time.'

The dear old lady smiled. 'Call it what you like. It's the body telling you to take a rest, and the mind is part of the body after all. That's not New Age, I should probably make clear. It's basic common sense, like doing house calls when it's needed. Of all the crises facing this world, in my opinion, it's a shortage of common sense that's far the worst.' She folded up her stethoscope and wrote a prescription in perfect copperplate. 'Blood pressure's on the low side, so don't skip meals. Send that large son of yours down to the chemist now, and come and see me in a couple of weeks. Or not, just as you choose. If the iron pills don't work, you'll know because you'll keep fainting.' She peered over her glasses like a friendly bantam. 'The best prescription would be a total holiday. Two weeks without the house and kids. Best advice I've got, and I suppose you can't or will not take it. I'll sneak out this way.'

With a matter-of-fact smile, she let herself out the back door.

Sophie had sat up during the doctor's examination. Now she lay down again. Her mind and body needed a rest? With luck, the others would think the doctor was still here, and leave her alone until they realised she wasn't. Clever doctor. What was she going to get them all for dinner? Hang on, if she were having a breakdown she shouldn't have to get them anything.

If Sophie had the strength, she'd scarper like the rabbit. A life in the greenwood eating greens — though she'd need red meat, if she had anaemia. She ought to have told the doctor about the angel and the ghost. She really had seen them, or she really thought she did. But the iron pills might get rid of the hallucinations. It was faeries who didn't like iron. She hadn't seen faeries, unless that angel was an elf. Elves were angels who were too slow deciding whether to side with Satan or the other lot. She did feel weird. The room was faint gold round the edges as if someone had sprinkled Tinkerbell dust.

It was a pity about the angel. She'd have liked to see that again. He was much more beautiful than those chicken-winged cherubs and the angry eagle bookstand, and he'd smelled like the breath of all flowers.

What did Uncle Todd say about his angel? It wore a boilersuit and a lemon-squeezer hat. It perched on the side of an overturned tank, one foot tap-tap-tapping: *Better get your backside moving, mate.* That was the battle when Todd met Dad, or so she thought. Todd knew where Dad had that other scar, but he and Dad never said. Mum never said either, really.

Uncle Todd said his angel was surrounded with a smell of fresh crunched apples.

If Sophie phoned the RSA, they might know how to find him. But at the moment she'd slur and be inarticulate. She could hold a pen, mind you. She could write to them instead. To hell with bloody Mother.

'Sorry,' said Sophie. 'I still feel too wobbly to cook.'

'Then Mary Jane can do it,' Mother said. 'I have that paper half-written.' Again, a glance between them, like rivals for the mayoralty in a wind-swept pioneer town. Mother *tched* and turned to Sophie. 'I see you've got your great-grandmother's chamber pot on display, along with some other little surprises which I won't ask about. In the hallway, Sophie? She'd turn in her grave.'

'How do ashes turn?' Sophie asked.

'It's got a fern in it,' Lisa said. 'It's antique kitsch. No one's going to use it, Grandma.'

'I remember it under Grandma Violet's bed,' Mother said.

'Do you remember it empty or full?' Lisa asked.

After a silent Baba Yaga stare at the female grandchild, Mother said, 'It's probably a Wedgwood.' She tugged the rug straight over Sophie, said goodbye and ruffled Rory's hair. Rory turned scarlet. Lisa mimed an up-chuck. Hugh kicked Rory.

'Fetch me the writing paper,' said Sophie once she'd heard her mother's car start up. 'And the phone book, I want an address.'

'You're too wobbly,' said Hugh.

'Bring me Todd's picture too, it's got his army number on the back.' If this was a silly thing to do she'd blame the faint, and all those gins.

Mary Jane poured her another. Time seemed to pass, somehow.

'I thought you put Grandma's picture up,' said Hugh.

'I did,' said Sophie, signing her letter. She made Hugh stick his tongue out so she could moisten the flap of the envelope: she couldn't stand the sour-egg taste of glue herself.

'Gone.' Hugh made a face at Lisa. 'I'm only a boy but I notice things.'

'You like the old crow so much you've got it under your pillow,' Lisa said.

'Don't bother your mother,' said Mary Jane when Hugh began to scream.

Rory or Lisa must have hidden the photo to annoy Hugh. Little toads. But Sophie didn't care a hoot. She'd quite enjoyed the by-play over the chamber pot and only wished Russell had been here to share it.

Lisa achieved a stroganoff, Hugh set the table, Rory made a stupendous amount of noise washing lettuce and banging the colander, and Mary Jane insisted on making baked apples which had always made Sophie feel sick when she was little: too soft, too squishy, too sour. They still did. *Stuffed with raisins, hot raisins, eugh!*

They all watched while she gulped down her first iron pill, and told her to go to bed.

'I haven't done the laundry,' she said. 'Someone has to do the sports gear.'

A few deep syllables came out of Rory. Everybody stared at him. Sophie realised he'd said he'd do it, it was his muck.

'Upstairs with you,' said Mary Jane to Sophie. 'Early nights all round.'

Everyone hesitated and glanced at the ceiling. Didn't anybody like this house but Sophie?

'Well,' said Lisa, 'as long as we're all going up . . .'

Sophie lay in bed and thought of the Balmoral garden. That house had been small, only three bedrooms, but along the back fence grew guavas, grapefruit, bright crabapples. Mostly, her memories were of scents, sunshine, sometimes of waiting outside while it grew dark. She remembered the new school there and hating it even though — because? — she'd already changed so often.

'Get out your green exercise books,' said the teacher. Sophie lifted the lid of her desk and pretended she was taking ages to find her book. She was really having a secret weep because the new school was horrible, awful. The girl who'd been told to mind her was obviously, *obviously* the most gormless twit in the class.

She remembered saying to her (her name was Judy that time), 'I wish I was a boy.' The twit's mouth dropped open, more gormless than ever. 'Boys can get dirty and be noisy, girls can't.

'Yeth,' said Judy.

Sophie thought Judy was mad to believe what Sophie said, though Sophie had seen for herself how true it was.

Sophie lay in the dark and smiled. Kids were funny little beasts. How could you know what went on inside their heads? *Stuff* went on, a weird mix, a complicated recipe for what they'd be like when they grew up. Scary. Funny, sad.

She turned over and stretched out. Such a luxurious bed, such an opulent bedroom all to herself. Poor Russell was probably cocooned in a smelly sleeping bag on a leaking air mattress on a rat-infested rock in the ocean beset by equinoctial gales. Though it wasn't the equinox right now. That was March and September. He'd be home by September, please God.

What was the equinox precisely? A time and a place. But did she know where the place was? This luxurious bedroom lacked a good dictionary.

The equinox was both a time and place, she was sure of it. *You're quite right, Soph, now go to sleep*, said Russell.

But mumbling to the absent Russell about equinoxes didn't help. Russell in the flesh would have known the answer. Other men always said they knew when they didn't. Or they fudged, and changed the subject. What a recipe men were, firm and chewy outside, while inside was tangy squish to revel in. Fragile creatures, and didn't they think they hid it well, beneath the triceps and testosterone, slugs and snails and puppy dogs' tails?

Russell would have wrapped her in his arms and made her forget about the equinox.

The absent Matthew would have reached down to nest her little heel in the base of his belly, growling a promising growl.

Sophie buffeted her pillow. She should take the half sleeping pill Mary Jane had given her. *You need a total rest. Overdoing things. A lot of strain. I'm hooked on these damn, things but a half won't hurt you. Sophie. Just this once.*

She wouldn't take the pill.

She lay there.

She reached out in the dark and found the tiny half-oval on top of the bedside cabinet. How long would it take to work?

She lay there.

Equinox. Dictionary. Blast.

Sophie slipped out of bed and into her dressing gown. The bedside clock blinked from 11:52 to 11:53.

No sound along the second-floor corridor, just the wind sneaking round outside. The kids must be asleep: no lights under their doors. Mary Jane would be dreaming whatever she dreamt up in the guest room, or lying awake fretting over Steven. Sophie snuck downstairs, through a curdled patch of moonlight from the stained glass. There was the gap in the alcove, above the chamber pot, where Mother's picture should be. Wretched kids.

In the living room, she turned on the lamp on a side table. The *Shorter Oxford* wasn't where it ought to be in the main book shelf, but the funny old red *Chambers* was. She liked it best anyway, with its spotty pages and list of The More Common English Christian Names which, by and large, were as Hebrew as you please. Outside, the wind breathed as if it gathered power for a sleek and deadly pounce.

She was absolutely right. The equinox was two times, in March and September. The definition went on to say the belief in equinoctial gales was unsupported. Though this was a 1947 edition. Who knew what might be supported a whole half century later? And the equinox was also a place, right again: a great circle in the heavens corresponding to the equator of the earth. An imaginary place, then. Angels probably skated on it when they weren't trying to shove each other off the head of a pin.

Sophie yawned. The sleeping pill was doing its stuff at last. She slid the book back on the shelf, switched off the lamp and turned to creep back to bed.

As she reached the foot of the stairs, the wind gusted and a sound came from the dining room. The kitchen? Perhaps Mary Jane had the midnight munchies. But that was the back door creaking.

Rory? Hugh?

The rabbit?

I do not want to see a ghost again, said Sophie to herself, I don't want to see an angel either at the moment. She realised her nose was cold: another migraine coming. She should never have had any gin. But she knew she wouldn't fall asleep even with Mary Jane's chemical help if she didn't know for certain that the back door was locked and everyone safe in their beds.

She wished that she were different, damn it. But she wasn't. Damn.

Hhhn-hnnn. Sophie jerked with fright. Darth Vader was outside. Blast the possums. Even when you knew what the noise must be, it still freaked you out.

She turned on the kitchen light. Her heart jinked again when she saw the back door slightly ajar. The extension cord to the washing machine snaked through the gap. She followed it with her eyes back to the wall socket. Turned on. Rory. He had done his washing but it was probably still in the machine.

Hhhnn. Hhhhnnn. Horrible noise. The blasted animal might wake Hugh and she couldn't bear having to be the perfect mother again at midnight. Well, possum, she decided, your cousins in New South Wales might be protected animals, but that is in another country. You're a pest to me and I am going to get you.

She tied her dressing gown tightly, pretended she wasn't scared and pushed the back door wide. A gust of wind tried to barrel her headlong off the verandah.

Two wide round eyes glimmered low down in the darkness just this side of the laundry.

'Oh shit. Piss off,' hissed Sophie.

The fat furry creature shuffled backwards along the porch and sat up like a miniature sumo wrestler.

The effect of the gins, the sleeping pill, early migraine and terror whirled together in Sophie's head. The animal had three choices: over the railing, into the laundry through its open door, or straight for her. Possums had fearsome claws. They could bite. They were reputed to carry rabies and TB. She understood why Mary Jane had leapt on to the sofa at the thought of rabbit bugs.

With a sudden thumping scramble the possum disappeared into the laundry. Sophie sprang to close the door, but something stopped it. The electric cord.

This was no good. Even if she did trap it, she'd have to get it out eventually. No one else would care a skerrick that a rabid animal might bite her children if they came in to use the outside loo. Mrs Nice Guy. Mummy Fix It.

She jerked the door open again. 'Come on out!'

What an idiot. As if a possum would understand English.

Anger and panic rose inside her. She needed a miracle now, not a migraine. Where was Russell? How could she cope with the daily crises of three kids, a crumbling Gothic house to restore, and bloody midnight possums?

But she had to, had to cope.

She snuck her hand around the door jamb and found the light switch. A feeble yellow glow showed the end of the extension lead in the middle of the floor, unplugged from the machine, the old-fashioned toilet with its seat up, the pile of chain beside it, one loop still dangling in the bowl. On top of the pile squatted the burly possum.

'I've had just about enough!' she said.

The wind beat against the house and made it rattle. The possum stayed there, squatting.

Sophie reached out slowly and gripped the broom leaning against the wall.

'Enough!'

She lunged and swiped at the same time. The possum leapt, but by some fluke she hit it. The broom twisted from her hand and clunked under the tubs, the possum fell back, landed on the toilet rim and, pointy ears first, slid in. Of their own accord, the seat and lid slammed down. Sophie flung herself across the heavy oak.

A *crunch* of chain, a *crack* of wood, a *screech*, a furry tail dangling out, a jerk as it zipped past her eyes into the toilet.

A moment's silence. Now what? The sleeping pill fought for control of Sophie; the migraine tried to push her down.

The possum began to snort and grunt, to splash, to scratch and bump the lid beneath her belly. She remembered the scene in Orwell's *1984*, where the caged rats were desperate to gnaw their way into the hero's face.

Do something, Sophie!

She clambered off the lid, kept one arm over it and crouched beside the toilet. Eyes squinched almost closed with migraine, she scrabbled on the floor to find a weapon. She had to fight to keep the seat down: the possum's claws were scraping on the porcelain. One tiny frantic hand stuck through the gap, flexing its sharp black talons.

At utmost stretch, she grappled the extension lead into her fingers. She would scare the animal, she thought, give it a fright so it would vault for the door. She eased the end of the cord, the plug, into her palm, and slithered up to sit on the toilet lid. More scrabbling: she bent over and peered between the seat and rim. The possum eyeballed her.

Oh, reader, don't try this at home! Sophie leapt up, heaved the lid back, tossed the plug into the bowl and hurled herself at the far corner.

A *sizzle*, blue-green *flash*, deafening *bang*! and the light went out.

For a moment, the outline of a possum's head was limned in flame. Splashing, a dreadful hiss (the possum), a scream (hers), the lid crashed down again.

Spectacular.

One big whoosh, really.

If that hadn't woken Hugh, nothing would.

She crouched there, panting, dazed amidst the wettish singe of possum fur. She had not handled that with startling competence.

What now, dear God, what now?

After several deep breaths which didn't help at all, she heard scratching on the verandah by the fuse box.

'In the laundry,' a voice said softly. 'Take a look.'

The smell of unwashed bodies seeped towards her in the gloom.

Sophie began to faint: maybe it was the pill at work at last. There was a pair of legs in the doorway, male legs and, oh, that awful reek. It had to be possum pee, it was too foul to be a human being's smell or even the smell of a grave. *Sorry, very sorry*, came a low, shaky voice. *Excuse me, please be careful, oh Lord help me, sorry.* The light was very poor, her sight was blurred, but the shape moving towards her was the ragged ghost she'd encountered in the kitchen. And the smell, the foetid choking smell. Dear Lord. Fear rose and tried to swamp her.

Sorry, it said again. *Sorry, sorry.* Its hair was long and tangled like a Viking's, and even in the midnight murk it had very anxious body language. *Excuse me, sorry, sorry.*

'Christ!' whispered a voice outside. Another male voice. A pure strong voice, although it was a whisper. 'Is *she* in there? Oh, Christ!' A white shape appeared in the doorway. The ghostly Viking shrank from it and its highly scented aura.

'If we go away, she'll find her own way out,' breathed the angel — elf — whatever.

Her own way out? Back to bed or — up to heaven? Had she died? Sophie blinked at the dim white figure. She swayed, kneeling, and steadied herself with one hand on the floor. Hang on, the possum hadn't bitten or scratched her, had it? Or had she been electrocuted too? She was only fainting, surely. She struggled with the blurring, on-coming swoon, with the reek and the rich strong perfume.

'What shall we tell the boss?' whispered Sorry Please the Viking. The boss? Could that be God?

Her head swooped and circled inside, just like the wind as it swooped and dived outside. Now hang on, just a minute, please. If this was a near-death experience, she should be up on the ceiling watching it all. And where was the long white tunnel people came back and talked to magazines about? She might meet Dad and Todd. They might tell her to go back. That could be because they didn't want her to horn in on the fun they were having up there. Mum never liked it when the men had fun without her. The men didn't like her going gadding, either; they didn't like that glitter in her eye.

'God, we can't leave her like this. We promised Russell we'd keep an eye on them.' The angel.

'Shit. Excuse me. Oh, I'm sorry.' The Viking hissed and hunched and writhed.

Inside her head, the dreadful swooping sensation swam, but steadied with her still relatively upright.

We promised Russell we'd keep an eye on them?

'What the hell is going on?' Sophie demanded.

It was pitch dark. Sophie rummaged in the odds and ends drawer: the egg beater, the giant runcible spoon, the Donald Duck eggcups the kids insisted made the eggs taste funny. When she found the kitchen torch, it let out a feeble light which flickered across the Viking's grimed and cadaveric fingers. She passed it over, and he went back out to the fuse box.

Still in the dark, she filled the kettle. The lights came on. She winced and covered her eyes, but upstairs someone whooped with relief.

Hugh. Damn it.

Sorry Please crept back into the kitchen like a timid spider and glanced at Sophie sideways. The angel glided in from the back yard: he wore silver and white Nikes, of course.

'I threw the possum on to the lawn,' the angel said. 'Do you want me to bury it?'

Footsteps padded through the dining room. Rory and Hugh edged in, both bleary-eyed, Hugh clasping the hem of Rory's pyjama jacket, Rory with a protective hand on his little brother's head.

'Mum?' said Hugh. 'What was the noise?'

Lisa hurtled into them from behind, dressing gown half on. 'You didn't wait! I hate it when you don't wait for me. What's going on?' She saw the angel and the Viking. 'Fuck,' she said.

'Shit! Oh. Sorry,' said Sorry Please.

'Pong!' Hugh wrinkled his nose and stared at him. 'Mum! A real computer nerd!'

'Hey.' The Viking gave a twitchy, anxious smile. 'Systems engineer. Or hacker, maybe. Even freak. Not nerd.' His eyes seemed bright with tears.

'Wow!' Hugh cried. 'Can I see your CPU? I bet it's gigabytes!'

'The flat,' said Sophie. 'The part of the house that's rewired. You're in there, aren't you? Russell knew.' A wave of fury washed in. 'He put you there? You work for him? But his new lab is at the university.'

'Oh, that never was an option,' the angel said with a glorious Botticelli stare. 'Your electrician gave us a hell of a fright, but the projects are on track. It's amazing, working for your husband. He is hot.'

The Viking's hands slid round each other, feebly grovelling.

'He's in the mid-Pacific,' Sophie said.

'Atlantic, now.' The angel glowed with fervent worship. 'E-mail. Voice-net too. When he can get a connection, it's like he's right at my shoulder. He can travel for months with this new hook-up.'

'He isn't going to travel any more,' she said.

The angel glanced at the Viking, and the Viking glanced away.

A tidal wave of anger rolled towards her. The latest radio equipment might be buggered, as per usual, but — e-mail, internet, voice communication. The locked flat of her house given over to God knows what without her knowledge. Russell. Bloody Russell hadn't taken that professorship at all. Not travel any more? Oh yeah?

The Viking, the angel and the children gave her uneasy looks, and a gust of wind rattled the roof tiles.

THE CAUTIONARY TALE OF A BUMPTIOUS LITTLE CAKE
Once upon a time, a little red-haired woman said to her little red-haired husband, 'It's time we had a child.'

'Whacko,' said the husband. 'Let's plant the turnip.'

'I like gingerbread better, and so do you,' said the wife firmly.

They set to and baked some gingerbread.

This was to be the best child ever. Instead of flour they used plenty of determination. For sugar, they used generous amounts of charm and, in with the ginger and spice, they sprinkled plenty of intelligence. They pounded the mixture, shaped the child just so, and into the oven it went. It grew and grew.

Out of the oven, plump and smooth it came, to be given curly red-icing hair on its head, green eyes as merry as angelica, and a smile as charming as you would ever wish to see.

But dough sure can keep rising. One day, the gingerbread child became a gingerbread man.

'Goodbye, little red-haired parents,' the gingerbread man said.

'Be careful,' they warned, 'it's a jungle out there.'

'I'll run and run as fast as I can. They won't catch me,' cried the gingerbread man.

The parents trotted behind, exhorting him to be careful until a truck zoomed out of a side street and knocked them into a ditch. So that's them out of the story.

Away went the gingerbread man, lickety-split.

Towards the university he raced. The tutors, lined up in the quadrangle, begged him to come and learn about the birds in the forest, the mushrooms in the meadow, and study all manner of mathematical formulae. The gingerbread man, who was utterly charming, obliged. He learned all there was to learn and then some.

'Be careful!' called the tutors as he sprinted off again. 'It's a jungle out there.'

'I'll run and run as fast as I can. It won't stop me, I'm the gingerbread man,' cried the gingerbread man.

He ran into the city where an office building towered to the sky. Starting at the bottom, he worked his way to the top. He ran round and round the boardroom, and the business people clapped and cheered like anything. They were still clapping as he gathered up the letters of recommendation they had written him and sprinted down again.

'It's a jungle out there,' they cautioned, waving their filofaxes and dialling their cell phones.

'I'll run, I'll run as fast as I can, so you can't stop me, I'm the gingerbread man!'

At last, the gingerbread man came to a lake. Even he couldn't run across it, nor even walk, without getting wet and crumbling.

He smiled at the creatures on the lake shore. 'Who will help me?' asked the gingerbread man. 'Who will let me cross the river on their back?'

'I will,' said a little blonde silky-furred fox. 'But I must get back to feed my foxlings.' (*It should be cubs, said Hugh, not foxlings. Shut up, said Sophie, this is in my head so bug off out, thank you.*) 'And please,' said the little fox, 'promise not to push my nose underwater for I would surely choke.'

The gingerbread man promised and hopped on to the vixen's back. Into the water she crept, carefully, so the handsome cookie would stay dry.

'How clever and charming I am! Everybody is my friend!' cried the gingerbread man, so excited he could not refrain from bouncing up and down.

A ripple of water splashed into the vixen's mouth: *coff, coff*.

'Faster, pretty creature,' the gingerbread man cried through his charming smile. 'I'm nearly halfway there!'

The vixen could not bear to repress his enthusiasm. But her exhaustion was growing, and so was her anxiety for the three little foxlings.

Still the gingerbread man smiled his charming smile, still he jumped about, and still waves splashed into the vixen's mouth, larger waves and stronger.

A log floated by.

What the heck, thought the vixen, and clung to it to rest.

'I see the other side!' cried the gingerbread man. 'Banners and balloons are there to greet me!'

The vixen tried to swim further, but her stamina was failing.

Ah, what the heck, she thought again, grabbed the log a second time and climbed on.

The gingerbread man peeped over her shoulder and smiled his charming smile. 'Hurry,' he said. 'We Renaissance men do not have time to waste.'

Ah, what the *hell*, thought the vixen.

With her tail, she swished him off her back and dunked him in the lake to soften him. The determination was chewy, the intelligence was full of zest, but by the third bite the charm was very sickly.

Tough, here in the jungle, the vixen thought, and paddled back to shore.

Compromise, did Mother say? Give and take?

A ferocious north-westerly howled at the house and battered it. The windows shook, the ceilings creaked, floors shuddered.

Anger thudded into Sophie, left her breathless. She always thought the gingerbread man was a smug little arsehole.

Oh, Russell. Bloody Russell. My God. Just watch her snap.

Part Two

SHAME & DELIGHT

Framed by the hotel room's thermal drapes, the tinge of sunset glowed on the Sydney skyline. Dr Stern hadn't prescribed Matthew, but at least Sophie was having a rest. So was Matthew. The bedclothes were a rumple on the floor.

She turned her head on the pillow. He had his hands clasped over his belly like a Plantagenet earl lying in state, but the smile meant he was exceedingly satisfied, exhausted for an excellent reason.

So was Sophie, for many excellent reasons, Matthew just the last of them.

What a day: whirlwinds punctuated by cyclones of the different kinds of passion. Mostly fury. Rage made her feel extremely sexy. Russell had pushed her to the edge, and it was great out here. Old Testament justice suited Sophie fine. An eye for an eye, a betrayal for a monumental let-down. Leave Russell guessing. Yes. The stinky Viking and pretty-boy cupid were on the job back home to tell bossman she'd bolted. Mary Jane had promised to be mysterious about the destination. Hand on heart, sour little twitch on her wide lips, Mary Jane had also pledged not to tell Russell about Matthew.

Matthew's face was flushed too, like the skyline. Was he all right? She nudged him.

'Darling,' he rumbled, so he probably was okay.

How she'd learned to love the frivvelling of his moustache as it tickled her instep. She nudged him again.

He groaned, but with appreciation because he rolled over and confirmed that he was fine. Never mind the ebb of his roundish belly when she pressed her own against it (his firm chest had slipped a little in the last few weeks): she nibbled on one of his biceps, appetising as a baked potato.

Matthew lay flat on his back again with his jaw slightly open. You couldn't blame her for wondering if an older lover was the right idea, no matter how firm or otherwise his arms and upper chest. That is, it mightn't be good for him. The Chinese recommended men over a certain age to conserve their emissions. It made them sound like cars in need of a tune-up. Sophie ought not to keep testing him; if she could mix a few metaphors again, it was like torch batteries. The more you checked, the more likely they were to conk out when you seriously needed power.

As he dozed, she lay and watched. The delectable curve of scalp where his hair had thinned. Grey and black hairs, perky on his earlobes. Men's ears seemed to do that as they aged, the secret beast becoming visible. So panda bear. Tame Yeti. He took a deeper breath than usual. *Pop*, his lips said faintly, *pop*, and his moustache flexed up towards his nose.

Mary Jane was right about one thing: older men were uncommonly appreciative. This one was, anyway. He took his time over things. Sophie stretched her legs out and smoothed a hand to her stomach, smiling with satiny all-over satisfaction.

Mind you, Russell was appreciative, in a different way. His approach was energetic, zealous, all gung-ho when he was home between biological and botanical explorations which now, apparently, involved extensive and expensive computer projects too. In her own house. And he could have got in touch at any time. He'd set up e-mail for his projects but not even given an itinerary to his wife and kids.

Utterly concentrated by rage and betrayal (Russell's, not hers), Sophie drew her legs up and grabbed Matthew's arm again. No response.

Didn't he know he was here to be used as a sex object? She tickled his chest hair and blew into his armpit.

His voice was not as deep as usual when he murmured that he thought it should be getting on for dinner time.

She bounded off the bed to have a shower. It didn't matter how tangled these sheets were: the room had another king-sized nearer the door, for later.

Two king-sized beds, a view of Darling Harbour: what more could a furious woman want? A view of the Opera House from the restaurant they taxied to; gigantic prawns and hunks of dory dripping with spicy lemon sauce; an excellent white Burgundy; and a stagger back to the hotel with arms around each other in the warm night air. So much wine she couldn't remember what happened again, if anything, on either bed. They'd both had a very long day.

Next on the menu of the furious woman: breakfast in bed with chunky pungent marmalade. Flakes of croissant lodged in Matthew's chest hair. Tame Yeti, garnished, though you sneezed when you tried to lick the crumbs. With a series of cordial rumblings, Matthew heaved himself away and into the bathroom.

Sophie lay and relaxed. Or tried to. Two images kept flipping through her mind. Mary Jane, mouth open like a funfair clown, ready for a ping-pong ball: she had swallowed at last. 'All right, Soph. To hell with Steven, I'm okay about minding the kids. But only because you look like total shit; no Sophie, truly, total shit.'

The second image was the possum. A tatty lump of rigor mortis in the cold morning light of the back yard. The long fur on its tail rippled in the wind. Dead. Exploded. Whooshed. Suddenly the creature lurched to all fours. Tail awkwardly off-centre, it made a weaving dash for the pine trees and Sophie blazed upstairs to pack.

It would be odd, sharing a hotel room with Matthew for more than just an afternoon. (It had been just the once in a hotel, the day they'd begun their affair, when they'd run out of his office, into a shoe shop, then over the road to the Travelodge. After that, they'd dashed up to the river cabin, Wednesdays, and she'd always been back home before Hugh was out of school.) Would he mind if she left toothpaste all over the taps? Would she mind moustache trimmings in the basin? Would they argue over nasty things like coat hangers? Surely not. They'd share. Just for ten days, after all. That was the plan. Her plan.

A ripple of guilt tickled the soles of her feet and travelled slowly upwards. Matthew came out of the bathroom, a towel about his newly roundish waist.

Oh, Soph, you're meant to be ashamed of shame, but look, you can enjoy it! Especially with a man's bare chest on view, the softish lumps and hairy bits of it. Guilt is meat and yeast to you, a Cornish pasty feeling, multi-textured, the perfect accompaniment to freshly showered panda and the sweet and sour savour of her rage.

Of course it wasn't love. It would be a bloody nuisance if it were. But in the meantime, this was very filling, thank you.

Sophie watched him pull on his socks and boxers. She loved to watch men dress. Matthew in particular seemed to wrestle with his clothes. It was another of Mother Nature's clever things with men, the way strength compensated for a want of flexibility.

Each visit to his office, the hairy patches on the backs of his fingers, the black and white moustache, the dimple winking at her from his chin. Brown eyes, twinkly, pouchy. Unethical but, oh, to rest your head on a big wide chest and feel a heart pounding like a bulldozer in a cavern.

This is becoming very personal, said Matthew.

Well, well. And so it was.

Eucalyptus trees marched off into the distance and she'd always liked the smell of rental cars. She counted six dead kangaroos. They lay like overcoats flung from car windows. And now, a small town on an arm of land, lake on one side, ocean on the other, in the afternoon simmer of the sun. No wind. None! Who needs a ritzy holiday resort with waiters and free suntan cream? It would have been accepted gratefully, but this would do just fine.

The fronds of the palm trees drooped, reminding Sophie of the ostrich-feather fan Great Grandma Violet used to keep in mothballs. She'd always hoped they were feathers from the rogue cock who'd tromped Great Grandad. A wicked family rumour had it Violet might have trained the ostrich. Guilt could turn anyone towards religion.

'It's a very quiet motel. We don't need much space, do we?' Matthew turned off the main road at a corner where one sign pointing on said *Cemetery* and the other said *Motel, cheap rates, free breakfast*.

'We only need a bed,' said Sophie. 'A kettle for a cup of tea.'

'That's my girl,' said Matthew as they pulled under the shade of a florid bougainvillea wreathed into overhead trellis.

She hadn't expected a motel that existed in a time warp. The place needed serious painting. The shade of blue was very seventies. But this would do, Dr Stern, truly.

Matthew told her to wait while he checked with the office. A wiry shape appeared in the obscurity behind the counter. Another shape was faintly visible in the deeper darkness of the room beyond. Insubstantial, the figures floated back and forth while Matthew's reassuring bulk stood signing forms.

He emerged, the key in hand. At ankle height behind him a wizened face snarled briefly and pattered back into the gloom: a twitch of a whip-thin tail. Some strange pet rodent or marsupial? Not a gargoyle: they belonged on church balconies and drainpipes. At Notre Dame, you peer upwards, right through their mouths to open sky. This was a dog, surely. Sophie shuddered at how nature could be twisted.

Their room was on a second storey; they carried their luggage along the verandah. Behind the drapes and net curtains of other units, large formless figures bulked in the shadows.

'Gidday,' one wheezed as they passed an open doorway, and raised a foaming can of Fosters past its naked chest. 'Great place. You'll love it here.'

Matthew unzipped his suitcase with one firm tearing sound. 'Which drawers do you want? Is the kitchen big enough?'

How big a kitchen did you need, to put a teabag in a tea cup? Sophie sank her teeth gently into his shoulder, let go and flopped on the bed.

'Lovely girl.' His voice resounded with appreciation.

The bed seemed big enough as well, and the gloom inside the unit was a relief, in fact, after the bright afternoon sun. She was a little dazed: that migraine had never completely vanished. Now and then its fuzzy shape lurked through her head. She ought to take her iron pill now lest she forget.

'What's that?' She pointed to a hatch beside the door. It had a bolt on, and a deep shelf.

'You order breakfast,' Matthew said, not looking. 'They serve it there on trays.'

Like a prison. Well, she did feel a little bad about leaving the kids, though it was only for ten days. You could have breakfast in bed at any rate.

What if, through some mental hiccup, you decided to use the minuscule, one-element cooker? There was no dining table, just a narrow ledge along the wall between the little sets of drawers.

Matthew held a pile of t-shirts in one hand, a pair of striped pyjamas still in cellophane wrapping in the other.

'You won't need those,' she said.

He twitched a shoulder and his head ducked down.

'Will you?' She laughed.

Matthew reddened across his firm plump cheeks. 'When my uncles had their heart attacks, neither of them had a decent pair of pyjamas.' He stuffed them in the bottom drawer. 'I always pack them just in case.'

She decided to take it as a disconcerting compliment. She was feeling very odd: sleepy, disoriented, agitated too. Part of that fuzzy shape prowling round had a hint of bloody Mother. Way back when, Mum had worn stiletto heels and she didn't prowl; she'd give Soph a quick peck and dart out the back door, chin in the air and *I'll show you*, and the men didn't say *Yep*, not even talk with wordless looks because they were in the dog box.

Sophie had probably been sitting in the car for far too long.

She hauled her bathing suit out of her case. 'It's warm enough for swimming. Do you want to try the pool here or go to the beach? I'm not sure about those pelicans, mind you. They're everywhere. Their beaks are like barbecue tongs.'

If Hugh were here, he'd love the pelicans. Lisa would loathe them and say so very loudly. Rory would bowl right through, as if they didn't exist: poor pelicans if they didn't waddle quick.

A shuddery sigh rose in her throat: she choked it down.

Rage, Sophie. Bite on anger, think of Russell, that's the ticket.

If Russell were here, he'd bore the kids to hell-and-gone with a string of facts. *Pelicans are the only birds (along with boobies, gannets and allies) with all four toes webbed. Their eggs are incubated by both the female and the male bird* (well, har-de-har, Russell, come again?). *Did you know the pelican is host to a peculiar kind of monocyte . . .*

The kids would have rushed screaming for the far edges of jetties and cliff faces to get away from him, pitching Sophie into a constant state of nerves.

Matthew straightened up from unpacking and hugged her. Her nose rested near his armpit. She sighed again and her nose prickled, not from tears but from aromatic man. So brave: he didn't wear deodorant or pungent aftershave, not like the angel. A real man, in the flesh, with her.

'We're going to do all kinds of things while I've got you to myself,' he rumbled in his great big chest. 'But first I want to organise the little wallaroo.'

She hadn't known he had a pet name for it. A modest name, too. She managed not to laugh. Matthew sat her down on the bed and found the phone on the wall behind the door. Thank goodness she hadn't said anything. The little wallaroo turned out to be the *Little Wallaroo*, four metres and a 40 horsepower engine.

When they are two weeks old, pelican chicks stand in the parent's huge throat pouch to feed on regurgitated food.

She had imagined the beach would be a curve of golden sand decorated by lithe bronzed bodies, perhaps with a row of cocktail tables, a waiter or two in running shorts.

The beach was the curve of golden sand. The bodies on the beach were very bronzed, but hardly lithe. No waiters. Two elderly women had a thermos on a tartan beach rug. Compared to the other people lying around or strolling to their cars, Matthew looked super-sprightly.

He stretched and flexed his limbs: panda bear aerobics. But, instead of splashing into the waves, he tugged her towards a sort of outdoor pool walled off by a low concrete barrier. Groups of swimmers stirred around in calm salt water. He patted her bare shoulder, tossed his towel down, inhaled noisily, swept his arms above his head and lurched forwards with a splendid splash. Up he came several metres away: the panda bear had turned into a porpoise. Agile for a man with a thick torso, though porpoises have thick chests too.

More lurking shapes slunk in her mental undercurrents: once, when she'd cooked Sicilian fish with pine nuts, Russell had sprung out of his chair as if he'd just been born again. 'The dolphin swims twice as fast as man,' he said. 'That's top speed. In a sprint.'

'It figures, Dad, they have more practice,' Lisa answered.

Apart from Matthew, the swimmers here were twice as slow as seaweed. Sophie sat and splashed her feet over the side. An elderly woman, round as a tea cosy in a purple-flowered bathing cap, bobbed past in a breast stroke. Beyond the saltwater pool, an endless stretch of ocean, paint-box blue.

Matthew ploughed on. He reached the barrier and clung there, talking to a cluster of other men already hanging on to the wall. Their heads flung back in laughter. The two women on the beach rug shared a comfortable belly laugh as well. Behind her, a rattling shriek came from a grove of eucalyptus. Kookaburra. Horrible birds.

You couldn't truly say they laughed; it was more like the racket of machinegun fire.

Sophie had to be the youngest here by years. She began to feel ridiculous not swimming, so she jumped into the shock of water colder than blood heat and set off in an overarm. Her shadow dodged before her on the sandy bottom. She ducked under, tried to touch it and came up spluttering. Fun at the beach. It was meant to be fun at the beach. It was sixteen years since she'd had a no-strings no-kids holiday, and this was wonderful, not having to cook or worry about a thing. Just for a day or so. Just till Russell heard about her absence over e-mail and had time to get worried sick, worried queasy, worried desperate.

Oh God. The kids. Alone with Mary Jane. What had she done?

Shut up, Soph. Mary Jane has three kids of her own.

All grown, though. She hasn't managed a ten-year-old for ages. She's never had a daughter. Rory's not as confident as he looks.

Shut up and swim, Soph. Swim.

One width of the pool and she was bushed. Painting hadn't made her fit, and lack of sleep hadn't helped. Iron pills did not an instant difference make. She staggered out of the water and huddled up like a folded jelly baby while elderly swimmers churned back and forth before her. Several of them nodded as if they knew just who she was.

Huffing and puffing, smiling and towelling his armpits, Matthew joined her. A vision of *From Here to Eternity* rolled through her mind: the long lean lovers tumbled by the surf (what would they do about their bathing suits, with sand all gritty in the creases?). Sophie towelled her face to hide a laugh. Comparisons were odious as well as most misleading. She longed to run back to the motel and gluttonise completely on her Matthew.

It doesn't matter if you eat too much of something far too rich. To recall how sick it made you feel can be enormous fun.

Dusk seeped around the streets like the grainy grey of old movies about Western townships, and scatters of birds flew over the power lines to their roosts. Matthew seemed to know where there'd be a good restaurant. Sophie's little hand in his big grasp, they strolled through the village to the harbour.

A pair of middle-aged shapes, their hands clasped too, moved heavily towards them in the mainstreet shadows. The man nodded at Matthew as if he might recognise him; the woman smiled, seemed curious as they passed. Sophie glanced over her shoulder. The couple, outside the ill-lit window of a store for bowling clothes, stared back at them.

Sophie nestled her hand more firmly into Matthew's. They stopped in front of a shoe shop but there was nothing there that really sung out hi-jinks, only sensible heels, round toes and comfort soles. Dr Scholls. Even the neon signs seemed faded here. Something different about this place was whispering at her: so many chemist shops, financial service centres. Chiropodists side by side with physiotherapists. Clothes shops, unchanged since the 1950s, displaying pearlised jewellery, cardigans and muu-muus. As they turned a corner, a modern car rolled by. Somehow it reassured her.

The restaurant, overlooking the sea, was not elderly so much as dated. The silver-service waiter glided round their table, so young his skin seemed made of plastic. The silver hair of other diners shone waxily in muted candle flames which flickered in the plate-glass window.

The reflections of herself and Matthew looked so much in love.

Why not? Relax. Imagine Russell standing out there, seething, at a loss.

Matthew offered her a bite of artichoke. 'Remember those little picnics by the river? Darling. Mmm.'

Sophie's belly did that wicked melting thing. She remembered very well, if you counted being in a cabin by the river as a picnic. After the first couple of visits she'd made new curtains, a rosy tie-dyed silk, for the tiny bedroom window. He'd said his wife hated the river, so there wasn't much chance of her seeing new drapes and wondering where they'd come from. Anyway, it seemed their marriage was like an old dog, at the staggering stage when it would be kindest to have it put down. Sophie and Matthew had lain in bed: he ate grapes from between her toes. They nibbled kisses from each other between bites of black olives she had marinated herself, her own sherry and macadamia nut paté, tiny pikelets topped with caviar, blueberry vol au vents that dissolved upon your tongue. How happy she had been, baking the secret mouthfuls, packing them into the little cane hamper she'd bought before her bank account began to squeak too pitifully post-Russell.

Humming to herself. *If you go down to the river today we're sure of a big surprise.*

The waiter moved to Sophie's elbow and silently poured more wine. This was what you ordered, Dr Stern: peace and quiet, stars emerging over the dark ocean, luminous curves of surf rolling for ever beyond the reflected candles. She hoped Russell was cramped in a tent beset by giant cockroaches, waiting for his pemmican to soak to a chewable state, imagining exactly what was happening here with Sophie while he tried frantically to fire up his portable communications equipment so he could connect his modem with an overloaded internet.

She also hoped Mary Jane was feeding the kids.

With a mixture of guilt, bliss and fright, she said yes, another bottle of Shiraz Malbec would be delicious, thank you, Matthew.

You shouldn't want to fall asleep by ten, not on a prolonged, all-expenses-paid-by-him assignation with a lover. But it was after the swim, the long drive up here, the energetic night in the king-sized beds, the dash away from home. And it was a long walk back from the restaurant.

Sophie could hardly make it up the stairs to their verandah. Some sort of night bird clicked and whirred in the palm trees, another answered, *blip-blip*, like an electronic car key. Muted TVs babbled behind the curtained windows. A rattle of claws on the patio below: she glanced over the rail. The gargoyle micro-dog bared its teeth and scuttled like a rat into the jasmine.

The room was stuffy, but she was far too tired to care. She wanted to phone Mary Jane but, vaguely, felt Matthew take her shoulders and ease her to the bed. She managed to slip off her own shoes.

'Curl up,' he said. 'My lovely girl.' The warm tickle of his moustache stroked her instep. Then the bed creaked, he turned on his bedside lamp and there was a rustling as if he were unfolding a newspaper. 'Off to sleep,' he said.

'Sorry,' she mumbled.

As she began to slide down into deep black, she heard him answer, chuckling. 'The river bank was glorious, sweetheart . . . wouldn't have to do so much of that if we could . . .' (growly chuckle, and a brief scrummage by her feet again, a moistness like a sea anemone around her little toe) '. . . propose tonight, my girl, but we don't have to go through all that, either. It's you and me, my love.' She felt him pat her shoulder as if she were a family pet.

Even as the deep black sleep came over her, she felt the shock of it. Oh shit. That wasn't what she'd meant at all. Marry your divorce lawyer? How soap opera could you get! But what exactly did he mean? He wanted to get married, or he didn't? Wasn't it eye-crossing enough to have an affair with him? Sophie lifted up the deep black sleep and struggled as far beneath it as she could.

Bang. Slither-slither. *Crash*!

She opened her eyes and lay rigid in a dim grey light. The bed jiggled as Matthew climbed off.

'What the hell was that?' she croaked.

'Breakfast,' said Matthew. 'I hope you want a generous one.'

The prisoner ate a hearty. . . Guilty on all counts, y'r Honour. . .

She sat up. She must have undressed at some stage. Right, she remembered wrestling with a twisted bra strap, half-tied up with a dream about shis-ke-babbing Russell in a sleeping bag, and flinging the damned thing somewhere in the dark.

Matthew picked an enormous tray up from the breakfast hatch and brought it to the bed. 'I'll be off about ten. Sure you don't want to come? Probably best if you have a quiet day, though. We must let you relax. Bacon? Two tomatoes?'

And fried eggs, staring up like two stunned yellow eyes.

They sat in bed and ate in silence. Further along the verandah, breakfast hatches crashed open and closed.

'You didn't answer me last night,' Matthew rumbled.

She jumped and her coffee cup rattled. That's right, he'd — had he?

'But darling, you don't have to answer.' He gripped her free hand in his and lifted a forkful of tomato to his mouth. Oh shit. It seemed as if he might have.

'The kids,' she began.

'Boarding school,' said Matthew.

She couldn't have heard him properly. Her children, stifled, bound down by rules and strictures? Over her dead . . .

'Russell,' she said: it came out like a bark from a miniature dachshund.

His shaggy head tossed in lawyerly disdain. 'Guilt by non-association. He's had his second chance. The man's a fool.' He loaded his fork with bacon. 'Sophie? You seem disconcerted. You must have realised what this is all about.' He gestured with his knife, indicating the motel, the holiday, them being side by side in bed with their tomatoes.

Her jaw seemed very wobbly. Don't let him say it, she prayed; if he doesn't say the actual words, I can pretend it hasn't happened.

'Darling, I never closed your file.' He sprinkled pepper on his eggs. 'Do you really think I'd let you slip away? A woman like you? That first day you walked into my office. You sat there telling me about giving up your doctorate for Russell's sake, then wanting to do accounting, how you'd done the painting and wallpapering in every home you'd had, your hopes for the antique shop, the little bits and bobs you wrote for the suburban paper to earn an extra dollar. I couldn't believe my luck. I thought, why didn't I come upon this woman years ago? And those little hampers by the river. Darling.' He picked up her hand again and kissed it. 'Sorry.' He licked the drop of egg yolk off her thumb.

There was absolutely nothing she could find to say. The overwhelming sense of *déjà vu*.

It might be the bacon, or the eggs. Todd used to hoe into huge breakfasts before he and Dad went off fishing. They were first best fishermen. They came home with grins as big as pumpkin wedges, and always got plenty of fish. They had fishing hooks and floats and lures in fascinating little cans and boxes, but they never let Sophie play with them in case she hurt herself. Sometimes, when no one was about, she'd sneak into the workshop and have a private rummage on her own.

Matthew put his fork down at last and wiped his moustache with the white paper napkin. 'A day to yourself, my darling. Do you want to come and see me off?'

On the *Little Wallaroo*. Why not?

Matthew made a marvellous fisherman too, with an ear-to-ear glow on just like Dad and Todd. Sophie still seemed speechless, a Little Mermaid who'd brought it on herself, struck dumb and treading on knives. But he did look gorgeous in a t-shirt and baseball cap, there on the jetty in the warm spring breeze, smearing sun protector on his neck and arms. He looked just like all the other fishermen, gorgeous every one, organising themselves with bags and rods, boxes of tackle, floppy canvas hats, and sunnies on their noses, with tummies firm and round like footballs hidden beneath their t-shirts in case there was a chance to have a game together later. Sun, salt sea breeze, the smell of male excitement. Their energy, their eagerness for hooks and bait burst through in every thigh movement, in the way their feet trod the grey planks of the jetty, in the sprightly curl of leg hair just above their socks. Sophie wished that she could bottle it and hide it away for secret tastes — that boyishness whatever their age might be, enthusiasm, earnestness all foamed through with laughter.

Matthew waved as the *Little Wallaroo* nosed into the channel. He'd promised to bring back a delicious something for their dinner. That meant they could take his barramundi or dory to a restaurant and ask the chef to cook it however he thought best. Matthew still hadn't seemed to notice she was mute: the Prince had liked the Little Mermaid speechless, after all.

She sat under a tree along from the jetty and watched the movement in the channel. Slow movement. Ripples on the great salt lake. A retired couple in their dinghy floated by, basking side by side as if they were in bed, rods in their hands, hats firmly on, noses smothered with zinc ointment. Such contented lazy style: *Here's who we are, here's what we do*.

A pelican drifted to the water's edge. In one movement, *woop*, it put its feet down and began to waddle past. The long ungainly bill, the huge fat belly. She raised an arm to shade her forehead. The pelican turned to stare. Its round black eye had an acerbic look. *And what are you here for?* it said.

God. Marriage. Give and take. She squeezed her eyes shut for a moment. She'd been married twice already. Even if it was to the same man.

When she opened them again, the pelican had lumbered closer.

It still looked sour. She picked up a dead gum leaf and threw it to the bird. The long bill caught it deftly but bounced it out at once. The large bird waddled backwards, sat down and stared.

'To hell with you too,' Sophie said.

Hey, Soph, when they're courting, they flap their bill pouches like flags in the wind. I've seen the male and female clap their bills in unison, Soph, amazing!

Like very awkward castanets. Great applause, cheering, bravo for the wedding of the pelican, peli-can't.

Wish you'd been there, Soph. Couldn't get a good shot. Ran out of film. Damn equipment. This life isn't glamorous, it's damn hard sweat doing fifty things at once. But God, I love it, Soph!

Pelicans have nasty tufty heads like badly combed old men. If Soph had made cross and childish comments, Russell would have been dreadfully hurt, but she'd just been dumb with admiration. Bloody Russell. Cheating, miserable sod. If she found out he'd been into the little design assistant Sophie had once found fluttering smiles at him, she'd make sausages out of his intestines. It would be a minor betrayal beside what he'd done already, but the absolute last straw all the same: camels put up with so much, no wonder they've got filthy tempers.

SMUDGE HAS A DAY AT THE BEACH

The waves were foldy splashes on the sand, like doll-sized waves. Uncle Todd put his big hand firm under her tummy so she was safe as safe, and she lifted her legs till she was floating. Her swimming togs had a tiny skirt, blue checks with a bow on the front, and she was like a ballerina with her skirt floating out, but Mum wouldn't look. Dad stood near the picnic basket with his hands round his head like he tried to hold it on. His eyes were screwed up and his ribs were bony as bony.

Mum had a big shady hat and a yellow sundress that showed her curvy chest. She closed her book and took the hat off slowly, and lay on the rug with her arms over her head like a film star. She looked like she was resting, but Sophie knew that Mum was fierce inside, all bursting hot ready to hiss and didn't care what the men said.

Mum rolled over and her skirt blew up in the breeze. If that happened to Sophie, Mum growled, but no one growled at Mum. Mum's legs were dimply, and people always stared as if they liked them. Dad stared at Mum's legs now as if he didn't want to but he couldn't look away, but then he did look away and sat down and held his head tighter. He was being mean because he didn't watch his little Smudge even though she waved and kicked her legs like anything to show him *she* wasn't bursting angry, and Todd said, 'Good-oh, kid, you're a bobby dazzler.'

'Look at me, look!' cried Smudge.

'Leave a man be,' said Todd. 'He's having a wonky day.'

Dad was hunched on the edge of the rug now. A big truck roared by up on the highway and he jammed his hands on his head again.

Mum was being mean too, just because she was angry. There'd been big rows last night when Sophie was in bed and Mum came home from gadding. Todd yelled and even Dad did, too. Mum had yelled and laughed but the laugh wasn't a funny one. And now she wouldn't look at Sophie doing a swim.

Todd swapped hands under her tummy and nearly dropped her under the water.

'Uncle Todd,' screamed Sophie because she got a fright, 'don't be mean! Stop looking at Mum, you're not swimming me!'

And Dad looked at Todd, and Mum rolled over slowly, pretending to be lazy. She lay on her side with her back to the men, and flicked her book open, and her hip stuck up like a yellow sand hill. And Dad didn't look at Mum, he looked at Todd and looked and looked, and he looked a bit fierce too, and pretty wonky. But he looked more than that, too, sad and sick in his tummy the way Sophie did when she was going to cry and trying not to.

Todd picked Sophie out of the water with his big hands under her armpits and popped her back on the sand. She tried to hang on to his muscle-bone arm so he'd do the squeezy strong thing to wriggle her hands off, but he ran up the beach past Dad and slapped him on the shoulder.

'Give you a head start, Jack!' Todd ran back and slapped him again.

Todd slapped Dad one more time, and Dad jumped up and shook his head and gave a short laugh, *ha*!, and the men raced down the sand. Their legs, even Dad's skinny ones, pumped like engines, and their feet hit the sand *thud thud* to the water. Their arms worked high and out to sea, till their heads were lost in the waves, and Sophie cried.

'Be quiet,' said Mum. 'They're nothing but puff and muscle, the pair of them. They're only showing off.'

Sophie wanted to scream *So are you*, but she didn't want to throw up on the beach. So she snatched all the shells around the rug, even the best ones she'd chosen to take home, and threw them at the seagulls and made the horriblest faces till her mouth was aching sore.

More interesting facts about pelicans.

The males hold their heads up and fling their bills from side to side. They can toss things in the air and catch them.

Showing off? Thanks, Russell. Gosh, you know a lot. Do you want to hear how the kids are getting on at school? Do you want to know about Rory's blocked eustachian tubes and how one of us has to take him to the Ear Nose and Throat man and there's the likelihood of them doing what they call invasive procedures? Do you want to hear what the doctor said about me being pregnant again? Do you know your daughter's name?

When pelicans take off from the water, they kick both feet at once.

Interesting fact about Sophie, which she doesn't care who knows.

She hasn't grown up at all and it's damn well not her fault.

Or it is her fault. Who cares. So bloody what.

By four in the afternoon she felt peculiar. She'd rested, bought a paperback at the newsagent's, looked at Tarot decks, crystals and essential oils in an over-scented shop where the owner talked loudly about the need for meditation, had a nap in the heat of the day, a walk on the beach to help digest the enormous breakfast, and a slightly better swim than yesterday. But her arms and legs were twitchy. Like trickles of vinegar inside the muscles: shocks and jumps. She was unwinding, like a clock. Except every time she thought of Matthew, marriage, Russell, she tightened up again. And she couldn't think of anything but Matthew, marriage, Russell.

Back at the motel, she had a shower to rinse the sand and stickiness off, fluffed her hair dry, dropped a cotton sundress over her head and zipped it, slipped into her sandals, then drove the rental to the jetty. Matthew should be back soon. With luck he'd be too tired to speak at all. No mention of the M word, please.

Todd and Dad had always been so proud of what they caught: *kahawai, schnapper, that one there's a kingfish.* They'd gut them, cutting heads and fins off, laughing. They'd talk cryptic man-talk and pretend to throw the innards at Sophie if they saw her being curious. They cooked it themselves too. At least Todd made batter and sauce. He fried and turned the golden slices while Dad stood watching with a look on his face that might, might not, grow wonky. Mum kept out of the kitchen where she wasn't wanted, and Sophie thought she ought to be pleased she didn't have to do the work, but Mum had her mouth closed tight.

'Let me check your piece for bones, Soph.' Todd with his rough head of hair bent near her plate.

'She's old enough to do the bones herself,' Mum said. 'And where are the fish knives?'

Dad, tired by then, so tired with his head down, picked at the creamy flakes, breathed deep at the clean new scent of groper as if he'd never smelt anything so wonderful, his arms around the plate to shield it.

'Eat up, Jack, plenty more,' said Todd, but it was like Dad never believed it when he got so tired, just never.

Once Mum hissed at Todd. 'So don't you dare to criticise me!' The men didn't look anywhere but at their plates, and that night no one ate much except Sophie.

She drove to the jetty. Dinghies and chartered launches glided in at the end of the day. As the *Little Wallaroo* nosed up to the jetty, he waved, a victory punch, so happy that she had to smile. He swung down the gangway with a swagger, a strut, a heavy bag of fish. She told him he was stinky just like Dad and Todd. He seemed annoyed until she said how much she loved it.

Sweaty, salty, windblown man. All of a sudden she could drown in him, longed to be alone with him, pull the curtains tight, burrow into him, feast over every millimetre of this muscle-bear, most palatable man.

Soph, you have to wait.

People from the dinghies and the launches gathered round tables near the jetty to gut their catch and toss the doings to a patient crowd of pelicans. Sophie gave Matthew a little push towards the others and leaned against a tree. She didn't mind watching while he talked bait and currents, local weather habits and the temperament of fish. Anticipation was a larger part of pleasure. Her insteps tingled, her toes flexed inside her sandals.

A white-haired, smooth-skinned woman with gold chains around her neck drove up in a Rover and joined the fishermen to admire the catch. She pointed to something in a pile of entrails. Three plump men, their heads as bald and brown as eggs, bent over, nodding. Matthew smiled and gestured, and a man with a white beard raised a benedictory hand above them all, eerily like Ricci's second and more successful *Mystic Nativity* except that there were Range Rovers instead of camels for the Magi. One by one, the three bald men glanced at Sophie and put their hats on. They were tanned and fit, stout and content. She felt alien, adrift.

An elderly woman in a wide sunhat left the group and crossed to stand with Sophie in the shade. After a moment, very softly, the woman spoke. 'So what do you think?'

Think of what? 'It's very peaceful,' Sophie answered.

'He'd be an asset to the bridge club.' The woman half turned her head to inspect Sophie, up and down. 'The girls might sharpen their claws on you though, pet.' This was the way people had eyed Sophie last night in the motel, the street, assessing, wondering, appraising. 'He's keen, dear. He's earned it, too. Well, we all have,' the woman murmured. 'Maybe it's third time lucky, after all.' The crinkly eyes smiled, so motherly that Sophie felt she hadn't heard it right. Third time? But the woman said no more.

The afternoon sun flowed down like fine spun gold and the salt lake whispered *hush, hush, hush*. Sophie smiled. And smiled. Her outside felt the comfort of it all, but her inside tangled with misery. Did Matthew want to live here? He wouldn't throw up his city law practice for this, not yet, not till he was well into his sixties. Would he? Had he brought Jenny here? And — someone else? The office assistant? Someone Sophie didn't know about?

Anyway, how dare a total stranger infer that he and Sophie wouldn't make a match? It wasn't being contradictory to think that Matthew would make a pretty good husband, better than Russell. He'd be on-the-spot as a male role model for the boys at least, which was more than Russell had ever been. Role model? *Russell?* An absent model of the king-sized ego. She'd like her boys to learn that men could play an active part in family life. She'd like Lisa to learn that men could be friends with you, and . . . well, Lisa would learn *something*, if the family had a father figure who was present more than ten percent of the time. Wouldn't she?

Matthew packed up his gear, said hearty goodbyes to the elderly fish gutters and signalled Sophie. As they walked towards the car she stroked the soft little ditch of his inner elbow.

'What did that woman mean, *third time lucky*?'

He put his hand out for the keys. 'What a day. I'm weary. I've caught enough for a good feed, sweetheart. You'll be up to cooking, now you've had a rest.'

Up to cooking. Well. Butter and a sprig of parsley could damn well do

Third time: he hadn't answered.

Well. She liked cooking simple meals sometimes. This would be extremely simple: fresh bread, plain lettuce, tomatoes, avocado. You couldn't do anything but basic with fish, in those conditions. Besides, when it's been dead only five hours, simple fish is far the best.

Simple words are sometimes best too. Like well.

Like *fuck*.

Paradise, to Sophie, did not include a one-element cooker with a dubious temperature setting, a lover who, now she'd like him to talk, still hadn't answered her question and didn't reply when she told him how Todd used to cook fish either, and who lay flat out on the bed snoring while, with a partly melted plastic spatula, she turned fillets of just-dead fish to an audience of fat black blowflies.

You have to see the funny side, said Mother, *you can't let it beat you, you have to stick with it, but by heaven, they'd better not cross me*.

When Mother talked about the funny side she wasn't smiling; she was putting on Guardsman Red lipstick and stilettos, stuffing a nightie into a train case, and Dad and Todd were in the workshop, not talking, not even *yep, yep, good-oh*, not saying a single only word.

When Great Grandma Violet talked about the funny side, she

139

used to pat her ostrich-feather fan.

The sun began to lower in the sky. The motel owner scuttled past along the balcony, and the cumbrous shapes of other guests drifted by and murmured greetings, lifted foaming cans of beer in slow salute. Matthew snored.

THE THREE LITTLE COOKS

'Who will bake me a big fishy pie?' asked the lawyer. 'Who will live with me in retirement paradise where I shall win trophies at the bridge club and install an automatic sprinkler for my lawn?'

'Not I,' said his wife. 'I have a grown-up family and I want to enrol at university and qualify in marketing. You want a cook? Buy pizza.'

'Who will fry me steak and onions?' asked the handsome middle-aged lawyer. 'Who will arrange dahlias in vases and potter with me in the conservatory tying up my Italian tomatoes as the sun sinks in the west?'

'Not I,' said the dolly-bird receptionist. 'I'm into high-fibre health food and aerobics. But I will take you for what I can get because I'm Generation X, and we'll have plenty of sex because I'm proud of my firm high breasts and insteps. But don't ask me to give up other men, especially young ones. Frying pans? Get real.'

'Who will simmer me a chicken stew with basmati rice and aromatic herbs?' beseeched the lawyer who had a grizzled moustache and shoulders sprinkled with pure white body hair. 'Who will glide beside me like a pelican into the twilight years and warm my bed and ego? Who will be restful and compliant? Whose foot will fit this shoe?'

'Me! Me! Oh, maybe me!' cried the home-loving woman who was only nearly forty-five. 'I will pretend my foot's just dinky in that slipper. I will refuse to notice blood dripping from the heel and amputated toe. I'll just mop it off the tiles in the conservatory, and animal protein is perfect nourishment for a thick, springy, easily tended lawn.'

Sophie didn't like being bitter for long. She rinsed the lettuce, diced the tomato and avocado, chuckled at Matthew's louder snores and killed another blowfly.

It was comical, when the fish was ready and she'd woken Matthew, eating at the long narrow dressing table, side by side like people in a cramped café. As far as love nests went, it was definitely basic, but she preferred it to Russell's sodden tent, the cockroaches, pemmican and the possibility of equinoctial gales.

'More wine?' Matthew held the bottle up. He poured some slowly, as if he was sore from all that holding rods and gutting things. It was dusky outside now; they'd need a lamp on soon.

As she took another bite of groper, a snorting made her jump. For a second she thought it was the gargoyle dog attracted by the scent of cooking. It was Matthew, eyes closed, upright at the counter. He gave a second snore and woke himself. He cleared his throat.

'Starting to relax. I've worked up a damn good appetite. Very tasty, Sophie. Damn good. Any more?'

She served another slice, a perfect golden brown, and sat down again.

'A clove of garlic in the butter would have made it absolutely right,' he said.

Sophie dropped her fork and let out a wail.

Matthew froze for a moment, arms out as if he was about to play a piano with his knife and fork. He jerked, tried to put an arm round her, jabbed her with his fork instead, fumbled the cutlery down and led her to the bed. 'Sweetheart!' he mumbled. 'Sweetheart.'

God, she sounded like a wounded cat. It was completely out of proportion, the way she shook and cried, the way her elbows pressed into her sides, the way she curled up. She didn't know what would have been in proportion, because it all came out of nowhere like an Act of God. If she heard an animal yowl like this, she'd want to turn a hose on it.

A shape bulked along the balcony in the dusk. 'Aah. Little woman tearful?' And a glint in the gloaming as it raised a can of Fosters.

Her shuddering grew less. Matthew, saying *um* and *ah*, lifted her bodily to lie her on the pillows. His face, when she managed a glance, said *Blown it*, but for a while his voice said nothing. Finally he said again, 'Um.'

Sophie wiped her nose on the skirt of her dress. How disgusting. (Who cared.) Matthew reached for the bottle, poured the rest of the wine into their glasses and handed hers across. Outside, various birds cawed, *chick-chicked*. Palm fronds shuffled in the wind. The gargoyle dog scuttled to the open door and sniffed.

'Piss off!' said Matthew. The dog edged out of sight. She suspected it skulked just behind the door jamb.

The air outside had faded to grainy grey. He got up off the bed. Pop. A burble of wine. Good, he'd opened another bottle. A nasty noise as she blew her nose properly on a tissue.

He lay beside her. They sipped, watching the last edge of sunset through the narrow window over the sink. Speechless, the pair of them. She rested her head on his shoulder, and he patted her small round knee with his big man hand.

Something cold pressed Sophie's ankle on the door side of the bed.

'Piss off!' repeated Matthew. A *yip*!, a caper of something ugly off the bed and out of the unit, and a rattle of claws along the verandah.

'If you hadn't boned the fish so well, we could give it a piece and watch it choke,' said Sophie.

She could give in, and they could just sign up at the bridge club too. Hell. She hated bridge.

At the rock pool that afternoon, she'd seen a nuggetty old man ease his wife into the water, his old slow wife with her pretty round anxious face. The way he held her arm, a hand on her waist, a series of little helps and encouragements as if the plump shape of her with the yellow bathing cap on top was the most cherished treasure he'd ever found in this wide world. When she was safely in, the husband swam off vigorously. But he always returned to make sure she was all right, and they shared lovely smiles.

Sophie's chest rose and fell in a great sigh. Hey ho. So did Matthew's.

'You didn't answer me last night,' he said.

Hell, nor did she mean to. 'You didn't answer me before,' Sophie said. 'Third time lucky.'

'Anyway,' he said. 'I mean — I haven't met your kids.'

She looked at the way her toes lined up on the ends of her feet: it seemed as useful a thing to do as any at the moment. Her feet didn't seem to want to run on out of here. The rest of her was far too tired to make them.

He grumbled an awkward kind of cough. 'I could cope with Rory. And Lisa. I'm not sure I could manage Hugh.'

'He's cute,' said Sophie. 'It makes him an astonishing pain.'

'Mmm,' said Matthew as if he'd met Hugh. 'So your m . . .' He stopped abruptly. Sophie turned her head. His face said *Blown it* again.

'My mother?'

'Um,' said Matthew.

'So my mother said?'

'Um,' he said again. For a lawyer, he was inarticulate this evening.

'You've talked about my kids with my *mother*?' God, sometimes the mental lights flashed on and showed all kinds of gargoyles squinting in the corners. The motherly woman eyeing Matthew this afternoon. Mother's reluctance to visit Sophie after her trip. The gleam as she smiled at Hugh's teacher.

'Bloody hell! Matthew! You haven't had an affair with my mother, have you? Did you bring her up here? Jenny, my mother, then me?'

Matthew choked. He wheezed and coughed, shook his head and struggled to put his glass on the bedside table.

She was up on her knees on the bed. Wine sloshed out of her glass and she flung the whole lot at him. 'What did you do with my mother!' She beat his chest with her fists, but the harder she thumped, the more he wheezed. At last she scrambled off the bed to fetch a glass of water. He held his hand out, but she threw that at him too. Back to the sink, and this time she did offer it for him to sip, but only when he did at last shut up.

He wiped his hands over his face, giving an extra rub at the dimple on his chin. It always took longest to dry. She was starting to see the funny side and might have rubbed it herself, but it would have turned into a punch. She tucked her hands into her armpits, sat away from the bed on the plastic motel armchair, and waited.

'No, I didn't have an . . .' It looked as if he was going to be the one to laugh, but his moustache worked over it, and he didn't. 'Your mother. Um. When she stayed with you last year, she came into my office. She . . .' He spread his hands in a pacifying gesture. 'She was worried for you, that's all.'

'She's an interfering witch.'

His panda paw rubbed over his forehead. 'It's a shame to waste the wine. How much is left?'

'Damn the wine. Third time, Matthew. Tell me, or I'm out of here!'

Even in the dusk, she saw him flush. 'A failed relationship which was but a dream of you, darling. Then Jenny, trying to mend things. Now you.' He held his hand out. 'Let's sit by the pool, sweetheart. Give the bed a chance to dry.'

Trying for confidence again? You really have blown it, Matthew. But what do you want from him, Soph?

Not him having a chat with Baba Yaga.

She longed to curl up and disappear entirely. She wanted everything to go away.

The terrible thing about love, or almost-love, is when you know it's the right thing, and it's also utterly wrong. No wonder she didn't like growing up. Or that it took so long to do, as well.

He shrugged, refilled the glasses and stood in the doorway to the balcony.

'All right, sweetheart. We'd better sort this out.'

She huddled on a pool lounger. The cool breeze curled the scents of night time past her.

'How dare my mother try to be my moral policewoman. She can lecture the academic feminists all she likes, but she's no right to try messing round with me.'

'Your hus— ' Matthew stopped with a *phwa* as if he'd bitten something nasty. A moth in his mouth, maybe. 'Russell. She came to warn me how difficult he is to pin down and to take no nonsense, get the divorce moving. I'm sure she was genuinely worried for you, Sophie.' The shape of his hand lifted and fell in the dark.

'I'm not going to raise my voice again because we'd be thrown out of the motel,' she hissed through the darkness. 'Matthew, what happened?'

'She is quite sexy, for a woman her age. It threw me, rather. Um.'

'What happened!' Something scuttled in the jasmine.

'I don't know how she guessed about you and me, but she did. She said I was a complete irrelevance, apart from what legal use I could be for you. She had nothing against you having some amusement, but romantics had to grow up some time and she still had every hope you would. I've never felt more dismissed in all my life. I had to cancel the rest of my appointments and go for a whisky in the Park Royal.' He sounded so offended and confused that Sophie was glad of the dark: it would not do for him to see her struggling not to laugh. 'I wanted to say she should leave us alone and get herself a darn good helping of old-age sex before she carked it. I restrained myself, of course.

'But — ' He stopped to swig some wine. 'A couple of weeks ago, she turned up at the hotel I was at in Chinatown. She completely ignored me. I — um — had Jenny with me. But your mother — Sophie, she was with a young man. Trendy as they come. Forty at the most. He was all over her. Of course he might have been a conference organiser.' He seemed even more confused. 'She looked remarkably like Betty Grable, quite a glow on.' He gulped the rest of his chablis: she heard the gurgle. 'Sauce for the old goose, Sophie. Ah, what the hell, why not?'

The secret life of Mother. No toys for Hugh, but a toy boy for herself. 'Good on her,' Sophie heard herself say before she'd finished thinking about it. 'Good on the tart old crow.'

The various night birds yipped and squalled.

Romantic Mother of the photograph: grow up some time? A glow on?

Sophie remembered Mother dusting the narrow black frame of Dad's picture.

'Dad was in the war?' Smudge asked.

Mum nodded.

Smudge frowned. 'Why?' Her little-girl fingers touched the glass over his eyebrows, down to his secret, handsome smile. 'I like that, Mum. Do you?'

Mum breathed in, short and soft. Sophie looked up and Mum's eyes were shiny, glowing like she might have tears. She put her hand on Sophie's head and tucked Sophie against her. Then she was kneeling down, to soft-bite Sophie's ear, and Sophie soft-bit Mum's. They knelt there hugging, Mum sniffing Smudge, Smudge floating in the warm sweet scent of Mum.

Dad, Mother, Todd. It had been curling at the back of her mind since the first night in the Gothic ruin, the trap Russell had set into which she'd walked so blissfully unconscious, and the weight of which still loomed and longed to squinch her.

I do have standards, she wanted to say, I truly do, though it seems I make them up now as I go along. But what were the rules, with Dad-Todd-Mum? Who wrote the rule book? When did it get written?

The rules. The rules got broken.

The rough head of hair against the light in the hallway as she came awake. The knock again on her door jamb. 'Soph!'

What?

'Wake up, Soph. Y'mother wants you. In the kitchen, Soph.' Todd's voice strange, empty of whatever made it his.

Dr Doolittle and her *Tales of King Arthur* slid off the bed as she pushed the blanket back. Groggy, confused. She nearly knocked the copper magic witch eye off her bedside table, but it rolled safely back.

Todd handed her the dressing gown she kept on the bedroom chair. What? Voices. All right, in the kitchen. She stumbled, blinking and tying her belt, Todd with a hand at her back, and saw the scared face of a young policeman and the patient face of an older one. Something had happened and they all knew. They'd woken her up to tell her.

Mum's skin looked flat, smoothed out by shock: she sat on one of the dining chairs that shouldn't be in the kitchen; someone had brought it in for her.

Todd put Sophie next to Mum like he thought Mum would hold her, but Mum's arms looked dead. Her mouth moved; Mum was telling Sophie, but she couldn't take it in, she didn't have to because she knew.

'He was too quick f'me.' Todd touched Sophie's shoulder for a moment but his hand fell off. 'We were heading for the bus, a quiet walk along the Quay, nice and peaceful.' Todd's big shoulders shook and he was crumpled. 'All of a sudden, a burglar alarm, clattering and shrieking overhead like God's bloody knackers. Christ, sorry, Kathleen, Sophie.'

'Watch your language,' said the older policeman quietly. 'Sir.'

'Your Dad. Jack.' Todd held his hand palm up. Sophie waited. She knew before he said; she pictured it. Dad would have started with a tremble, then a quake, then trying hardest not to move at all, but exploded into movement, a scramble for the nearest cover, so ashamed, so taken over, helpless. Her Dad.

Todd raised his head and looked at her. 'Sorry, Soph. My best just wasn't good enough.'

As simple as this: in the shriek of the alarm, a heavy diesel roaring past as Dad dived for a doorway over the road. Sophie felt the moment splinter. No, it couldn't happen, but it has. He'd been much better lately, smiling at her school report and joshing Uncle Todd for being a nursemaid. She'd seen him kiss Mum on the ear and Mum brush him off but with a wee smile at the corner of her mouth, and it was Todd who did the moping in corners when he thought that no one saw.

But now. A visit to the pictures with his mate. But now.

Mother cleared her throat. 'You did your best, Todd. For years. You did your best.'

'Kathleen, my Katie-Kate,' said Todd. Both of them had a look in their eyes that said so much, that said how much they'd done. Sophie hadn't seen them look at each other like that before.

The young policeman glanced at the older one, and the older one glanced back: his look said, *Son, I've seen it all before, you'll learn.*

How odd that Sophie should notice the policemen when time had stopped on one dark awful splintered moment, but all the same it shook you like an earthquake, whirred by, racing, black, no, every beat of blood in your ears warning soon you'd have to know how terrible, no, how terrible, my Dad.

'You can't wear that.' Mum hung the dress back in Sophie's wardrobe. 'School uniform.'

No use arguing that Dad had liked the dress and smiled when he saw her in it. Put it on, the horrible navy tunic, white socks and brown school shoes. Who cared.

Mum was a widow. People were meant to be crushed by grief, but Mum stood thin and straight. When did Mum grow thin? In one night. She melted to a woman made of bones.

'Todd will do the eulogy,' Mum said. 'No one else. It's the last thing he'll do for us.'

Sophie began to ask what a eulogy was, but words hadn't got far in her over the last few days. *Why* faded somewhere near the top of her throat.

Todd left his pew and stood beside the long dark box. For a touch of time it seemed as if he'd pat it, but his arms went to his sides, thumb on the trouser seam, hands straight. His voice came tattered. Sophie heard things for the first time, but things she'd somehow always known: she also heard what no one ever said, not even Todd at this moment. The battles in North Africa, smoke and confusion under the hard Egyptian sun, the way Jack rescued Todd through tracer fire, shell fire, the burning ammo trucks, smoke, explosion, shrapnel. Little Jack and burly Todd, too big for Jack to lift, you'd think. The injury he didn't tell about, the flaming idiot, but what can y'do? A ripple of understanding through the church then, among the older people anyway. Todd's voice, ragged and strong: skinny Jack, even back home after months of good plain cooking; how Todd had urged, *Get sorted out, mate.* How they met Kathleen, the look in her eyes when she knew Jack had been wounded in action. Jack, good quiet worker, what a good wife Kathleen was, how proud he was of Sophie.

Words, some full, but more of them empty, washed by Sophie in the cave of the church. Dust specks drifted in a ray of sun slanting through some coloured glass, a picture of Jesus as a shepherd and a silly-faced sheep. Jesus and the sheep both had cross-eyes.

If Mum told Todd to leave, if Todd didn't live with them any more, Mum wouldn't have anyone. What would she do? Sophie wouldn't have anyone, either.

They followed the coffin out of the church and Smudge thought, *Goodbye, Dad, goodbye from Smudge,* and stood not blinking while the pall bearers with their RSA badges and their medals slid it into the big black car. Not even blinking in case she missed the last of him. It was like she was floating, a dust speck but so heavy. Like she would faint soon, or had already fainted and there'd only be this moment evermore.

'Chin up,' said Mum standing next to her. 'No silly nonsense, Sophie.'

People shook Mum by the hand. Mum nodded and said thank

149

you, then people nodded at Sophie and said things, so she nodded too. No one expected her to speak, but she bent her mouth so it might look like a smile.

Some girls from school were standing by the blue hydrangeas at the church gate, staring, serious; she was glad they didn't come over, because what would she do? She felt guilty; not that she could have stopped what happened, no one could have stopped it. It had been no use, all this time, when Mum and Todd and Sophie had gone from day to day, moving to a new place when Dad grew too wonky, not saying, never saying. If you said, it made it real. Learning: don't grizzle, no matter how awful it was going to new schools, trying to fit in.

Later, back home, after everyone had drunk their glass of beer or sherry, and the sandwiches and lamingtons had disappeared and so had all the people, Sophie felt as if she were covered by a veil of iron, solid but invisible. The house was like a box they were caught in.

She heard Todd and Mum together in the kitchen. Todd's quiet rumble, 'Now, Kathleen. We won't rush things.' Then sudden, hard, short words from Mum, bricks, blocks, chunks of rubble, *thud* on the iron veil round her.

Sophie put her hand on the wall, to help her move down to her bedroom. Put the other hand over your ear because you don't want to listen. Sophie, you'll be all right, as long as you keep one hand against the wall, the other hard against your ear, your eyes squeezed tight.

She was going to have to go to boarding school, because Mum wouldn't have time any more. Sophie didn't know for what.

But it didn't matter. Home was nowhere now, because her Dad was gone.

Something snuffled at ground level on the other side of the pool fence. The breeze nudged the jasmine, rustling, sneaking through it.

Matthew's lounger creaked as he stood up. 'You've gone quiet. Darling. I know I haven't been straight with you . . .'

Sophie reached for his hand and tugged so he pulled her up to standing. 'Sorry. Just thinking. Children are bizarre.' She had to clear her throat, and disguised it by toppling against his chest.

'Oof,' said Matthew. 'I'll go mad if I lose you, sweetheart. Darling — I have something else to tell you.'

She sniffed his neck but her mind wouldn't play along with her. Why had she felt ashamed when Dad died? Kids are so weird. She hadn't done anything she should feel bad about. She must have sensed the undercurrents. Dad had been — what? Forty, forty-five? Much younger than Matthew. Matthew, who was probably wondering if he'd have to wear his pyjamas tonight. She sniffed harder, the soft skin underneath his ear.

'*Mmph*,' he said now into her hair.

Ah well, he was comforting. That's why she'd picnicked with him in the first place. He didn't push her round, bully in the ways that other people tried to — not as obviously as others, though sometimes he sat and watched her as you might observe a strange new household pet. The pet that cooks.

'I own a piece of land here, Sophie. I want to build.'

She heard him, but God, this was too much for one night. In a skitter of headache behind her eyes she caught a flash of Mother the day of the funeral, motionless as she stared at the old double bed. Another flash of Todd, a frown black across his forehead, filling his car with his gear and heaving his big cabin trunk into a van driven by a mate of his. Sophie asking Mother where he was going, what would his address be? No answer. Todd coming back from the van to stand in front of Mother, great towering man, neither speaking now, another look between them, Todd disbelieving, a shake of his rough curls. Mother with her chin up: she was still smoothed out with shock and grief, but there was another smoothness too, a toughness, confidence.

Todd took one step backwards. Long legs. His strength was no use to him, seemed to confuse him. Big shoulders, stooped. He didn't know Sophie was there. He jerked his arm to the mate in the van, the van drove off, and Todd slammed into his car. The empty street.

'Sophie?' Matthew tightened his grip and jiggled her. 'Building. Here. I've got a clifftop site. Open plan, I thought, with a mezzanine and a big conservatory. We'll have a deck overlooking the ocean.' Under her ear, his deep chest *thumpa-da-thumped*. His stomach complained gently. 'You could design your own kitchen.'

She remembered stealing the photographs a few days after the funeral. She'd found them in a heap by the rubbish tin: Dad and Todd grinning with the clear, eager faces of early war time, and Mother, soft-lit as a movie still, the year she became a child bride, coquettish. Romantic excitement. Three framed photos. The thin black frame of Mum's was broken at one corner.

Sophie smuggled the photographs into her schoolbag. Next day in the park she dumped the glass and backing, and sneaked the pictures round with her till she could hide them safely. They nagged at her, those secret thoughts, past hopes behind their eyes, hidden in her locker with the magic dancing eye during all the frozen years that she endured at boarding school.

'Sweetheart?' asked Matthew. 'You'd like a walk-in pantry.'

The wind off the sea licked with a cold tongue, and there were tiny flying bitie-things about.

'Sweetheart,' Matthew said, 'you're shivering.' He kept an arm wound around her as they climbed the concrete steps to the balcony, past the snuffling gargoyle out for its last sniff and widdle before lights out.

The bedside clock blinked in the gloom, red numbers that reminded her it would more or less be dinner time at home, depending on who was there to eat it (soccer, drama practice, sulks, music, detentions, tantrums) and who was doing the cooking. And *boarding school*, he thought? For *her kids?*

Matthew shut the door. 'Darling. Sophie? I'm sorry I kept it from you. I played it wrong. But God, let's not forget the basics: you and me.' His chocolate gravel voice, the one that shook her marrow.

The gingerbread man was so excited that the vixen could not bear to repress his enthusiasm.

Ah, what the heck.

Matthew was as savoury as anchovies.

But.

He reached for the zip on her dress.

Stuff that.

She reached for the phone. 'What's the area code for home?'

His arms lurched into a grab for the whisky bottle. He turned on the bedside light.

The phone burped at least seven times before Mary Jane said hello, sounding very controlled. That on its own was worrying.

'Don't be — ' Mary Jane seemed to search the dredgings of her brain for what to say next. 'Disquieted,' she almost shouted. 'Don't be. Enjoy yourself. Wherever you are.'

'Why should I be disquieted? Have you heard from Russell?'

'Don't fret at all,' said Mary Jane in her bossiest voice. 'We're absolutely fine. Stay as long as you can. I mean, long as you like.'

'Have you got in touch with Steven yet?'

'Like hell. We visited your mother yesterday. Hugh insisted. I don't think she trusts me with the kids. I told her for the fifty-fifth time that I had to resign from the English Department because I was pregnant. Those were the rules back then, she ought to know, even though she was in another department. By the way, none us will use the outside loo. The bowl is a nasty shade of yellow since you blew it up.'

'What's happening? Have you been driving Hugh to school? Is he happier?'

'Don't fuss. He and I are fine, har-de, you know. Though I can't do midnight horror recipes the way you can. I tried Hugh with "Pygmalion" and he told me to go back to bed. Those young men are still here, you know.'

Matthew's hand came in front of her with a glass in it, offering a whisky. She brushed him away. 'Mary Jane, what about Lisa? How is Rory?'

'They haven't been inside again, so that's something. The *men*, Sophie, not the kids. I'm trying to insist the hairy one has a shower. I tried to make him have a bath as well. I don't think he understands.'

'At home? Our bathroom?'

'He had a perfunctory wash, I think. The handbasin turned ungodly shades of greyish-brown. Hugh was captivated. I gave him some of Russell's clothes, I chucked his out. Not Hugh's, the hairy one's. No one wanted to wash them. The one who looks like a Botticelli has been in and out of the back door like a yoyo.'

'You said they hadn't been inside again.'

'I lied,' said Mary Jane. 'But I can't keep it up. Not — to a friend.' She was definitely hiding something. When it's a friend, you can tell.

'Have they tried to unlock the passage doors inside? Call the police if they do, Mary Jane.'

'Some would say that Botticelli's a fantasy on two legs,' continued

Mary Jane. 'Too pretty for me, though. Intelligent, of course. He's charmed your mother. She fascinates him too. I hadn't realised before, she's archetypal. Phaedra was after her stepson, wasn't she? The crone as *femme fatale*.'

'Mary Jane,' Sophie said loudly. 'You're stalling. Have you heard from Russell!'

'The kids are fine,' Mary Jane shouted.

'Mum!' said Hugh's voice somewhere away from the phone. 'I want to talk to Mum!'

There seemed to be a scuffle: thumps, Mary Jane hissing and a yell from Hugh.

'*Grunt*,' said Rory's voice and added three unintelligible syllables. The pitch and rhythm indicted he was fine, or he hoped she was.

'Mum?' Lisa. God, they must be standing on top of each other like the ass, the dog and the chicken in the fairy tale. 'Mum, it's incredible, I don't think I'm a lesbian after all. I like dresses. Quit that, Hugh, you'll get a turn. Ow! Quit that, I said!'

'Where is Mary Jane?' asked Sophie. 'Lisa, let me talk to her. I can't talk to you all at once.'

'I posted your letter!' cried Hugh. 'What's Returned Services Association? Do they give things back? What are we getting, Mum?'

'Have a good break,' said Mary Jane. 'Don't worry. Oh Christ!'

'When are you coming home?' Hugh shouted in the distance. 'The food's become very disturbing!'

The phone went dead. Sophie slammed it back on the rest and stood biting the side of her thumb.

'Something going on?' asked Matthew.

'Several things, I expect.' She started on her second finger.

'They can manage without you.' He stood, jaw tight, and gestured, whisky glass in hand. 'Take care of yourself. Let me take care of you.' She stopped nibbling and stared at him. 'All right. Sophie. My timing's wrong, that's all. I'm desperate for a quiet life, but you need a chance to think. I'll take you home, sweetheart, and from a distance you'll see how right this place would be for us, how right you are for — ' He sipped the whisky; gulped it rather, for a drop fell off his moustache. 'I mustn't rush you. But we can't go home tonight.'

If he kept his jaw rigid like that, he'd get a headache. He looked angry: rather tempting, truth be told.

'I'll pay my share of the tickets and things,' she said. But how? Not unless the money from the gallery had come through, because you couldn't use your husband's money to pay for a trip with your lover. Could you?

Matthew's face had taken on a purple tinge. He downed some whisky and sat back hard in the ghastly vinyl chair, bottle in one hand, tumbler in the other. 'I had a kitchen consultant lined up.' He looked like an eggplant, definitely angry. Fair enough. It's not as if she were calm as butter either; her own headache was grimacing round a corner of her mind. She'd like to pounce on him and jab her claws in, have them tumble all round the room, and her end up on top.

'I've been a dreamer,' she said. 'My timing's all wrong too. When I was little, I used to have awful dreams till Uncle Todd told me not to be frightened. He said, tell yourself it's a dream and then enjoy it. Because the thing about dreams is, whether they're good or bad, they're sure to be interesting stories.'

'Your Uncle Todd sounds too good to be true. Weird set-up if you ask me. He was probably gay, and probably screwing your mother as well.'

Something hit Sophie in her stomach from inside. She wanted to shout at him, but zipped her mouth closed and snatched up the dirty dinner plates still perching on the counter. She stalked the three full paces you could in the barely adequate space, and clattered everything into the sink. The frying pan was speckled with dead midges. She wrenched the tap on and water splashed all over her. For a moment she stood stiff with anger.

Matthew stood up, a paler purple now, and stared as if he thought she was about to detonate.

She'd come away with him to rest. Time out. To use him as a sex object, how shameful to admit. And look at him. Tall. Barrel-chested. Nice round haunches. Scared of her. Magnificent. And my God, was she lathered up with fury.

She stepped forward and yanked open the first button of his shirt. He looked even more shocked, and stood absolutely still. Very sexy, thank you, yes, that's luscious. She undid his second button. He seemed to realise she wasn't being dangerous. His breathing quickened as he let her undo buttons three and four, work her fingers into his belt buckle and release the big brass button of his Levis. At last he got excited enough to put the whisky down. It had taken him long enough, but then he was nearing sixty, had drunk too much tonight, and had looked scared.

While he heeled his shoes off and hurriedly trod out of his jeans (*adorable*, the way men did that) she unzipped her saturated dress, let it fall to the carpet, undid her bra, dropped that, and turned her back on him. His hands came up and rounded over her; she grabbed them and pressed her nails in. He chuckled deep in his chest, began to rub his foot on hers.

Shameful, yes. Delicious, yes. What, after all, had she come here for? He was so good at this.

Together, sideways, they slid on to the bed and tangled inextricably in all the ways there were to tangle. The nipping on her little toe, the taste of hairy earlobe, the plump and textured bits, firm haunches, scratchy chin, the whiffly moustache, big hands on her heels, and woops! to his earlobes again. How scrumptious, juicy, with the excellent seasoning of rage. Wasn't it lucky that Mother Nature designed a man to be useful, that everything fitted just so?

She wept half the way in from the airport, with tiredness as well as unwanted yearnings for her aging Yeti-panda-man: how dare he be so presumptuous, how dare he turn out to be no better than bloody Russell and so much fun in bed.

When the taxi swung into the drive and she saw the house, her heart plunged further. Bluebeard's wife comes home. Har-de-har. So she can rescue the kids? Or does she still want Bluebeard? At least Matthew's methods of home decorating had points to recommend them.

'I didn't expect you for at least another week.' Mary Jane opened the front door in her gypsy patchwork velvet and a cheated expression. Did she want to be the lady of this manor? For all Sophie cared, she could have it.

Mary Jane hunched down to peer at Sophie's face. 'You look no better than when you went away.'

'Nor does the house.' Sophie heaved her case to the foot of the stairs. 'The taxi driver said, "Rather you than me, love," when I told him this was home.'

With the frayed carpet gone, their voices echoed in the hallway. Lisa and Rory hadn't put Grandma Kathleen's picture back and the fern in the chamber pot was scrawny from not enough light. An anorexic wind rustled the tatters of wallpaper at the end of the corridor where the ladder and the heat gun sat. The locked door still looked thoroughly locked, and that at least she was glad about. She pushed the front door to, and the gloom of the hallway murked about her.

She'd had a nasty moment at the airport when she'd tried to get some money out of the housekeeping account from a cash machine: insufficient funds, it said. She'd have to talk to Russell, damn it. There'd be a message from him by now, she was sure, but she wouldn't show her uncertainty by being the first to mention it. And how do you fight the hand that feeds?

Oh Sophie, you've dug your hole and you might have to fall in it. Unless you can jump over.

What an exhausting notion.

'Coffee?' asked Mary Jane too brightly after just too long a pause.

Sophie opened her mouth to tell Mary Jane about the coffee shop they'd found in Sydney. But she had to try to forget Matthew. No; not *try*, just *do it*. The last thing she needed was a handful of brochures about Swedish kitchen appliances. She still couldn't quite believe what he'd murmured leading up to his last orgasm: *Sophie — ah — like I said the other night — we won't need to — ah! — do this so often when we're marrie . . . ah!* He hadn't seemed to hear a word she'd said: It's over, Matthew. Over.

This was not a great start. 'I am gasping for it,' Sophie said. 'For coffee.' She slid her jacket off, hung it over the end of the banisters and fumbled past Mary Jane, through the dining room and into the kitchen.

Someone had been potting what looked like tomato plants on the bench. Too early in the year, unless you had a greenhouse. Three rows of infant plants in dinky pots with labels. Black seed-raising mix was sprinkled all over the formica. She glanced at Mary Jane, who avoided her eyes.

Sophie filled the electric jug and found just enough coffee beans, not in the usual place which was the freezer but on the shelf with the teabags. The plunger had vanished. Maybe she was so tired she couldn't see properly. The tomato plants didn't look right either.

'It'll have to be instant.' Mary Jane's eyes grazed past the back door. Sophie opened it. The broken plunger pot rested on top of the overfull recycling bin on the back porch. She closed the door and leaned on the bench. The artificial sunflowers smiled vacantly as sunflowers do; she wanted to hit them, but it would have used up too much strength.

'Sit down,' said Mary Jane. 'Have you been taking your pills?' She busied around the kitchen. Sophie's legs crumpled her on to the pyjama-striped sofa. She accepted the mug of instant from Mary Jane. Mary Jane sat at the table, hands squirreled round the mug decorated with fishes. Hugh had bought it the year he'd been into things religious because he thought they were Christian symbols. Rory reckoned they were sperm. Lisa said he'd know.

Sophie looked at the bench, the tomato plants. 'School project?' For which child?

Mary Jane shook her head, shot a look at the window and back again. Russell's helpers? She couldn't mean the plants belonged to them.

The front door opened and a gust of wind pumped through the house. Footsteps came into the dining room at a pace Sophie could only call lugubrious. Too light to be Rory. Hugh or Lisa? She couldn't tell.

Mary Jane eyed Sophie over the rim of her mug. Just as Sophie warned herself to be resolute no matter what appeared, a total stranger walked in and dumped — her? — schoolbag on the kitchen table. Her: it wore a school skirt. Lisa's school. It had Lisa's legs too, the figure eight scar under the knee from the time she'd lammed into a bully on the school bus and the driver had been so impressed he'd driven her home, off his route. But it didn't have Lisa's mane of candyfloss strawberry blonde. It had a shaved scalp like a tennis ball, and a triplet of minute furry pink plaits dangling over each ear.

Mary Jane made a sound like a mew. 'I did make her wait for you to come back before she got her nose pierced,' she said.

'Hello, Mum,' Lisa said.

'Her grandmother's not pleased,' said Mary Jane.

'It doesn't matter what anyone looks like on the outside,' Lisa said, 'it's the force of their personality and their determination to make a mark in the world that counts. Grandma should approve.' She collected the biscuit barrel from the pantry cupboard. 'So, Mum. Have you got yourself a life yet?'

'Her school dean wants a word with you as soon as you're back,' said Mary Jane. Sophie flinched: trouble at school, oh God.

'Be thankful I didn't get it tattooed,' Lisa said. 'But I can't decide between a lemon or an *I love Mum*. Or a Princess Di tiara. Everyone would copy me. Want a cracker?'

Sophie didn't want to speak in case she should weep. All she could think of was her principal at boarding school, a tiny grey woman as nasty as a ferret. Oh, Lisa, Lisa, Lisa . . .

Lisa prepared cheese and tomato crackers, gave three to Mary Jane and four to Sophie. 'I still hate it upstairs,' she said, 'but you two need to talk.' She gathered up her schoolbag and took her plateful of crackers away.

'You're very quiet,' said Mary Jane.

The front door opened again. Another billow of wind. Hugh this time. A normally dirty day-at-school face and normal tousled hair.

'Cool, you're back.' He plumped on the sofa beside Sophie. He seemed fine, on the surface anyway. 'Did you hear about my trial?'

'Ah, they're your tomato plants.' Sophie stole a sniff of his hair and skin: her boy. She felt like weeping still. 'Nature study, how many flowers and tomatoes.'

He wrinkled his nose. 'Nah. That's Dad's stuff from the attic. My trial, Mum. I'm going to be tried. I'm scared. I'm off my food.' He sprang up, plugged in the toastie sandwich machine and fetched bread, cheese, knives and butter to the bench.

So the tomato plants were Russell's stuff. Sophie could not ask.

Hugh carried his toasted sandwich to the back door and looked at Sophie, wide eyed. 'For stealing the rabbit,' he said. 'Angie

Smenovich is the persecutor.'

'Prosecutor.' The correction slipped out, involuntary as a hiccup.

'Heck no.' His eyes grew wider. 'She's really vicious.' He was out and thudding down the steps.

'I suspect he's poignantly in love with her,' said Mary Jane. 'She's a year ahead of him but they combine classes for social interplay. There are two charges against him, in fact. Angie Smenovich is persecuting him for stealing the rabbit, and Buron Smith has brought a second charge of damage to the environment. For letting the rabbit out.'

'But I let it out,' said Sophie.

'Hugh decided to take the rap. Good kid,' said Mary Jane. 'They're all good kids really, Sophie. Even Lisa, though Lord, she looks terrible now.'

The phone rang and Sophie grabbed it before she could think. 'Yes!' she snapped.

'Sorry, but it's me,' breathed a quiet ravaged voice. 'Sorry, can I have another look at that . . . thing. Like, shower? I really feel that maybe this is it.'

Sophie snatched the receiver from her ear as if it was a call from outer space. 'Excuse Me Please?'

Mary Jane grimaced and took the telephone. 'What? Sure. Door's open.' She shrugged as she put the phone down. 'Well, what can you do?'

'It's my house!'

Mary Jane shrugged again. 'That's another thing, Sophie.' Her face twisted as if she was about to say something appalling. 'Not.'

The meaning of the word unfolded slowly.

'Not? Not my house?'

Mary Jane screwed her face up tighter as she nodded.

'Don't be silly. The house has always been in both our names. Russell told me. Matthew said the papers were . . . Russell swore.' *Oh, Sophie, I've missed you, can't live without you, oh God, yes, I promise to spend more time — mmm, yes, Sopheeeee.*

'He lied.' Mary Jane gnawed her lower lip. 'I've talked to him. A terrible phone connection from somewhere very foreign. I refused to read those boring-looking e-mail printouts and we're not allowed in the flat. Oh, Sophie! God, I'm sorry.'

'You can't have been taking your iron pills,' said Mary Jane. 'I've never seen anyone keel over sitting down before.'

Sophie lay with her feet on the arm of the sofa, head down on the seat. The tartan rug was spread across her: *déjà vu*, except with *déjà vu* you only thought it had happened before. This had definitely happened before, about six days ago.

Get a life? Now wouldn't that be nice.

'It's not my house.' Husky with disbelief, faint with incredulity. Mary Jane shook her head.

'Not my house.' Sophie filled her lungs with a shudder of air. 'I need a lawyer.'

'Matthew,' said Mary Jane.

'A property lawyer, you idiot. Matthew is a divorce lawyer.'

'That's the one,' said Mary Jane. 'Russell has gone too far. He needs a damn good shock.'

There was a tap, the back door squeaked open and Excuse Me sidled through with a bundle under his arm. The foetid reek sidled in too. He squinted at Sophie: he was either shy, very short-sighted or the smell of his snaky locks made his eyes water. 'And can I look — you know? The cupboard. In it.'

'A towel,' Mary Jane explained. 'Second shelf. Of course.'

He skirted the table and sofa, and slipped surprisingly quickly into the dining room.

'Lock the door this time, whether you have a shower or not!' yelled Mary Jane. Already his footsteps were padding up the staircase.

'He doesn't know what to call a towel?' Sophie tried to sit up. Her limbs were weighted with shock and confusion. Mary Jane pushed her down and tugged the rug up to her neck.

'It's all that marijuana, his brain's completely smogged. Lord knows how it fits with being a computer whiz. It's certainly played havoc with his verbal skills.'

Two and two made — oh my God. Sophie shoved Mary Jane aside, raised herself enough to see the tomato plants more clearly, and collapsed on the cushions again.

Mary Jane pulled the rug back over her. 'I'm assured that it's not for smoking. The attic's been adapted as a controlled environment — perfect, apparently, till you lot moved in and they could only check it when you were all out of the house. Russell was concerned what you might say, what the kids might do. But, apparently again, there is a problem with who is permitted to know about it. Red tape. Ethics committee. Foundation of Research something. It was a hell of a job keeping the poor things watered.'

Sophie remembered how the electricians had talked about red tape and the attic. Even her thoughts were speechless.

Mary Jane tucked the rug tighter round Sophie and swaddled her arms in. 'I'll do some potatoes.' She cocked her head. 'Bugger that.' From the pantry, she fetched a gin bottle. 'I've been drinking it with water, to make less calories. But bugger that, too; some men like cellulite.' She released one of Sophie's arms and handed her a tumbler with tonic bubbles winking at the brim. 'Cheers.'

At least Mary Jane knew where Russell was. So Sophie could talk to him about all this. She took a gulp of gin — pungent and sour, Mary Jane's brand again — and began to struggle up. 'I'll bury those plants while you get dinner. Then I'm going to phone Mum.'

'Stay!' Mary Jane pointed as if she were training a dog. Sophie did stay, on the sofa's edge, and Mary Jane heaved a plastic sack of potatoes out of the vegetable rack in the pantry. 'The marijuana is part of a double-blind-crossover trial. There's a rare fungus involved and some connection with the psychiatric health of — mollyhawks?' She shrugged again. 'The Botticelli showed me the authorisation. A blue stamp from a government agency, and a scrummy-sized grant from some scientific film commission.'

'So there's money in it.' Though no money in the cheque account this month. 'But marijuana with the kids around? Not even Russell . . .'

'Who cares, really, if it keeps him happy and out of your hair. Though you really need him home.' For once, Mary Jane seemed to realise her own contradictions: she frowned, at any rate.

'Yes, in fact, I'd like him to come home.' Damn, she'd said it aloud. Change tack. 'Mary Jane, I have three children here. I do not want marijuana plants in my house. My house. Because for good or ill, at the moment I am married to that man, whatever the situation might be like if I gather up my wits and strength.'

Mary Jane, potato peeler in one hand, tumbler of gin in the other, lifted a shoulder and sighed. 'I really would phone Matthew.'

Sophie closed her eyes. Thank goodness she'd come home. But home was not her home. Russell had swithered it out of her legal possession. It had to be some kind of oversight, but even so . . . Blood pummelled through her veins again. The thoughtless, lying, egotistical . . .

'Mum warned me! All the work he's got out of me, not just the decorating and the solo mothering while he's been doing his *meanwhile, deep in the jungle* in his shirts with lots of pockets. Rewriting his scripts. Those scientific papers. He's useless with dangling participles. He's long on charm but very short on syntax.' Sophie put a hand over her eyes but it didn't black out the memories. 'Ant farms in the garage. I fed him and five soil scientists soup and stroganoff all hours of the day and night. The car got stolen because we had to leave it in the street.'

'That's when I met up with you again,' said Mary Jane. 'You looked like death walking. You were so starry-eyed about your clever husband, it made me want to puke.'

'Hugh and Lisa did the puking,' said Sophie. 'Three months of gastric upset.'

'Mind you, he won awards for the ant stuff. He is incredibly brilliant . . .'

Sophie thrust the rug off and found her arms flailing, fingers jabbing the air as she was up and storming round the kitchen. 'I am such a fool. Five years of following him round the globe so I didn't finish my degree. Then the babies. Rory and the job up north. Lisa, when I'd signed up for the course at polytech. Hugh, even though the bastard had promised me he'd have the snip. But he vanished into the fiords for a week looking at giant tree ferns, and came back so excited that I couldn't bring myself to sulk.'

She pulled up short and leaned against the fridge, gasping. 'That means I didn't want any of my children, that I thought they were mistakes. That's terrible. No, it's mitigated, surely, by the fact I want them now.' And loved them so much it was like little volcanoes going off inside her. That was one of the dreadful things about kids: no matter how awful they were, you did end up loving them. No matter if you were a bad mother or not, you loved them till it hurt.

It was a hell of a bind. Her children needed a home. This house was not her house until she'd sorted out the legalities. What the hell was Russell thinking of!

Mary Jane was trying to peel potatoes and watch Sophie at the same time: she'd skin herself if she wasn't careful. Sophie grabbed her gin, raised it in a little toast and took another swallow. She lay down on the sofa again and pulled the rug up. Rage wasn't making her feel sexy this time; it made her dizzy and the room tilt to and fro.

Hugh pattered up the back steps, came in and peered into the sink over Mary Jane's arm. 'Oh,' he said. 'You're cooking again.'

'The casserole you liked so much two nights ago.'

'I was being polite,' Hugh said.

'Serves you right, then.' Mary Jane flicked peel at him.

Hugh scrabbled in the pot cupboard for a bowl and scooped the peelings into it.

'The rabbit won't eat peelings,' said Mary Jane. 'Besides, it's long gone. It won't come out of the trees, you know that.'

'It did one time.' He eyed the rows of marijuana plants. 'D'you reckon?'

'Go for it,' said Sophie. The room steadied then tipped around like a carousel.

'That's your father's experiment,' said Mary Jane.

'A boy has to obey his mother. I am a loyal child.'

'You're a pain in the behind.' Mary Jane skewered an eye out of a potato.

Excuse Me reappeared, possibly with fresh clothes on: it was difficult to tell. He smelled just as bad, though he trailed a towel with a corner that seemed damp. It was a luxurious peach-coloured bath sheet, one of a pair someone had given her and Russell for a wedding present (recently). Smiling and blinking, he eased his skinny body through and out. After a moment came the dull thud Sophie had heard before. So that's what it was: the forbidden door to the prohibited flat of the house that was not her house.

She sipped more gin. When the dizziness had become the fuzz of alcohol and not the fuzz of fainting any more, she climbed off the sofa. 'So the rabbit's still around? I hope it has a name now, Hugh.'

Mottled red spread up his cheek. 'Angie.'

'That will sound odd, in the trial,' said Mary Jane.

Hugh bit his lip and managed a skew-wiff grin.

The persecutor and the rabbit. Nice idea. Well, Sophie'd been a rabbit long enough.

'How do I get hold of Russell?' she asked.

Mary Jane waved the peeler at the back door. 'The hairy one will send an e-mail. We can't call him at all. He might call us.'

Walking to the bench was an effort, but Sophie made the distance. 'Here.' She uprooted the marijuana, scattering more potting mix, and dumped the plants into Hugh's bowl. 'Go, rabbit, go,' she said.

'You've destroyed government property,' said Mary Jane.

'If I replanted them, they'd grow. Angie's going to destroy them for me. Scoot!' She tapped Hugh's bottom, and he scooted. 'Are you going to get me another gin before or after I call Mother?'

'Why the devil do you want to talk to her?'

'I'm tired of being fobbed off and fooled by everyone, and ending up doing the wrong thing.' The sob in her own voice shocked her. 'Besides, she told me to.'

'Oh Christ,' said Mary Jane. 'Deep psycho stuff with mothers. Have more gin now. There's another bottle stowed away for after.'

Sophie hung up the phone, clattering it because her hands were shaky.

'She will never do it,' said Mary Jane. 'Your mother won't bring fish and chips around.'

'You heard what I asked her.'

Mary Jane gathered up all the knives on the bench and flung them, clean or dirty, in the drawer and shut it. 'It's a waste of these peeled potatoes.'

'Boil them and we'll have potato salad tomorrow.' Sophie tugged the tartan rug over her shoulders. 'I've got time to see the flat before she gets here. Are you coming?'

'It's not a good idea for you to — '

Sophie glared. Mary Jane shut up, wiped her hands on a tea towel and followed her out the door.

The wind was bitter. How Sophie loathed it. A gust tried to buffet her towards the pine trees; their needles whished and shimmied. Hugh, sitting against a pine, dangled a limp marijuana plant in his outstretched hand.

'Angie. Angieee.' A plaintive call, no beast in sight. Hugh was learning about love a darn sight earlier than Sophie had.

She forced herself to stand as straight as Mother in her mid-life-acquired PhD gown and rapped on the door of the flat. Mary Jane huddled behind her, shivering and trying to get a corner of the rug. She rapped harder.

Behind the door was a rattle and the rasp of bolts. At last it opened, a three-inch gap. She stuck her foot in. 'I'm here to talk to you,' she ordered.

She was prepared for a fight, and would have called the cops if she'd thought she needed to. She would have loved to call the cops.

But the door sprang wide. The angel, smiling, teeth as white as his perfect shirt, spread his arms in salutation.

'Sophie! Mrs Redlove. I'm really not supposed to let you in, but I'm sure we can stretch a point. Russell has been damned worried about the effect on you guys, but hey, the red tape to get through before he could concentrate on family things. You know what it's like before one of his expeditions, the hassle with bureaucracy. But he says, family first.' The angel punched a fist into his other hand like a coach before a rugby game. 'Mrs Redlove, d'you mind if I call you Sophie? It must be exciting, married to a revolutionary thinker like your husband.'

'I wouldn't bother my head about it,' Sophie said and entered Bluebeard's den.

It stank. A long room full of stale body odour and a sickening aftershave. In one very messy corner was a bench with an electric jug, a hot plate with an open can of baked beans sitting on it. Under the bench was pair of muddy gumboots. One saturated running shoe. A mattress with a rumpled blanket. Otherwise, the room was clean, dirt-free: fresh paint, efficient modern fittings, three state-of-the-art computers. Two big office phones. A fax machine spewing sheets covered in numbers. A heating thermostat on one wall, screens over the windows, the latest in strip lighting on the ceiling. Sophie's bath sheet over the back of an office chair. And the room had carpet. New. Cut-pile wool, oatmeal shadings, a hundred and fifty bucks a metre at a guess.

She blinked and looked again. No grime. No cobwebs. A thoroughly controlled environment. Money had been spent, a lot of it. Blood, sweat and tears had been expended here. She could be in another country, another continent, even on another planet. The far wall was covered with a soundproof panel, bolted on.

An *oop* came from floor level.

Excuse Me scrabbled, bottom up, underneath a work station. He peered at her through his matted hair, bared his teeth — an apology? — and wriggled backwards, a cable in each hand.

'You'll get dirty again down there,' she said. His eyes widened, fascinated and aghast.

'Russell got through a couple of hours ago,' the angel said. 'He says I can explain it to you now.'

Sophie inclined her head and waited. Mary Jane hovered, letting Sophie know by little intakes of breath that she was right beside her. A support, a buddy.

As she'd expected, it was a typical enthusiastic expert's explanation: interminable.

Of Russell's many current projects, one had been current for a decade. Tree frogs and entomogenous fungi. He'd made at least three films on the existence or otherwise of an interface between them. None had been shown to more than one small audience of spotty-necked botanists wearing t-shirts that pleaded *Save the Digynia*, which apparently was an in-house joke. But somehow he kept hauling in funding for it, and increasing his stunning reputation for originality. The new computer project, apart from involving these two sidekicks who had abetted his duplicity in luxury while she scrubbed, sanded and painted in the dream house (hollow laughter) next door, concerned statistical work on cellular clocks in a particular kind of mushroom, and how long it took proteins to accumulate and enter the nucleus. There was something to do with an exceptionally complicated form of photography, which was why Russell had found it too difficult to get local funding and had been granted two years' support from an international outfit Sophie'd never heard of and why he was forced to use these less than perfect facilities. (Extremely empty laughter.)

'The job at the university,' she said. 'Was he actually offered it? Did he turn it down? Or did they turn him down?'

'He's too advanced for them,' the angel said.

Which meant, they turned him down. She glimpsed the angle of her head reflected in a blank computer screen and recognised the tilt of grim scepticism as her mother's.

'I bet the local research foundation would be interested in this,' she said, with a gesture at the room.

'It has no actual control,' said the angel quickly. 'Overseas funding, anyway, for this one.'

'But I could have a little chat with it, as to whether someone's a dodgy operator,' Sophie said. 'The scientific grapevine. Useful tool.'

Botticelli-man proved her right by darting to another topic: the marijuana plants were something to do with psychological patterning in, not mollyhawks, but mollymawks: there was an excruciatingly large difference. This was funded locally but not through the university which had decided . . .

The explanation tailed away, which Sophie took to mean that one official hand had not a clue that the other hand was making vigorous signals to *stop it, stop it right away, before somebody goes blind*.

'Yeah, um — frontiers of science — ' Excuse Me spidered off the floor at last and untangled one ankle from coils of cabling. 'Bringing it to the common thing. Man. Person.'

'Why?' Sophie asked.

The men seemed disconcerted. 'It's obvious. People want to know,' said Botticelli.

'B-but — ' Excuse Me's hands waved fitfully, and so did his snaky hair. 'I only do the numbers. Wow. Oh wow. These numbers.' His head swung slowly towards one of the computers.

'Rats loose in the attic,' muttered Mary Jane. 'Mind you, Russell is an international name. He was globally impressive on the cover of *People*. Steven kept it lying round for weeks so he could show off to his friends.'

'Shut up, it was only an inset,' Sophie muttered back. Her strength had begun to leak away again. 'When will you hear from Russell next?' she asked the sidekicks.

Botticelli elbowed the Viking: it looked a spiteful jab to Sophie, but the Viking seemed to find it normal prompting. He found his balance again, dropped his lower jaw and sneaked up to stab a keyboard. Manifold messages flashed across the screen. 'Midday

tomorrow . . . no . . . seven hours from . . . now. No.' The screen
went dead. 'Sorry.'

'That would be the middle of the night,' said Mary Jane.

'We'll be here.' The angel, standing proud. 'The chance to work
with Russell, chance of a lifetime. Eh, Conga?'

''Scuse me,' said Excuse Me. His nose didn't move from the
screen.

'I'm going to send a message back,' said Sophie. 'I'll give it to
you later.'

'We're not to use the funding for personal messages,' declared
the angel.

Sophie was going to fall over any minute and probably be sick
too if she didn't keep a very firm control. 'Have you got a name?'
she asked.

The muscles of his face flickered. Aha, the clever little acolyte
had realised how furious she was.

'Russell hasn't told you?' he said.

'I haven't talked to Russell for weeks, as you well know. Your
name!' Wrapped in a rug like a caterpillar, Sophie didn't expect to
be obeyed. But the angel snapped to attention.

'Damon.'

Damon and Conga. It figured, though she'd rather expected
Tonto and Sancho Panza. 'So tell me about this house. Or is that a
state secret too?'

'Not *state* secret,' said Damon. 'It's just, if anyone hears what
Russell's up to, there'll be objections, or . . . '

'I knew it. The ethics committee.'

'No!' Damon looked as if a naughty little imp had darted over
the ramparts of Heaven and pinched him.

'Industrial — what's it? You know — looking,' Conga said. 'Stuffs
the equivalent of — uh? — Pulitzer for scientific — bugger. Sorry,
spying.' He disappeared under a computer again.

'Thick as a brick pot-head.' Damon's face took on a bitter cast.
'If I wasn't working for Russell, I wouldn't put up with it. But, hey!

No way would I turn down the chance to work on a Redlove.' The seraphic air returned; he clicked his fingers energetically. 'How many jobs are there, these days, for a PhD in mycelial enzymes?'

Sophie couldn't stand the way his enthusiasm made his aftershave more pungent. Her insides were very queasy.

'The house,' she said. 'Explain.'

Damon's eyelashes twitched. 'It's Russell's but it was mortgaged to the — they actually — hey, this is personal detail, you need to hear it from him.'

Sophie turned for the door.

'Sophie!' Botticelli seemed to materialise in front of her, skin radiant with the ardour and dedication she'd seen in the face of a Bellini angel (Gabriel) who appeared in front of poor stunned Virgin Mary and waggled a lily at her: *Tonight you're getting pregnant, kid, great news!* 'He raised money on the house to finance this expedition to the — he's after the source of a fungi that was meant to be extinct, but there are traces in N'zeto.'

'Angola,' said Mary Jane. 'Page ninety-eight of your atlas, B across, 3 down.' Her eyes flicked from Damon to Conga, Conga to Damon, wary but firm.

It would be impossible to cope, if Sophie didn't have a friend like her. Gratitude rose through her, helped her stand straight and quell the coils of invective boiling up inside.

Damon spread his hands. The situation was so obvious, his gesture said: no reasonable person could object now, could they? And Sophie, Mrs Redlove, was reasonable. Of course she was.

Conga snaked up from beneath a computer by a boarded-up window. 'You're a hell of an understanding —' He frowned, momentarily cross-eyed. 'Woman. And you've got things. In cupboards. Helpmeet.'

'It's obvious why Russell's a success.' Damon still gazed at Sophie as if she were the Madonna and, wearing his archangelic toe-peeper red lace-up boots (go look at the painting, it's somewhere in Venice), he'd brought that courier message from God which, these days, would be woefully wrong, politically.

For crying out loud.

Sophie unwrapped the rug enough to tug at Mary Jane. Mother would be here soon.

The side door shut behind them and the bolt slammed. Sophie gulped fresh cold air, the scent of pine trees and wind from the sea.

'What now?' asked Mary Jane. 'What are you going to say to Russell?'

'I haven't got a clue.' Sophie stumbled towards the back door. 'I suspect there's more to this house business than even you know. I have to make it to the ensuite. I am definitely going to be sick.'

HOW LONG IT TAKES AN ANGEL TO FALL, OR HOW LONG IT TAKES A WORM TO TURN

It depends on the distance from Heaven to the other place, or from one end of the worm to the other.

According to Milton, who was meant to be a genius (though Sophie'd only found two of the twelve books of *Paradise Lost* entertaining, in fact had skipped the scenes in Heaven, who doesn't?), Satan took nine days to plummet all the way.

Sophie did not like to be gazed at as if she were the Madonna. Anglicans had never gone much for the Virgin. At the moment, everything she knew about the Madonna had vanished from her head, except for one line in a Christmas hymn which said how terrific God was because he *abhor-or'd not the Virgin's womb*. That's pretty suspect, isn't it? If she'd been chosen because she was the perfect woman, why should anyone abhor her womb? You'd be rotten if you did, not special if you didn't. How could you be born if not from a womb, and who the hell put Jesus there in the first place? Give Soph a break.

These days, if any sensible woman was minding her perfect and virginal business, and an angel popped around the doorpost to announce, *The Holy Ghost shall come upon thee, and the power of the*

Highest shall overshadow thee. Whoosh! Baby time!, the right answer was: *Forget it, creep, go take your medication, what the heck's in it for me?*

So: angel-face and the Viking thought Soph was Holy-Holy because she'd been such a brick for Russell all these years.

Time to fall, indeed; long past time to turn. No more Mrs Goody Two Shoes. Time to stop kneeling at the foot of the resident genius.

Resident? Well, choose your words.

How much more would she, could she take before she'd changed completely from sweetness and light; fallen, turned, transformed?

In some ways, she'd fallen in an instant when she'd learned how devious Russell had been about the house. In others, she'd had one abortive leap and was back for a second go, teetering on the edge of the high dive board, summoning the gumption to hurl herself off, starting with the equally abortive try at having a sexy holiday. Well, ho ho ho.

Satan had plenty of time to contemplate his problem during the nine days' plunge that Milton reckoned on. Satan's problem was really the lack of consensus in Heaven. Consensus between her and Russell? Ho again.

What did the other angels think as they watched their previous buddy go hurtling? *Well, there goes spice. Well, so long, Mister Mischief. Hey ho, let's hang out on the shores of the silver sea of paradise. What say we chuck our golden crowns again, guys, and we'll do it tomorrow as well (whoopee, I don't think), and again the next day. Ooh, your back gives you gip from all that bending. Isn't the weight of your wings hell (oops)?*

What did Satan think during his nine-day fall? *No more Mister Bossy Boots. So long, I'll do it my way.*

But what was Soph's way, what? How long till Russell came rampaging home? Would she withstand, this time, the buckets of urgency and boyish glee, the effect on her of his male sex hormones?

Was it better for the kids if she did withstand it, or if she crumbled and gave up forevermore?

Oh, Satan, help her, help her.

Well, that's one reason she'd called Mother.

She finished being sick, and cleaned her teeth.

A grind of brakes outside, and a car door slammed.

'Dr Briddleton, we presume,' said Mary Jane without glancing through the window.

Trit-trot up the concrete steps. Rat-tat. Remind her, quick: why the hell had she called Mother?

'I'll get it!' Lisa yelled from the stairs.

Mary Jane puffed her lips and sat at the kitchen table. Sophie grabbed the gin bottle and stuck it in the bottom of the pantry behind the onion sack. Her head swooped inside as she straightened up. Her heart would have liked to run and hide in the pantry too.

As they entered, Lisa and Mother didn't look prize-winning family portrait. And Mary Jane was right about one thing: Mother hadn't brought fish and chips. Just as well, because Rory wasn't home yet

'What are you going to do about this?' Mother pointed to Lisa's scalp.

'She can't do anything.' Lisa sulked to the fridge and yanked it open.

'She'll get freckles on it,' Mother said.

'Then glory be to God for dappled things,' said Sophie. Mother's head tilted a little, as if she might be thinking that was funny. 'If you're looking for tea, Lisa, it's Mary Jane's special casserole.'

Lisa brightened. 'Excellent. Hugh hates it. So do I, but I'm going veg.'

'Pardon?' Mother squinted.

'Eat nothing with a face,' said Lisa. 'See, I can't be an anarchist yet, I still need my mum. I'm kind of disappointed. But there's other ways to make political statements.'

Mother sat down, holding her handbag on her lap. 'I was never allowed to be an impulsive child,' she said. 'I made up for it later and made some big mistakes as a result. But don't we all.' She eyed

Mary Jane's glass in the middle of the bench. 'I had a wine with lunch. Is that gin, or something for indigestion?'

Mary Jane retrieved the gin from the pantry, thrust a glass into Mother's hands and began to cube a slab of beef.

'So what kind of political statement is that hair?' Mother poured for herself. 'I'm interested.'

'Actually,' said Sophie, 'I've got something more serious to worry about than anybody's shaven scalp. Besides, I like the little cat tails.'

Lisa grinned.

Sophie's hands had begun to wring themselves together: she straightened them so she wouldn't look too nervous. 'Mother, I've just found that this house isn't in joint ownership. Russell promised me it was. I still don't know where he is. He's been growing illegal substances in the attic, though he calls it science. I have to do something.'

'I said you should have gone ahead with the divorce.' The surface of Mother's gin gave a quiver, just a faint one.

'I've got the children to think about. I've mucked them about so much. What's best for them?' Sophie badly wanted to snap the words but forced them to edge out smoothly. But she knew — oh how she knew! — that asking Mother's help had been a very bad idea. 'I mean, you and Dad had problems but you always managed, really.'

Lisa's eyes were round as dinner plates. Mary Jane paused mid-chop.

Oh, Sophie, bad idea. Hey, Soph, here's a brick wall, let's bang your head against it gently for a while. Her throat hurt, from being sick in the ensuite and also because of asking for Mother's help when Mother was sitting like a disconcerted effigy from Egypt, gin in hand instead of a ceremonial flail.

'And Mary Jane, I don't know what's up with you and Steven, but basically you're happy, right? There's no one else to turn to but you two.'

Mary Jane clattered the knife into the sink, pressed both hands to her face and gulped noisily. 'Mother-daughter, one on one?' she suggested with the brightest smile. She yanked at Lisa and left the kitchen.

Lisa pulled her fish-bottom face and followed. The slant of her shoulders said, *Grown-ups!*

Mother took a sip from her glass and put it on the table. 'You don't look any better than before you went away. Not much of a holiday, then.'

Sydney. Chinatown. Matthew, and Mother visiting his office. 'Bits of it were very good.' Sophie sat down across from Mother. Please, Soph, get it right, you haven't asked her help for years. 'But you had a good time, when you were away, Mum?'

Mother glanced at her with a tiny frown.

'I hope you did, actually.' Sophie rested her head on one hand. 'Oh, Mother, it's a mess. What am I going to do? I can't be content with just some gadding.'

Mother picked up her handbag. She looked at the catch as she clicked it open and closed, open and closed.

'Mum. Mary Jane must have told you about the two men in the flat.' Thank goodness she'd been sick already. She held back the sting of tears. 'I wanted to make my marriage work. I don't know if I can or if I still want to. Mum, what can I do?'

'The problem is. . .' Mother's brow knitted. *Click*! went the clasp on the handbag. *Click*! 'Well, you just decide, and stick to it. Good heavens, that's what men do. Sophie, I said we all make mistakes. I mean, look at me, healing the wounded hero: what a let-down. But if you make your bed, then you simply do what it takes to keep things on an even keel. You meet your responsibilities.' She must have had more than one wine at lunch, her face had flushed, and she didn't always use so many clichés. Mother took the glass again and sipped. 'Do you invariably have gin in the house?'

Sophie began to speak, though she had no idea what she would say. But after another mouthful Mother was on a fast horse, overriding like the dickens. Harpy time, though harpies don't ride horses: they've got their own moth-eaten wings to whizz around on.

'*Tch*, Sophie, I don't know about you.' Another swallow of gin: the flush was fading. 'Your daughter's gender expectations are thoroughly scrambled, Hugh is wandering round outside without a coat and, from the glances you've given the clock, it's obvious you haven't got a clue where Rory is. If you'd learnt from me, and you had plenty of opportunity to do so before you went to boarding school, yours would be a well-run household. The dinner would be cooking, and everyone would sit down at 6.30 sharp. We'd all know where we were.' She set the empty glass down with a bang. The pinched hiss became an exasperated purr. 'But I have to say, I'm pleased you're asking for my help at last instead of simply flying off the handle.'

Sophie felt as if something bumped her sideways. 'Yes,' she said, 'we all knew where we were. Dinner at 6.30 sharp. A normal happy family? Dad, hardly able to eat but still wanting to dive headlong into his plate; Todd rattling off cheery conversation to hide the vibrations in the air between the three of you.' The hiss was in her own voice now, and God, did it feel good. 'There's more to being a good mother than placemats and folded napkins and packing your daughter off when you had no time for her. There is more to a good male-female relationship that picking up a hot little toy boy in Chinatown. You hardly seem to practise what you preach, oh sorry, lecture.'

'You've been speaking to your lawyer friend.' Mother's voice was like a vege knife; the skin around her mouth was white, compressed.

'I had a hot time myself, which did me not an earthly ounce of good.' Sophie tried to calm down before she shuddered into open frantic tears. 'Mum, what can I do?'

With a jolt, she realised Mother's eyes were filled with tears as well. For a shiver of a moment it seemed she might give Sophie a hug. But she tucked the handbag under her elbow, stood up and walked to the back door. 'I'll say it again. We all make mistakes. I accept that. There's no point in regret.' She picked up Mary Jane's gin and downed it. 'But let me tell you this. Old age is the last chance you'll have to whoop it up and not have anything on your conscience.' Mother's voice quivered. She opened the door and was gone into the dark.

Rage pushed Sophie to the back verandah. 'What help to me is that? I learned to be a good mother all right, but not from you. It was from watching Uncle Todd!' Mother's dim shape turned on the path that led to the front of the house. Sophie stumbled down the steps. The southerly whined and grizzled in the pines. 'It's a pity you didn't learn from him too,' she shouted. 'Poor Todd worked like a demon to make you happy. Why the hell? Was he sweet on you? He carried a torch for you, didn't he? Are they the coy clichés you used in those days?'

The side door opened and a wedge of light shone over the barren back yard. Mother continued to walk backwards to her car.

'I didn't have a chance to say goodbye to him,' Sophie screamed. 'Where did he go when Dad died? Where is he now? Where's he buried, then!'

'The man made some impudent assumptions.' No quiver in Mother's voice now. 'They do, of course, I'm satisfied that it's genetic. Next time you buy gin, make it Beefeaters. That stuff you've got in there is kerosene. It can't be good for you.'

She turned and disappeared.

Sophie's fists balled up and pressed into her stomach, but just as she was on the edge of weeping she sensed someone behind her: the angel, Damon, in the wing of light. After a moment, he shrugged and vanished too. The wedge of light closed up and was gone.

Her legs were soft as jam. She took hold of the rail to pull herself up the back steps, and two male shapes came out of the pines and whirled towards her. A short one waltzing with a hunchbacked tall one. Hugh, and Rory home at last. The hunch was Rory's backpack.

'*Mmgh*,' said Rory. (Hello Mum, love you, missed you.) She patted his shoulder: broader than when she went away.

'Are you all right?' she asked.

A deeper *mmgh* was all she got, and she couldn't interpret this one.

'Angie didn't come,' Hugh said. 'Those plants tasted awful, anyway. I'd hate her to be sick.'

Sophie shooed them inside and followed. The warmth of the kitchen soothed her chilled face. Please don't let fungi-influenced marijuana plants affect ten-year-old boys, she prayed. Please don't faint again, and remember to take your damned iron pill.

The beginnings of a meal, deserted by Mary Jane, lay like a still life on the bench: chunks of blade steak streaked with fat; peeled potatoes with most of their eyes left in; an onion with a tinge of pale green mould, the palest green that ballerinas might be draped in if they danced the Wilis in *Giselle*.

'Anyhow, I feel sick,' said Hugh.

'You do not,' Sophie said.

'It's hunger,' said Hugh. 'Do one of your recipes, Mum.'

Mary Jane shut the dishwasher and turned the knob. 'I didn't mean you to end up cooking but I couldn't stop bawling.' Her eyes were still red-rimmed. 'That was a dreadful piece of steak, how come you made it so delicious?'

Sophie huddled on the sofa, frozen though the heater was on high. 'It's the cast iron casserole. Black olives would have helped, but you ate them while I was away.' Her eyes would hardly stay open: if she stayed here much longer she wouldn't be able to get up.

Mary Jane seemed edgy. She chose the other end of the sofa and rested her hands on her stomach. 'Time to think about a message to Russell?' Her folded hands twitched.

Sometimes, the best thing to do was nothing. Like with a casserole, leave it to simmer. Was that what Sophie was doing, or was she being wimpy? Was the best message none at all?

But how else could she find out when the cheque account would fatten up again? How could she get her name on the ownership papers for the house? She was behaving like those incompetent generals in the Boer War who pretended everything was hunky dory because they couldn't face the truth about their limited talents and resources. She was frozen all right, physically and emotionally.

'So don't answer,' said Mary Jane. 'You're a mixture, these days. You're much more like your mother, if you'll pardon me for saying so.'

How horrible it was when scales fell from your eyes. How painful, growing up. The later you did it, the harder and deeper the pains. 'Mary Jane, forgetting your affairs for a moment because you don't seem to want to talk about yourself, is it worse to be unfaithful, or worse to lie and cheat like Russell's done?'

Mary Jane's face writhed for a second as if it too wanted to run and hide with the full gin bottles in the bottom of the pantry. Which meant Sophie had behaved the worst. She was the one who'd been unfaithful. She was the one who'd walked out on the kids.

Guilty as charged.

'You're doing fine.' Mary Jane looked as if, against her will, she might even believe what she'd just said. 'It's complicated, though. Hell, I'm reduced to stating the obvious. Shall I stay around for a while — um — to make sure you're okay?'

What a landslide of relief. 'I've been rotten to you, so selfish, and you're being marvellous.'

'I'm possibly trying to go back to Steven,' said Mary Jane.

'Pardon?' Sophie asked.

'It was a terrible mistake, that last affair. It was very short. I promise it is absolutely over, but Steven did find out. He had been — what shall we say? Oh dear. Very limp on it for a while. And learning about the younger man did his ego zero good, as Lisa might have it. Abominable squared! I mean, he was abominable in a way you would expect at first. But I just could not believe what happened after he'd thought about it for a while.' She wiped her eyes and nose on the hem of her sweater. 'I still can't talk about it. We've finished that bottle. Damn and blast. Kathleen was right, it isn't very good gin either. I heard her shouting.' Her shoulders shook and a series of wails escaped her, each one longer and involving more of her body. 'Damn!' She curled up like an armadillo. 'I should go back to him. I might. Tissues! Tish-issues!'

Sophie tumbled off the sofa and grabbed a tea towel, only slightly used.

Mary Jane mumbled a wet thank you through the waffle-weave.

At last she looked up with little red eyes. 'I came to stay because I wanted to be sure you were all right. I hate this. Is everyone's marriage a screw-up? Oh, Sophie, you deserve to be happy, you and Russell.'

'Poor Steven,' said Sophie. 'Poor Mary Jane. It will all settle down. Just be here, that's enough.'

But happy? Oh dear me.

THE VERY BIG MISTAKES

Once upon a time, there was a little girl. She had a pretty mummy who wore clean aprons, and a daddy with shiny black hair. He kept his soldier medals in a wooden box in the wardrobe. The little girl used to search it out and look. Once her daddy found her looking, and he made a choking sound and sat on the big bed where he slept with mummy and held on to the edge and wouldn't move until the mummy phoned the little girl's uncle to come around and help.

Then the daddy and the uncle sat under the tree tomato, grunting man grunts and having a beer, and the mummy was pleased that the daddy was better, even though she stayed in the kitchen. The little girl tried to help the mummy with the dinner but got her hand slapped for wanting the lickings from the pudding mix. So the little girl stayed out of the way and truly everyone was happy. The sun shone down, and the sky was blue.

The uncle brought the little girl a guinea pig who very soon got fat and had three dear little piglets.

Well. The mummy and daddy and uncle said they were dear little piglets. That made the little girl cross because she had seen them come out of the mummy guinea pig's bottom, and that was a mess and an accident, and someone said once that a baby was an accident. The little girl didn't ask which baby, because a worm in her tummy said don't ask that question, Smudge, and don't remember which someone said it, either.

Anyway, the mummy went hissy when there were messes, and

the piglets must be a mistake because they were squirmy and bald like white grubs, not like guinea pigs at all. Besides, there couldn't be babies without a daddy guinea pig as well as a mummy one.

There wasn't a daddy one.

And it wasn't like Baby Jesus either because he had God and Mary and, besides, Joseph was around, and three wise old men, and plenty of shepherds, and an innkeeper.

The little girl was angry that people tried to trick and fool her. She tried to say how wrong and mean they were. They laughed.

That made her cross. Really truly big, fierce cross.

So cross and mad that she put the squirmy bald things down the toilet.

Eugh. Pooey. Eugh!

So there.

But then the little girl went and cried, in the bottom of the hall closet with all the smelly shoes, where no one saw at all.

Then the uncle came to stay all the time, and things were really happy. The uncle took the daddy to work each day and brought him home each night. The mummy kept everything clean and there was plenty of food. Sometimes the mummy was curly pink smiles, but sometimes she was thin-mouth, you just never knew, and sometimes she threw books across the room. When the mummy wasn't gadding, she listened to music and talks on the radio, and read library books that made her chuckle and chew her nails and write things. When no one was looking, she danced (but the little girl peeked). And as long as everything was quiet, everyone was happy.

So the little girl learned to be quiet, but she watched the uncle and the daddy do their man walk, strutting with their knees turned out, chests braced and their big hands curling loosely but so tough. She sneaked into the long grass under the grapefruit tree where they couldn't see. *Good day for it. Yep. Stone the crows.* It was like dogs or cattle-beasts she'd seen on the farm one time, noises to show the other animals they were there. When she came out from hiding and they cuddled her, their hearts went *thud-thud, thud*, and she loved to see them springy in their knees and the way their arms had bulges and went crisp like ropes when they showed how strong, how strong.

The little girl grew and grew, though she was smaller than most people in her class at school, and she was pale and curly blonde, not like her shiny dark-haired daddy and her brown-haired mummy who had such pink cheeks. But no matter how big she grew, she must have stayed stupid, because she only looked at what she saw. She didn't see what was underneath. Because how could people be upset underneath when the mummy wore aprons like in all the story books, and the daddy grew carrots in the garden, and there were heaps of roast potatoes and spicy cakes with icing and you had paper dolls to play with?

Being married and being a mummy and a daddy meant being happy and two people sleeping in the same bed with plenty of food on the table. That was the easiest thing to think.

If you thought that, you didn't think, and that was really easy.

Mary Jane sat up, scrubbed her eyes with the tea towel and blew her nose on it. 'I did want to see you were okay, you and Russell. But staying with you was meant to be a boost to me as well.' She gulped. 'To help me close the door on my past. Get over it. Oh, God.' She wailed briefly, though her nose woffled as if she remembered something. A particularly juicy young male lettuce. That might explain why she seemed traumatised. It could be awful, baring your body to a younger man if you're nearly fifty.

Sophie tried to warm her hands on the heater. 'You almost warned me off an older lover. So young ones aren't much chop either. Are you going to tell me who it was?' And how much younger, that was the unaskable question. Or how *many* younger ones there were?

Mary Jane yanked a sepia curl down over her forehead like camouflage. 'Honestly, Soph, I'd recommend celibacy if it weren't such an inactive alternative.' Another sob wobbled her throat, but she sniffed hard and a Mary Jane smile flowered bravely. 'But the other thing's so wearing, now I'm older. My vertebrae can't take the strain of holding my stomach in, let alone those acrobatics.' She shoved the curl back and began to examine another from over her ear. 'On a mattress or wherever. But some men do like cellulite.'

Lovers — *tcha*! All Sophie wanted was the happy-ever-after rosy glow. This enormously cheated feeling had hardened like a bruise, deep down inside.

Mary Jane let out a whiffly sigh. 'Floors are the worst.'

'Pardon?'

Mary Jane was hotting up, at least; a little daring made her cheeks glow. 'That's what gets me. Not mattresses; the floors. Why do men think it's sexy on the carpet? Apparently passion's meant to dull your senses to facts of life, like carpet burn, or skidding on the parquet so your head ends up bumping on the skirting board. Or the kitchen cupboard.' Mary Jane glowed like a naughty teenager.

'Har-de-har?' Sophie knelt on the floor and pressed closer to the heater.

'When you're scooting over the lino on your back, it dulls you to what else is going on. But you can't tell them. Think of the wound they'd get on their ego. More lasting than any abrasion on your own rear end.' She sighed. 'But oh, he was unflagging. Gorgeous. Just like chocolate. But I'm giving that up too.'

'At least my one old lover had some respect for his knees.' *We won't need to do this so much when we're married.* Sophie still could not believe he'd actually said it.

She glanced at the clock but she'd reached that pitch of tiredness when your eyes refuse to take things in. 'Russell can be a carpet caveman too, when he gets back from an expedition. All Iron John and inner child. Lovely, but is it worth it?' Maybe, if she still loved him. Did she? The bruise as hard as ice.

Mary Jane didn't look too pleased. Sophie can't have been sympathetic enough, but God, consider the circumstances. She checked again that the heater was on high.

There were several moments of uncompanionable silence, punctuated by the clacking of the dishwasher. Not like the silences little Soph had listened to, between Dad and Uncle Todd. Those had been rich with significance, punctuated with code phrases, *Got to stick with y'mates*, like bits of walnut deep inside a pudding. *Good day for it. Yep*. Like firm buttercrust pastry that, when you'd bitten it, disclosed sweet apple and the pungency of cloves. Smudge had tried to do the same with her friends: *Good mate, yep*. But the little girls laughed and went on the swing boats without her.

Her head jolted; she'd nearly fallen asleep against the heater.

Someone came up the back steps. Someone knocked. Mary Jane jumped and wriggled an eyebrow at Sophie. Sophie shook her head: her heart thumped like a jack hammer. Someone knocked again. She stayed beside the heater. The very best message was none. Was this revenge? Revenge is a dish best eaten cold, the saying went. Oh, she was cold enough tonight, but that was all.

After a few moments the handle turned, but Sophie had locked the door hours ago. 'Just a tick,' she called. At last, she unfroze her knees and opened the door.

'Russell,' said Damon. 'Russell's on the phone.'

'The phone that I didn't know about?' Sophie asked. 'Your line or Conga's?'

'He wants to talk to you.'

'If he's near a phone, he can call me here,' said Sophie.

'It took him hours to make this connection.' The sentence popped out of Damon, each syllable pure disbelief. Angel Gabriel, aware now, *Cripes! the damsel has an option*.

'You can pass on any news.' Her voice fluttered.

She shut the door. A pause, and footsteps walked away. She shoved her hands in her armpits so she wouldn't wrench at the knob and hurtle out.

'Russell will be very puzzled.' Mary Jane seemed close to tears again. 'When I talked to him, I said you'd give him merry hell. He didn't want to talk to me; he was almost rude, which is awful when he's usually so charming. That hurt me. Not that it should.' She shrugged. 'Although. Oh God, Soph. Men.'

'You said he was in Gambia three nights ago.' Sophie's stomach knotted with nerves. 'Is he still there, d'you think?'

'Maybe Boffa.' Mary Jane's lower lip trembled. 'Then Grand Bassam. Moving towards the mouths of the Niger on the crease between page ninety-five and ninety-six. It's going to be more and more difficult to get in touch with him and vice versa. Even if he is still in Gambia. It's such a skinny country, did you realise?' She seemed very worried. It was nice to have someone worried about Sophie.

Footsteps came running up the back steps. Somebody knocked briskly on the door.

'Sophie, it's urgent!' called Damon. 'He insists!'

Sophie waved at Mary Jane vigorously for help, which made her head ache.

'She's off to bed!' Suddenly, Mary Jane was screaming. 'She's on medication! The pills are huge! She must not be disturbed! Good night!'

Thank God for best friends. The great white fungi hunter could take care of himself. But what was Sophie doing? Burning bridges. Biting the hand that holds the chequebook.

Pause. Footsteps ran down the back steps.

'Nightcap?' Sophie asked like a little explosion.

'We've had too much gin,' said Mary Jane. 'So it's brandy and hot milk. Sophie, you should have gone to bed hours ago. You look like even worse shit than when you came home this afternoon.'

The children were asleep. They had been remarkably good. Homework, no grizzles, then bed. They sensed there was a crisis, trusted her to deal with it, and were keeping out of her hair. Which, with a nasty shock, reminded her that she had to check with Lisa's school tomorrow about the shaven head. She'd try to make appointments with all their schools at last, though she dreaded what she'd find.

Sophie hiccupped, changed into her nightie and fell into bed.

Mary Jane, in her green chenille with the crown of her hair sticking up like a duck's quiff, brought the hot milk in, and brandy.

'Love's a sort of safety device with your kids,' said Sophie, so tired she could hardly hear herself. 'It kicks in just when you need it, like that dead man's rudder they have on trains. Good old Mother Nature knew her onions. As long as I'm looking after the kids, I'm looking after me. Am I? Am I, Mary Jane? I'm terrified the kids are really unhappy. Lisa. Her dean. Oh, God.'

'You're squiffy enough without this brandy.' Mary Jane curled on the cane chaise-longue under the window and eyed the queen-sized bed, the dais. She raised her glass and sipped. A sharp sigh, more like a sob, came out of her, and a line cut between her eyebrows.

Sophie wanted to tell her she was marvellous but the right words wouldn't come. She tried to relax, just to enjoy companionship in silence. To leave things be, like men did. Yep. Har-de-har. Yep. Yep.

'This is the girls' school?' asked Mary Jane. Sophie gave a jitter, meaning yes. 'I'll stay in the car. Paint my nails.'

Fine by Sophie. Mary Jane had insisted on tagging along, but there were times when friends couldn't help. Still cold and hurting, as nervous as a child again, she walked along the main corridor to find the dean's room. It echoed, just like boarding school.

She remembered the ferret, oh Lord, sarcastic thing. Even the tallest girls had been terrified of the tiny grey headmistress. *Gels! Who rang the bell for earthquake drill? Though need I ask?* Lined up in the hall, the ferret's little face patched blue and black with light from the ornamental window as she stared Sophie right in the eye. Mother's name in firm gold letters on the walls around her, three times; count them, three: *Scholarship Roll. Duxes of the School. Head Prefects.*

The escape had been that Sophie grew to like the learning part of school: a release from the gloomy walls, the long dormitory, the misery of being cast into nowhere, ditched like an *eugh pooey* worthless guinea pig.

Feeling nauseous, she knocked on the dean's office door.

But the woman, no taller than the full-grown (still small) Sophie, clucked like a Buff Orpington when she saw her and stuffed her hands into the pockets of her long woollen cardigan. 'Goodness me, Mrs Redlove, you could easily have phoned for a chat, you didn't have to bother coming in.'

Sophie's heart dived round and up like a battered kite in the grip of the wind.

'Sit down, sit down. I did want a word, mainly to reassure you, Mrs Redlove. Some parents get upset about the hair, but we've got several little baldies at the moment.'

She opened a cabinet and found Lisa's file. 'Good marks in French and maths. Not terrific, though solid enough. She's doing fine.'

'What about friends?' Sophie asked. She knew Lisa had new ones, though she hadn't brought them home. But were they real friends? Sophie'd been so sit-in-the-corner at secondary school, except for the times she'd exploded into wickedness. Of *course* she'd called the earthquake drill, and five in the morning was obviously the best time to do it. She'd glued the dustbin lids on too in the hottest months of summer, and decorated the prefects' clean fawn gloves: question marks in indelible ink; ban the bomb signs; and pictures of a fat pig's bottom (try it: a circle, two fat stumpy legs, wee triangles for ears, and a curly tail right in the middle). That kind of thing had got her friends, if friends were what you called people who liked naughty little rebels who popped up now and then.

'Plenty of friends,' said the dean as if she could read Sophie's scrambled memories. 'They seek her out. Nice girls, the lot of them. She's a completely normal teenager. We ignore the hair or lack of, Mrs Redlove. If you make a fuss, it only makes them worse. They get so annoyed when we ignore them.' She spoke as if she sat in front of the fire with her slippers on. Sophie's eyes filled up with tears.

'She said something about a tattoo,' she said in a stifled voice.

The woman looked amused. 'I threatened to show her mine if I found out she'd got one. It works like magic, drives them nuts. They don't know whether I have one or not.'

'Do you?' Sophie asked. Where?

The dean laughed. 'And how are your sons? Brazening out the change in schools, or giving a glimpse of their marshmallow insides?'

Sophie managed a smile. 'I'm going to find out, I hope.'
'Sensible.'

'What if I have to move Lisa?' She hadn't meant to say it.

The dean tipped her head to one side. There was a warm and dusty smell about her. 'We'd hate to lose her. As they say, don't sweat the small stuff. Save it for big issues, dear.'

But it was all big issues. She was in a trap again, like school had been. No matter how well she'd done, no matter how she'd fought and banged the sides, Sophie had been stuck there. Stuck there. Stuck.

Mary Jane finished her nails while Sophie stopped at a cash machine. In a spatter of rain, a tug of wind, the chilly green message still flashed at her. *Insufficient funds.* The credit card was nearing its limit, too. She would have to visit the bank. Later. She would have to talk to Russell: pain moved in her like an ice floe, crushing and hard.

She shivered, and drove on to Rory's school. She went through two orange lights, clashed the gears, and didn't so much stop the car at last as stall it.

'You're not leaving me behind again like a sack of old potatoes.' Mary Jane was out of the car while it was still jerking.

'Make up your mind,' said Sophie.

Mary Jane didn't hear, or took no notice. It was irritating how she led the way into the foyer. *Excuse me*, Sophie wanted to say, *whose children are we worried about?* She felt like a rag doll, the last best doll with the squashed head, the one from the bottom of the toy box that she'd hung with a string noose on the grapefruit tree shortly after the horrible episode of the *eugh pooey* pigs.

Bloody Mother. Hell, it had been all right for her to take off whenever she'd got fed up with things, and then dump Sophie into boarding school. But none of it was right for Sophie. If only it were a different universe where the sins of the mothers were not visited upon the children.

These corridors resonated too, to footsteps, commands, thuds and suddenly, from somewhere up a wide polished staircase, a line of melody from a pure tenor voice.

And pestilence with rapid stride bestrews the land in death.

A door flung open just in front of Sophie and Mary Jane, and Rory's principal stuck his head out. He seemed startled. It might have been his permanent expression. He did up one button of his suit jacket, invited them in and offered Mary Jane a chair as if he thought she could be Rory's grandmother

With that nice full frontage, she'd make a good granny. Kiddies like grannies with a frontage, and plenty of women were grandmothers by the time they were late forties, though not too often with grandsons of sixteen. Oh, Mary Jane might have overstayed her welcome: Sophie was being inconsistent too.

She brushed her hair off her face, hoping it would wipe away the effects of last night's brandy and the annoying headache which had come to say hello again. All it did was to show the tremor in her hands.

The principal settled into his high-backed chair. Sunshine fell through a leadlight on to the carpet. She caught a whiff of foot odour: years of adolescent boys in front of the principal's desk.

The man clasped his hands across his chest, but then bobbed forward in his chair and frowned. 'You're not worried about Rory? No, no no. The staff can hardly keep up. I'm getting a lot of amusement at their expense; bad of me, I suppose, but there you are. He grabs everything we throw at him, we're delighted.' He smoothed the air as if he were patting a dog that had fetched him the paper.

Again Sophie remembered the ferret as she'd handed over Sophie's Fifth Form prizes. The grey acerbic face. *First in English and Science? Are you sure you didn't cheat? Mind you, you are your mother's child,* the eyes had said. Sophie had been sure it was all an embarrassing mistake. When they'd told her she was Dux, she'd nearly cried with fright. But all she had done academically was grab everything they threw as well, even when she'd known they didn't like her.

'Would you mind if we put him in a higher maths class?' asked the principal. 'Takes after his father, does he?'

'God forbid!' said Mary Jane. 'Sorry. Forget I'm here.'

The man pushed his glasses higher up his nose and squinted at Sophie, even more startled, as if he had in truth forgotten Mary Jane and wished he hadn't been reminded. Sophie's white-knuckled hands seemed to astound him further. 'Any problems, Mrs Redlove, um, please come straight to me.'

'I might not know if there are problems,' Sophie said. 'He doesn't say.'

'Of course not. He's a boy.' The man gave a bark, presumably mirth, then came out with a sympathetic smile. 'Mothers generally know if there are problems.'

Mary Jane rattled her bracelets as they walked back down to the car: the noise spiked Sophie's nerves.

'You'd better calculate when Russell could arrive,' said Mary Jane. 'I'd be right out of there. Give him a shock, like I said.'

'If your physios would come through with my hard cash, I would definitely do something.' Maybe. Leave Russell — again. Make a mess of things — again. How many times could you lie down in front of a bulldozer and expect to bob up with your limbs intact and functional?

'My money's come,' said Mary Jane. 'Yours must be there by now. I'm only saying be assertive.' But her eyebrows did a crochet stitch of doubt.

Who knew if Russell would arrive or not? And, if he did, after a particularly successful expedition — the charm, seductive energy. It was hard to take a breath, she felt so pulverised.

She scratched the key into the ignition. Hugh next, her little one, her pet abomination. *And Mum walked off, quick, quick, and didn't look back for a wave . . .*

But after visiting the primary school, of course she'd have to go on home. Where else to go but home to the wardrobe filled with lovely oversized clothes, to Bluebeard's sidekicks through the wall? Home to the weight of the house which was and was not hers. Home, to wrestle with this time of psychological plague like Jacob and the angel wrestled, night-long, hours and hours.

Sophie found a parking space and rested her head on the steering wheel. She hadn't been able to make an appointment with the deputy; she'd have to take pot luck.

Mary Jane twitched a shoulder and her bangles clashed like warning bells. 'Soph? Is Matthew still an option?'

'Do shut the hell up,' said Sophie in an undertone. She wasn't sure if the angel touched the hollow of Jacob's thigh or the other way round. The King James Version wasn't very clear on pronouns. What the devil was that angel up to, anyway? But she wanted very much to go off all men, the hollows of their thighs and their brains included. She opened the driver's door.

'That brandy kept me awake all night, worrying,' said Mary Jane. 'My mind changed every ten seconds, but I have to say, your Russell is a user.'

Either Mary Jane was goading her deliberately or she had lost several IQ points lately.

'God, at least my mother's opinion is consistent,' said Sophie, 'even if it sends me up the wall. So who's the user in your case? You or the youthful boyfriend? I hardly think it's Steven.' Mary Jane's face quivered. Damn, now Sophie had upset her. 'Sorry, sorry, but I don't know how to help you, Mary Jane. All you've told me is that Steven found out this time, and his ego was already labelled fragile. Or limp, you said. Reading between your lines, I gather that's hardly his ego.'

Mary Jane's nose turned red at the tip, but her lower lip stopped trembling. 'Shit. This is neither the time nor the place.' She leapt out and strode in the direction of the tennis courts. Sophie followed.

There was the deputy, with a crowd of children scattering across the asphalt.

'His name's Nick, right?' Mary Jane blew her nose and shoved her hands in her pockets.

Sophie joined her beside the base line and waited. The wind bustled back and forth. The deputy looked harassed, like a cowpoke with cattle on the brink of a stampede.

'You're into older men,' said Mary Jane. 'He's far too young for you.'

'He's at least thirty-four,' said Sophie, 'so he's years too old for *you*. And married.'

'Hugh said the Laura Ashley could be from his mother.' Mary Jane's mouth turned extravagantly hostile.

Sophie turned away. There at last was Hugh. He was circled by other children and seemed agitated: he was waving his hands round. Were they picking on him? If they were, she'd pounce right in — except that would embarrass him and make things worse. She hunched her jacket up around her neck.

'He's wearing my scarf!' Mary Jane muttered. 'Little toad, it's my leopard print Gucci.'

A girl about twelve appeared beside them. 'I hope you're here to judge our seventies contest.'

The seventies. That's why the children wore bell-bottoms (the polyester rustling sound), beads (the rattling) and the scarves around their foreheads. Velvet jackets, long obscuring wigs and garish colours. Sophie'd worn a leather and bead belt just like that one on a dear little fat girl. There was music too, seeping through the wind from a tape deck on a bench across the court.

The starlight glimmers in the air . . .

How on earth had Nick come upon a tape of this? Sophie felt that strange shrinking down inside. A band at the Student Union, white suits with gold trim, trying to imitate the Abba pose and smile, although there'd only been two male singers, one very tall, the other short. The Contrapuntals: nearly as banal as Abba, too, though in the seventies Sophie'd thought them fabulous. Dear God, what a confession. Dim lights, curls of perfumed smoke, low voices and the clink of cups in the common room. The hunch of shoulders over text books in a library carousel.

'I can't stand this,' she muttered. 'Too much *déjà vu*. I'll phone Nick later.'

'You can't run off,' said Mary Jane. 'He's seen us.' And didn't move except to hold her stomach in.

Nick loped over and stood in front of Sophie, legs apart, knees slightly bent, hands in hip pockets. His denim eyes gazed down as if she were a favourite mare. 'We've been stood up by the new city councillor — emergency meeting of the garbage division. Can you stand in and judge for us?'

Mary Jane bristled beside her. The deputy, with a curt nod, backed up half a pace. Had he worn spurs, they would have rung with a harsh little tink.

'Sophie can't waste any time here.' Mary Jane bristled even more. 'She's got serious problems on the Redlove front.'

'Hey, right, the documentaries.' Nick smiled at Sophie. 'Procellariformes, and ant farms. Hugh's filled us in. Look, if you can judge the contest now, it will only take a minute. And it would be great if I could persuade you to film Hugh's trial on Thursday. The professional touch. If you're half as awe-inspiring as your mother, the kids would learn a lot.'

There was a muffled yelp from Mary Jane.

Sophie felt like Alice in Wonderland: all those crazies with their own agendas, Mock Turtle, Tweedle Dum and Dee, March Hare, pulling, pushing this way and that. No, second thoughts: she felt as squinched and disregarded as the dormouse, dumped into the teapot. She didn't have the strength to heave up Russell's old camera even if it was in working order. She'd have worse backache than Mary Jane after a scoot across the lino. She opened her mouth to say no.

But the trial would be a chance to see Hugh in his new classroom, check for herself how he was coping . . .

'Sophie, you're a dream come true,' Nick drawled like a young Clint Eastwood. Though Clint hardly spoke at all.

Nor had Sophie: she certainly hadn't said yes, though her *bip* of confusion might have sounded like consent. The headache was back behind her eyes, and the ersatz Abba syruped on and on.

The soft night wind blows through our hair . . .

No, she thought, no. But she clamped her hands up her sleeves and looked at the milling, rustling crowd of kids.

For crying out loud. The thumping, oozing music and a jigsaw of images cluttered in her head. Weird stuff. The fizz of being nineteen, eager, unconstrained. Midnight rain sweet on your face under a street light as you recite the whole of 'Prufrock' to a group of drunken cheering friends. Mary Jane, bottle of cider spilling yellow in her hand, *I'll be the first woman in this country to get a Personal Chair in Literature, just watch me, Soph!*

The children wriggled and danced all over the courts, the music slid and coiled.

Our hopes and dreams will set us free.

Burning down inside, Sophie remembered: the unfolding of your mind as the Professor of History leans over his desk to give you back an essay, the one he's saved till last, the other students waiting: *Combine this material on social roles with the use of symbolism and iconography, and you've got something very interesting here, Sophie. I do hope that you're considering a doctorate.*

The tutorial overturns in your astonishment. While you listen, answer questions, argue with the others over points of this and that, the shock of his belief in what you can achieve is mounting through you. Finally your face flames with the warmth of it, the pure delight. You can accept it, Soph. You're sure. You know. You're there. Ideas like facets of a jewel a-glitter in a dance, and you can choose them, own them: the Russian Revolution, military philosophy, art history. Discoveries, learning, leaps of logic, intuition all combined, and trees outside the seminar window explode in a gust of wind, a wild escape of power.

You feel a deepening surge inside now, day by day, billowing, uplifting you to meet your own path as it shimmers into being in the intellectual world. You're reaching for your focus in the centre of the storm when:

W*hoosh*! comes Russell, comet-like across your vision.

W*hoosh*! You're high-tailing into his orbit.

Whoosh!

Come ride the fire, come stride the stars with me . . .

Whump.

All gone.

And you didn't even realise.

God stone the bloody crows.

The children pranced, the music slipped and rolled. The poised twelve-year-old, in a long Indian cotton skirt, high cork sandals and leather jewellery, danced as if she graced the day. Several little boys tried to catch her eye, but she refused to be distracted. Such single-mindedness: Sophie longed to creep away, to mope and mourn, dissolve.

Who is that efficient child? she tried to ask. She cleared her throat and asked again. The dancing queen was Angie Smenovich, of course.

The last notes echoed, died. Sophie held up her hands and called for silence, which didn't fall, it hung suspended. The little expectant faces smiling at her tore her heart.

'I know about the seventies, I was there.' She had no idea who'd get first place, just hoped to God she'd get through this without disgracing Hugh. 'The seventies were far too short on real rebels. We all thought we were, mind you. But, way deep down, we were terrified of being different. You're all much better than we ever were, I think you're all tremendous, and the prize must go to Angie Smenovich.'

All the little boys and girls cheered and smiled. Hugh's head was visible at the back of the crowd, down-turned. Angie smiled like Mother when she scored a point in a panel discussion. Nick got a fit of giggles like the far-off thundering of tiny hooves somewhere in his pectorals, which gave Mary Jane a shortness of breath. She hadn't changed a smidgen in over twenty years. Personal Chair in Literature? Give Soph a break. A floundering dilettante, more like.

And Sophie felt thoroughly, utterly squinched: the disjointed, last best doll. Poor Bluebell had even failed at being hung. The string broke, and a strange black dog had slobbered up and chewed her feet off. Smudge screamed and jumped with rage, and then threw up.

'You are digging yourself a very big hole,' Mary Jane warned as they drove to the supermarket.

'You should be packing,' Mary Jane warned as they drove back up the hill. 'Let him get home and see your cases packed.'

Sophie muffed a gear change and the engine groaned.

'You have three choices,' Mary Jane warned as they turned into the driveway. 'Stay and be a wimp. Pretend to go, to frighten him. Or really go. No, don't do that, Soph. Don't leave him, he'll come to his senses. He could be flying into Johannesburg by now.'

'I wish you would shut up,' Sophie whispered.

She pulled up outside the front steps and climbed out of the car. She wanted to run shrieking away down the hill. Wind swept the branches of the hedge over the old tiled garage roof; scritch, scratch, like someone doodling when they couldn't think at all.

She bit her nails at the kitchen sink while Mary Jane unloaded the groceries.

'Stop that,' said Mary Jane. She clattered in the pantry and rustled plastic shopping bags. 'That's where the olives went, behind the instant noodles. Hullo, Lisa. Good grief, is this your study afternoon? How is your day so far?'

'That should be Mum's line.' Lisa grabbed a cookie packet. 'Gross, marshmallow. Snail vomit, if you ask me. Mum, how long are those weird guys going to be around?'

'Ask your father.' Sophie'd hoped to sound angry, but her voice was like torn tissue paper.

Lisa pealed with laughter, launched across the kitchen and buried into Sophie's neck. 'You made us sound normal for a second! You're fabulous!' The soft prickles of blonde hair smelled of winter sunshine, the little cat tails tickled Sophie's chin. Lisa's arms pressed round her tight. 'Mum, I'm going to have a stud in my nose.'

Sophie shook her head.

'Okay.' Lisa let go and began another raid on the pantry.

'People with studs look as if they haven't wiped their bogies properly,' Mary Jane said. 'If anyone wants my opinion.'

'Frea-ky!' Lisa stared round-eyed over the cracker barrel clutched to her chest. 'For a second you sounded like Grandma.'

Freaky was right. Sophie'd never noticed that before. You can clear out now, go home, she thought, let me alone. But it was hard to tell a friend to bugger off. She couldn't even dredge up the energy to phone the bank. She sank on to a chair.

'What's the matter, Mum?' Lisa, on her way upstairs, offered a cracker for Sophie to bite.

'I want a life.'

'So get one,' Lisa said. 'Start with the study. Hell, Dad will never use it. He's never coming home.' Her lips curled down. 'It's creepy, it's a millstone round our necks. But you have to call it home.'

'Not coming home? Who told you?' Mary Jane stood as straight as a katydid. No, Greek column, caryatid, that's it: thick as a brick and as solid. Sophie pressed her fingers between her eyes.

Lisa looked surprised. 'He's been home for a total of three years in all the time since I've been born. There's an eighty-six percent probability of him not being home at any given point: I calculated it in maths. Mum, I know you're having problems. But why leave him? Just treat him like that thing that happens. A natural disaster, like a tidal wave. After it's finished, you tip the dead fish out of your gumboots and carry on as usual. Easy-peasy. But, hell.' For a second Lisa looked a lot older than fourteen. 'I would like to get rid of those two weirdos.' She swung out of the kitchen and curled back round the door. 'Yeah, another weird thing. Grandma's picture. She's got it tucked behind her bookshelf. Do her for nicking it, Mum.'

'I told you we went there while you were — um. On holiday,' said Mary Jane.

'It's all right,' Lisa said. 'I know Mum was off bonking.' She clattered upstairs.

Sophie remembered one of her principles when she was editing Russell's turgid sentences: if in doubt, cut. If something doesn't quite fit, you can't make sense of it, delete. She erased the last half minute from her memory, and wished she could delete an aeon more.

'Mother pinched that picture. Mind you, I stole it from her first. In fact, I stole it from the rubbish men thirty years or so ago.'

'It never pays a woman to try and understand her mother.' Mary Jane pressed the puffy patches under her eyes. 'I need to give myself a facial. I'm coming when you film the trial. When are you going to hunt out the camera?'

Sophie's stomach jolted. She would make an idiot of herself in front of Hugh's classmates. It would be no help to him. She should be the one in the dock: indecision was the least of all her crimes.

Shoulder raised in a very Mother manner, Mary Jane swanned off. Sophie tried to tidy the kitchen, to concentrate on mindless tasks. She ignored Hugh and Rory as they stepped in from the back yard in a slow gavotte, their whoops as they wrestled under the table, the return of Mary Jane with a squeaky-clean face, the sideways scuttle of smelly sorry Conga through the back door and up to the bathroom. The sideways scuttle out again of Conga (still unwashed) with his pile of dirty clothes, and the advent of Damon and his chiselled cheekbones, offering two pages of computer printout as if it were a holy conjuration.

'From Russell. I haven't read it.'

Such falsity. Angels are not supposed to lie, except for the good of humankind. Fallen angels, however, tell fibs constantly; they're meant to. Especially if they're fallen angels who serve as sidekicks to golden idols with riding boots of clay. Golden idols, whom you long to see, your heart a twist of frozen hurt and hope just in case, this time, they'll bring the miracle of solid love and honesty, show that they are, indeed, the other half of your jigsaw self.

So, turn the other cheek? Oh, sure, it's worked so well before. Oh, sure, lie down, roll over.

No.

Come on, worm, keep turning: get a life, become the golden angel with the outflung arm: *Want to come back in, Adam? No way, you snivelling sorry little piece, you know the story, piss off. Go on! Get!*

'Message from Russell?' Sophie asked in tissue paper. 'Stick it down somewhere.'

'From Russell!' said Damon, eyes like auger-holes of horror that she'd ignore the sacred missive.

Sophie flicked through a recipe book and coughed a frog of fright out of her throat. 'I've just formed a video company. I'm a bit preoccupied.'

The angel backed slowly from the kitchen.

She cooked up kidneys in white wine with the juice of one lemon and a mass of finely chopped parsley accompanied by hot noodles with pesto and followed by a thick moist carrot cake. Lots of stirring and beating and mixing, grating and chopping, the comforting wrap of warm smells. *We have to share, Soph . . . Blow me, those angels look exactly like a row of boiling fowl.*

She tried to imagine Todd replying to that letter, but couldn't.

Lisa complained about never finding any clean clothes and ate the kidneys with no reference to her latest political statement, going veg. It's obvious: kidneys do not have a face.

'You're in a funny mood, Mum,' said Hugh. 'Is it because you were a judge today? The kids thought you were cool. I had to say you were my mother.'

'What did Angie do?' Lisa asked.

Hugh blushed. 'She blushed,' he said.

'Hugh's blushing!' Lisa cried. 'He's pretty when he blushes!'

'Love.' Rory, *basso profundo*. 'Sucks.'

'You look as if you need another early night,' said Mary Jane.

'We're clearing out the study.' Sophie hadn't known she'd say that. Tip the fish out of your gumboots, Lisa said? But they're still damp inside.

'Cool!' Hugh jumped off his chair. 'I love Dad's junk. You're going to find the vid cam, too.'

'So you're not going to leave him,' muttered Mary Jane. 'And you can't chuck him out this time, since it's really not your house.'

A friend is like a clinging vine: in this case, poison ivy.

It was a temptation to get Rory to bash down the connecting door to the flat and pitch Russell's gear through. Rory would have enjoyed that, too. But she didn't have the courage to be quite so confrontational. Anyway it was beginning to rain and, with the wind starting up again, it was probably more subtle to dump it on the back verandah. This was, after all, to show herself she was not completely helpless, though she was shaking like a wraith.

Lisa picked up a heap of box files labelled Ant Farms; Task III. With a faint yelp, she glanced at Rory. He snorted.

'What?' Hugh wriggled under Lisa's arm to see.

Rory held up one hand like the host of a TV show. 'Unusual constant warring among members of the same colony,' he said in perfect English. A collective moment of shock: Sophie felt as if she'd seen a beetle pop out of a pupa-case. He gave another primitive snort and kicked a pile of boxes.

'I hate it when they leave me out!' Hugh screamed. 'That's Dad's stuff. Why are they laughing?'

Lisa tried to speak, Rory got her in a head lock: they wrestled and thumped.

The mixed-up feelings inside Sophie simmered, trembled, jumbled. War in the colony. Civil disobedience, revolt. Don't fire till you see the whites of their eyes. While you wait, dig trenches — in your gumboots? She swallowed a gulp of hysteria. Mums are meant to be conscientious objectors, not get involved in battles, and at least keep No Man's Land tidy and dusted, well polished.

Articles of War, George II, Seventeen Forty-something. Of not preparing for Fight, and encouraging the Men in time of Action: every Flag Officer, Captain (so forth, etcetera) who shall not make the necessary preparations for Fight shall suffer Death or such other Punishment as a Court Martial shall deem him to deserve.

Yet, how much easier to lie down and surrender. Or scarper, desert, go AWOL.

But she'd already scuttled off, first with Matthew, then away from him. Oh guilty and confused. Confused and guilty, guilty.

'Mum.' Hugh tugged her sweater. 'Your eyes are doing funny blinking.'

Mary Jane plumped on her haunches, crawled under the desk and tossed back the rickety portable typewriter. Sophie had clacked three versions of Russell's thesis out on it, while her own sat in a little box. Ninety thousand words of enthusiastic explanation plus footnotes and references. *Russell, Proust may have got away with sentences two pages long, but we'll have to cut yours up. You haven't read Proust, Soph. I read enough to realise I couldn't stand the sentences. Come here and have a cuddle, Sophie, you can finish all that later.*

'Got 'im,' said Mary Jane under the desk. She crawled out shoving a dusty box labelled *vid cam* in front of her.

It had been hopeless trying to hold that camera steady. Sophie'd been breastfeeding Hugh, and the demands of him and Russell had usually clashed.

'That one always broke down,' said Lisa.

'*Ungh,*' from Rory. The glance between them meant, *Why d'you think Dad made her use it?*

Sophie fought the window open and fumbled the typewriter over the sill. A *crash*, which made her nerves shriek.

She closed the window. She was on one of her plateaux of speechlessness, but no one seemed to notice.

'Chuck the camera too and claim the insurance,' suggested Mary

Jane. 'Might be the only way you get some ready cash if there's a screw-up at the bank.'

'That's naughty.' Hugh grinned.

'A boy about to be tried for stealing a rabbit will know all about naughty,' said Mary Jane.

'I'm innocent till proven guilty.'

'So how did the rabbit get here?' Lisa elbowed past him.

'The end justified something,' Hugh said. 'I won't say what.'

Screams, thumps, hilarity, but at last the room was cleared of Russell's gear. Sophie's tiny box sat neatly in the middle of the desk.

The phone rang.

If Russell could send an e-mail . . . Sophie hated herself for running to the kitchen. Her hands were sweaty on the receiver; both hands pressed it to her ear. She managed a smothered, 'Hello?'

'It's no good,' rumbled Matthew. 'God alive, we can't have meant it when we said that we were through.'

No, thought Sophie, meaning, Go away. Meaning, help me, decide for me, please. She was swimming in despair: lie down, surrender, right *now*.

'Jenny's definitely left me. I've signed the papers. I'm coming to see you as soon as I can.'

'No!' Sophie cried at last. Too late, because Matthew had gone.

'Ghastly day.' Mary Jane opened the front door. 'They'll have all the details at the bank. It's cold out there, you'd better fetch your coat.'

Sophie's nerves jangled. A burst of wind came through the dining room, and the front door nearly slammed on Mary Jane's fingers. Sophie thought she'd locked the back door: why did she try to fool herself that she could cope?

'Look, you won't want to hang round with me this morning,' she said. 'Take your own car into town, see the art gallery, go and have lunch or something.'

Mary Jane looked hurt. 'I'm here to keep you company. To help you.'

The only help Sophie wanted now was from an angel, in a boilersuit or red satanic wings — she wouldn't care as long as it was clearly an angel. She needed it to cry in a voice that held the sound of trumpets: *Stick a flaming sword into thy bossy friend or at least show her where to buy a ticket out of here. Fret not about the house, thy bank account. Ignore thy lying husband and his sidekicks, disregard thy importunate older lover. Sophie, happy tidings! You can make the users pay!* She needed an angel to tip its halo to her like Uncle Todd used to tip his hat to a lady. She needed, *whoosh!* a miracle.

All she could conjure in her mind was Great Grandma Violet, sour mouth, gnarly hands waving a little black book, sitting tight by the fire in her old black armchair while wind squalled outside and smoke billowed in a back blast down the chimney. While, no doubt, the chamber pot resided in the bedroom. *You don't need that on show, Sophie. I'll chuck it out then, Mother. Sophie, you can't do that, it's possibly a Doulton.*

Cope, Sophie. Make an effort.

'What will you want for lunch, then? Cracker and cheese, I hope, I can't be bothered doing anything else.'

'We can do better than a cracker. What would you fancy?' Mary Jane's bangles clashed and rang once too often.

'Your teeth down the back of your throat!' Sophie shouted. Her hands flew over her face.

'So. Well. That's it, I gather. Outstayed my welcome.' Mary Jane folded her arms. 'I shall have my things packed and . . .'

A thump fell on Sophie's back. Conga pushed through, a load of boxes in his arms. 'Excuse me. Wow, this's heavy, man.' He disappeared down to the study.

'What the hell are you doing!' Sophie was amazed she had the energy to shout a second time. 'Get out of here! Get out of here at once!'

Conga came back wiping his nose on his sleeve. Damon came through the dining room with another load, shoved it into Conga's arms and gestured to the study. Conga sloped off, obedient and smelly.

'Orders from Russell. We used our keys, don't worry.' Damon's curly diadem rioted above his glistening brow. 'No room for this stuff with us. He'll be here within the week if he can get the connections, he's on his way already. I've said you're slightly fragile. Hey, what happened to the marijuana? He's not too pleased about that.' A deep glow lit his eyes. 'We have to realise, Dr Redlove's keeping plenty of balls in the air.'

'Feedback loops,' Excuse Me said, returning. 'Biologically crucial. Um. Philosophical implications. 'Scuse me.'

Damon spread his shoulders to show how hard he was working.

'I'll whizz in after lunch and stick a bolt on that door. See you.'

One small box sat on the bare boards outside the closed study. *Sophie Redlove. Personal.*

Sophie didn't look at Mary Jane: she didn't look at anything, unless you counted the whirr of helpless rage that circled her.

'If he gets the connections,' said Mary Jane. 'Sophie, what will — you do?'

'You tell me,' she whispered. 'You're the bossy one.

'I feel sick,' said Mary Jane.

Sophie looked at the paint pots, the ladder, the can of turpentine. 'I wish I could graffiti the entire house with *Russell sucks*. Except Damon would have me done for damage to property that's not my own.'

'Philo-bloody-sophical.' Mary Jane sighed. 'Christ, Soph, you're trembling like a wounded cat. I'll forgive you. I'll get you down to the bank.'

Sophie hauled herself upstairs to fetch her coat, through the grisly glimmer of the stained-glass window.

'Letter for you, Mum,' said Lisa, furry blonde head bowed over her school books at the table. She looked different. Sophie couldn't pick why: her brain had enough to wrestle with, waiting for the bank assistant to phone her with some answers.

'Mum? Are you all right?'

Who knew?

Sophie dumped a couple of grocery bags on the bench. Mary Jane had gone upstairs for a lie-down: for this relief, much thanks. 'What are you doing home?'

'Sports afternoon. I'm wagging.'

'Most girls wag with their friends.'

Lisa shrugged. 'I've gone off girls. They giggle.' She glanced up from her homework. 'I'm still not into boys, though. They are gross. Hope you bought some more knickers. I put them on your list.'

Sophie tossed the package to her and picked the envelope up

from the table. The handwriting wasn't familiar.

'Maybe I'll be asexual,' said Lisa. 'Or, you know, split down the middle like an amoeba. Binary fission. Sex sounds too disgusting. Mum, why is there a bolt on the study door? Have those creepy guys have been in again? I hate that.'

'I'll get all the locks changed,' said Sophie. 'Or we'll leave. I don't know.' Lisa frowned. 'I'll change the locks anyway.'

'Good.' Lisa tucked her head determinedly over her book.

'Have they been bothering you?' Sophie pointed in the direction of the flat.

Lisa raised a shoulder briefly. Sophie watched her for a moment, but Lisa stayed busy with her homework. A French exercise. The pages of the dictionary flicked back and forth.

'Lisa, you've cut off your little cat tails.'

Lisa's mouth twitched.

Through the window, the needles of the pine trees swayed, a stir of wind tossed a bird across the sky. Sophie began to open the envelope. The letter inside was typed, from a rest home up the coast.

A note from Todd — about him, rather. Todd Deckler. A tiny shift: someone knew he had a surname. It made him take on a different shape, made him more strange and more real.

Unable to unfold the letter further just yet, she sat down, her back to Lisa. She'd never really expected this. Apart from his army number, she'd been able to put so little in her own letter. She thought he'd served mainly in Egypt, been wounded there at the same time her father was. She knew nothing, except he'd been her Dad's first best mate since before Sophie was born and she'd last seen him when she was twelve.

So many years ago, in this city, when he heaved his cabin trunk into the back of a mate's van, jumped into his own old car and took off with a burn of tyres, and Mother walked to her bedroom, not straight and neat, nor curvy like a dancer, but cramped, hands fisted to her stomach as if she'd been punched, in pain, bowed down at last by grief and loss yet something in her strong and grim, determined to climb up, powerful, passionate and resolute.

Sophie hadn't put that in her letter. She hadn't put anything about the angel in the white boilersuit, either.

Better get your backside moving, mate.

It's all right, Sophie love, I'll get old Edith out of here.

You're a bobby dazzler, Soph. Good kid, good-oh!

She managed to unfold the single page at last. Todd, it said, had wanted the rest home to reply to her query. Kathleen Briddleton was down as next of kin. It gave Mother's address and phone number, too. She had to read the letter twice before the shock struck into her.

He wasn't her uncle. Todd said he'd never known a child called Sophie.

Sophie stared past the jar of sunflowers to the pine trees but she knew she wasn't seeing them.

'Mum? Mum, phone,' Lisa said. 'You didn't even hear it.'

Sophie took the receiver and listened to the assistant from the bank. 'Thank you.' Her voice was no more than a thread. 'I understand. Oh, yes, I'm quite all . . .' She stood holding the receiver until Lisa took it out of her hands and hung it up.

This house was not her house. That had been bad enough.

But it wasn't Russell's, either. He'd set the house up as a trust. The deal was off. In Russell's mind, the deal had never existed. The kids and Sophie didn't have a home at all. He had used her money from the gallery to help him, to help him to fool her again.

The last worst hurt: the utter emptiness it left her in. His access to her cheque account. So easily done. So simply. *Sign this stuff, love, and hurry into bed. Dom Perignon and caviar, you're worth it, little fox, mmm, yes, we make a team.*

Part Three

THE SECRET LIFE
OF MEN

Sophie dialled three digits of Mother's number but let the phone slip from her hand. What would be the point? *Next of kin. Never known a child called Sophie. Good heavens, what a let-down, tch, purr. You just decide and stick to it. I said you should leave him.* She saw it all like a fractured Picasso again and again.

Lisa closed her dictionary and put an arm round Sophie. 'It's okay, little Mum.' The girl was taller than her, it must have happened overnight. It felt odd to lean against her daughter. 'The bad times always pass. What's that old bat done now?'

'Don't talk about Grandma like that,' whispered Sophie, because mothers are supposed to say such things. 'Actually, she's the incarnation of Baba Yaga,' she added, because mothers are not meant to. 'I used to want to catch the little running house and fry its chicken legs.'

'Bloody old hag.' Lisa eyed Sophie as if she were doing a mathematical calculation. 'Mrs Goody Two Shoes and *Grandmère le Loup*. That's wolf. She gobbles you for breakfast.'

Not a crumb left. Russell had gobbled it for lunch, dinner and supper-time snacks.

Lisa shrugged. 'Pity Dad's parents died, eh. We might have had one okay grandma.'

Sophie shook her head. 'She was a doormat to Russell and his dad. It used to drive me mental.'

'Well, you're a doormat sometimes.' Lisa grinned. 'But basically, you escaped.'

Loss, sorrow, the mistakes you've made: accept them, smell and taste them, find out what you have done, what you've left undone.

Damn it, the only way out was straight ahead even if it might be a dead end. Sophie picked up the Yellow Pages and found the locksmith section. Twenty-four-hour mobile service. Prompt attention.

But it was surprising when a van and two blue-overalled men arrived inside the hour. She told them there would be some opposition from the flat but, as the mother of three children, she didn't want oddballs traipsing through the house in dark or daylight. They looked perturbed and sympathetic, and installed new locks both front and back.

'How can I make sure the oddballs don't change the locks again?' she asked.

'You're joking!' The older locksmith's voice was like toffee with nuts in. His knuckly hand sprang up to scratch his forehead. 'But in that case, double bolts, I reckon, on the inside. And let the police know. Any funny business, we'll be back to help you out.' He trudged out to his van.

But Sophie expected at least one more major confrontation with Excuse Me and the Hallelujah Hero, and she doubted that a toffee-throated locksmith could do much, given Russell's charming, cheerful way of capturing the voters.

What can you do, Soph, when the enemy has taken all you've got, wears a smile and says he loves you? You can hardly pursue someone who, arms wide, is running straight towards you. It also seems impossible to shoot in those conditions.

How can you fight, when he ignores what you believe in?

She felt the shiny new lock. It was smooth and smelled of oil. Well, she'd try her best to keep the weirdos out for a while. She might have thirty-six hours, maybe less. Gambia to Cape Town, to

Sydney perhaps, then Russell would be on the tarmac, into a taxi, roaring up the hill.

Sophie, as she dreamed, thought it a very odd story: a scramble of Russell surfing from Africa towards home; Mary Jane's mouth open, silent, like Edvard Munch's *The Scream* when Sophie told her what had happened to the money from the gallery; and a circumcised rabbit (wasn't it meant to be female?) debating with the exploded possum how to manage painting ceilings. Haloed in fire, the possum, in the wordless way of dreams (and animals for that matter), said if you were into *cordon bleu* you didn't need to fret about ceilings, they were only there to keep spaghetti off the outside of the roof, but ovens could be really scary places. With a ceremonial flourish, it began to present a platinum whisk to Sophie.

She woke, warned a shivery fit of sobs to hold off until after Hugh's trial, took an iron pill with her first cup of coffee and set about dealing with school lunches.

'Do I have to go?' Hugh whimpered. 'I need a hearty breakfast. I'm a wreck.' She shoved a bowl of muesli in front of him.

She had no idea how to work that camera any more. Ten years ago, she'd simply followed Russell's shouted orders. She'd felt so proud being part of his projects, thrilled by his bulk against her shoulder as he showed her how to hold the camera steady. She'd refused to notice how she felt outside the cosy room called love. Squash the little twinges, hide them, Soph. He barks at you for doing something wrong? Pretend it doesn't matter. You're supposed to smile, so smile.

Wife = love = happy. Note the error here? Excuse me, shouldn't husband have a place in the equation? Good heavens, no, he's away dealing with your finances.

'Mum,' Hugh complained, 'you've left my sandwiches empty.'

She gave him five dollars for a school lunch and packed him off.

Mary Jane came down as if the slam of the front door was a breakfast gong. A pair of jeans on? Mary Jane had even tied her hair with a bandana. Frankly, Sophie would have preferred the bandana fastened to the end of a stick with Mary Jane's sponge bag inside it: off to seek her fortune, back to Steven.

'Have you looked at the camera yet?' asked Mary Jane. 'You should, if you're really going through with this. It might be broken. You'll make yourself a fool in front of Nick.' Her expression changed slightly. '*C'est la vie*. How trivia employs us.' Instead of sitting, she picked her muesli up to eat it standing.

Tight jeans.

Déjà vu again. Smudge and the Ranch Family: her paper cut-out dolls with a well-fed 1950s look about the face and torsos — healthy living, outdoor smiles. Matching brown leather jackets with tassels, denims for the man and boy dolls, full gingham skirts for the girl and lady dolls. Oh apple pie and rope them dogies!

Sophie'd loved those happy-family dolls. Mom and Pop so comfortable in love; the two kids with scrubbed red cheeks, obedient and able, helping out around the farm. She played with them under the grapefruit tree. While inside? The triangle of Mum, Todd, Dad. Triangles are made of metal. There's a hole near one corner and that's where Sophie used to wonder if the sound fell out.

Mary Jane tinked a fingernail on the rim of her coffee mug. 'Sophie?'

'Time warp. Sorry. You look great in jeans, just like the Mom at the Ponderosa.'

Mary Jane's chin tucked back like a Thanksgiving turkey's. 'There wasn't a Mom in *Bonanza*. They were all men together.' Her hand hovered near Sophie's forehead as if she'd like to detect a temperature. 'You're a very white shade of pale.' A version of responsibility showed in her eyes. 'You shouldn't go through with this, you look absolutely ghastly.'

'Hugh needs me. I've said I'll do it. You don't have to come.'

Mary Jane finished her muesli in odd silence; something grated Sophie's skin every time she looked at Mary Jane or her friend glanced over at her. They tidied up the kitchen, still not speaking, and Sophie ignored the knockings on the back door of Damon waving another e-mail message from On High.

'Did you read the last one?' he cried through the window. His beautiful eyes grew rounder as he saw Sophie snatch the printout from the bench where she'd dropped it last night, screw it up and toss it in the garbage. 'He wants to know how you got the money for a video company! You must reply soon as!' The halo of golden curls was awry, and seemed slightly greasy too. Maybe that was the window. Mom and the girl doll of the Ranch Family would have scrubbed it, smiling.

As they left the house, Mary Jane wore a worried look as well as her tight new jeans. She spoke at last as they drove through scutters of leaves whipped this and that way by a low, ground-hugging wind. 'If you're thinking of time warps, Sophie, you mean *Lost in Space*, not *Bonanza*.'

'The Mom in *Lost in Space* should have had a gingham space suit,' Sophie said. *Warning, warning. Danger,* said the Robot, every episode, as it waved its fat white arms and waddled closer. The worm in Sophie's insides nodded hard. Russell might be in the stratosphere right now.

Outside the classroom, wind rose and battled with the trees, sent clouds scudding beneath the watery sun. Inside, under paintings of dinosaurs, articles of raffia-work with no obvious use, a class motto in cut-out copper-foil letters (GO FOR IT!), and a scramble of children, the chairs and desks were shoved around to form the jury seats, a judge's bench, the prisoner's dock. Hugh wasn't in it yet. He wasn't even in the classroom.

A lanky boy popped up in front of Sophie and squinted at the lens of the old camera. 'Dad's got a hand-sized cam corder with digital zoom. It's got multi-angle shooting, we do seriously rude things with it.'

'This camera is antique,' said Mary Jane.

The rest of the class bundled round to figure how the antique worked. Sweaty hands poked and ferreted, and one of the buttons fell off. Sophie felt as if the last straw was being laid upon the camel's back and she was underneath its belly.

'Don't worry, it's not worth anything,' she said. She ought to leave, there was no reason for her presence any more.

But the lanky boy, breathing heavily through his nose, fixed the button back on, and tried to show her how to operate the camera too. He got it wrong. Angie Smenovich's chin tilted in a manner that suggested Marie Antoinette disdaining the peasants. There was an edge of Mother to the tilt as well. Angie looked a grim and vicious persecutor: no way she'd wear an apron, gingham or not.

'The accused's relatives should stay at the back of the courtroom,' said the persecutor.

Nick winked at the accused's mother: a wink that said, *You're Dr Briddleton's daughter, I'm a good teacher, please watch me.* A wash of anger helped to buoy her up. This cowboy, despite his brown bread and cheese exterior, was as much a user as any other adult male in her life. She was a fool to let herself be trapped into a morning here when Russell was high-tailing it back to the ranch.

But, Sophie, you did trap yourself. Again.

Next to Sophie, the friend of the accused's mother shifted to show her limbs to best advantage.

'Quit that!' Sophie hissed.

'Jeans are hell,' whispered Mary Jane. 'I'd forgotten how you have to hold your stomach in. Christ, no man's worth it.'

'Let your stomach out then,' Sophie said.

'Silence in court,' cried a fat little bailiff.

Crunch point. Sophie had to work the camera, or give it a darn good pretend. She closed her eyes, trusted instinct and pressed something. The camera blipped, and whirred.

Her eyes snapped open. Through the viewfinder, though it wavered, the jurors as they settled were so earnest. The judge, a pale child with curly hair in bunches like a spaniel's ears, was sedate, but with some mischief in her eye, she gave a friendly nod to Sophie.

The second charge against Hugh, damage to the environment, had been dropped. 'We don't have time and we reckon we'll get him on just one thing, anyhow,' the judge said. 'I'm impartial though. Okay?'

The defending counsel, draped in a black garment which looked like her mother's Indian cotton overshirt, angled her elbows like a mathematical compass. The persecutor stood as straight as an arrow.

Hugh was brought in by two more fat little bailiffs. When he caught sight of Sophie his face twisted with embarrassment. But as they put him in the dock his eyes sparkled, his mouth became grave and straight.

'Your Honour!' declared the defending counsel. Sophie swivelled to catch her in the frame. 'The defendant's heart wrenched at the plight of the rabbit. Hugh's bosom —' The defending counsel brandished her sleeves while all the little girls and boys snickered. 'His bosom, eh, was torn. Should he leave the rabbit in a rat-shit cage without —' The defending counsel checked her notes. 'The benefit of independent foraging? Or should he deprive his schoolmates of their pet, their entertainment?' (*Entertainment* seemed a very dirty word.) 'How would you like it, members of the jury, if you were cooped up and fed old lettuce? How would you like it, with kids who were heck of a bored with you anyway? The real bad-ass,' the defending counsel shouted, 'is the ones who caught the rabbit in the first place!'

Bravo, Sophie wanted to cry. The focus blurred, but she adjusted it.

'I haven't had my turn.' The persecutor's voice rang like a clash of cymbals. 'The prosecutor's meant to have first turn.'

'The court apologises,' Nick said. 'Be our guest,'

The persecutor, tall as a spear in the centre of the viewfinder, addressed the court. 'Not even the defending counsel can wriggle off the facts. Stealing means to take something from someone else without permission. Who said Hugh could take the rabbit?' She shot a fiery look at him. (Sophie did a quick swivel: he was demure.) 'Stealing is to take something unlawfully, especially in a secret manner.

We had a rabbit. Hugh stole it. We all saw him, so it wasn't really secret. But he didn't know we were watching! He is a rabbit thief and also he stole Mr Watson's bag.'

The jury, bailiffs, even Mr Watson looked impressed. Sophie captured them on tape. The soft whirr of the camera seemed to chuckle.

'I brought the bag back after Rory washed it,' Hugh said. 'It still smelled though.'

The small judge eyed Hugh with a wise and keen expression. 'So what about the rabbit? Have you a thing to say about your own defence?'

Hugh raised his head. *A Tale of Two Cities*: chin up, peaceful, sublime, a pint-sized Sydney Carton, hero, sacrifice.

'Don't call it "the rabbit", Your Honour,' said Hugh. 'It needed a name. I gave it a name. It's Angie.'

The court whooped. The persecutor flushed. The defending counsel hooked her thumbs into her armpits with a creditable male swagger. The camera jiggled but steadied, and Nick looked as if little horses stampeded through his pectorals again.

'The court reporter has to write it down,' a bailiff called. 'Angela Rabbit.'

'Is that Angel with a "a"?' asked the court reporter. 'Or is it "er"? Angeler?'

Sophie had to brace the camera on a desk by kneeling down.

Beneath her severe expression, the little judge was flushed with giggles. 'So tell the court why you stole the ra — stole Angie.'

'Steal is a very heavy word,' Hugh's cheeks were big red apples. 'If you really like something, you have to set it free. Angie bit me. Angie scratched. But I set Angie free.'

Laughter exploded from the children, Nick, even from the persecutor who glanced at Hugh beneath her lashes. The camera swooped over them all, the lens as much fun now as Smudge's copper dancing eye.

The judge whanged her gavel. When silence eventually fell she bashed out a last *rat-a-tat*!

'My client is guilty of a kind heart,' the defending counsel said. 'Guilty of getting the rabbit, I mean Angie, out of here. Anyhow, even Mr Watson was scared of it, it used to kick like heck.' The jury looked worried and nodded. 'Hugh's got guts. He's a new kid but he's cool.'

Hugh turned to his mother and winked. The viewfinder blurred: she focused it again. The friend of the accused's mother hiccupped behind her.

The bell rang, an Act of God, or at least of the timetable. Her Honour banged her gavel again. 'Members of the jury, hang on and do your verdict.'

'Right,' Nick said.

'We are animus consent,' announced the foreman.

'Unanimous,' Nick said.

'Okay,' the foreman said. 'He's guilty.'

'They've been told to say that!' Hugh cried. Sophie skimmed the eye around the room and caught his look of enjoyment centre frame.

Her Honour beamed with delight too and crashed the gavel down. 'I have to do a sentence, so all of you shut up.' The court did, more or less. 'Hugh Redlove, you are guilty!' She glowed like a sunburst. 'So you have to do a Pugslie. A Prettie Pugslie on how to roast rabbits.'

Cheers gusted from the court, along with screams of *yuck, gross, yuck*.

'Little toad,' said Mary Jane. 'Pinched the rabbit, nicked my Gucci scarf, now he's off with your stories as well.'

Hugh slipped out of the dock and out the door faster than the rabbit had loped into the pine trees. But Sophie had it all, on tape.

'I don't want to go home just yet.' She put the video camera carefully in the back seat of the car. A child in baggy shorts watched through the school fence and put its tongue out. Sophie made a face in return:

the child looked shocked and then impressed.

Mary Jane shrugged. 'Early lunch in town, then? I suppose I'd better pay for you.'

'I thought you wanted me to pack,' said Sophie. 'When are *you* going to pack? You can't stay there if I leave. Though I suppose you could, if you wanted.'

'Just make up your own mind.' Mary Jane busied about in her handbag. 'Don't worry about mine.'

Good. Sophie hadn't planned to. The bad times always pass? House guests who've grown irritating pass eventually as well, though it was possible that Sophie might be first out the door of Nightmare Abbey.

So, a coffee bar, intimate, half a dozen tables, abstracts by local artists round the walls. Buses groaned past, and the espresso machine roared like Mt Vesuvius.

Sophie stirred her coffee till it was lukewarm, and fiddled with the green salad she'd chosen in the hope it would boost her iron reserves.

'Does Nick fancy me, or you?' Mary Jane asked. 'Silly question. It's possible to fancy us both.'

Nick had looked almost as guilty as Hugh. 'Dodgy, plagiarising your mother.' He'd chewed his upper lip. 'This won't make me look good. I've sent the eggplant story off in a bunch of poems and what-nots for a competition.'

The eggplants. The story Hugh said sucked. The little brat.

Teeny whisperings like the wind crept round Ms Prettie's house.

'Who licks at my window panes made of frozen tomato sauce?' she called, as sweet as squishy Easter eggs. 'Who nibbles my door step fashioned of garlic?' She snuck to the keyhole and peeked.

There stood two plump and purple little aubergines. 'I'm Handsome, she's Grovel,' one cried. 'We're cold, all alone, and so hungry. Open the door and we'll play happy families.'

Ms Prettie waved her Diamond Spatula, and Handsome rolled over the threshold.

'*Warm up in this boiling olive oil, it's magic for your chilly bits,*' *Ms Prettie Pugslie screeched.*

'Let Hugh get away with that and he'll become a photocopy of his father,' said Mary Jane as she stabbed a squid ring. 'Nick had better do something.'

'It's not at all important. He said he'd sort it out.'

Nick's wholesome brown bread look had disappeared; in its place was rugged tenacity. His voice was powerful as bourbon, and as tanned. In stories, men with bourbon voices and trustworthy teeth could save the world, as long as they had enough time. Sophie had waited, to see. He furrowed his forehead in his prairie-searching manner, shot a thirsty cowpoke look at Mary Jane, then smiled at Sophie in his Wonders of Mother Nature way. Coming, married or not. Brown bread and bourbon. And a slathering of mustard about him of wishing to ingratiate himself with Mother.

'Yes, and I'm sure he'll come and tell you all about it.'

Mary Jane chased another squid ring, a smug curve momentarily on her lips. His body language had spoken of the saddle as he smiled at Mary Jane. Mary Jane's had indicated at least a little docey-do, a line dance straight towards another big — and young — mistake. She was riddled with bossiness for other people, but take her own counsel? Raucous laughter, slap your thigh.

Smudge would have wanted to shove Mary Jane into the oven with the witch. Heave Handsome in there too and let him burn.

Sophie ate a cherry tomato.

'Men can give very mixed messages,' said Mary Jane. 'Like, what sort of wife does Russell want?'

'What sort of wife does Steven want?' asked Sophie. 'A faithful one might do it.'

'For instance, take the clothes he brings back,' Mary Jane continued as if Sophie hadn't said a word. 'They're always for a larger woman. And the colours. Fuchsia. So depressing.'

There had been a black overall thing from Tokyo. *You'll look good enough to eat, Soph, mmm* . . . It made her look like a gnome.

Who wants to eat a gnome? She'd passed it on to a short mechanic at the local wreckers yard.

Mary Jane put her elbows on the table: her mouth was turned down now. 'It's all so awkward and confused. I feel absolutely terrible. You're right, I mustn't bottle it up.' She buried her face in her hands, and ran her fingers up through her sepia hair. The espresso machine choked and gargled in the background and made it hard to hear. 'I just can't sort him out, I never meant to be unfaithful to you, Sophie . . .'

'To Steven,' Sophie said.

'What?' She shook her head. 'God, I'm in a muddle. Steven, bloody Steven! Shit. I want to make him happy, I want him to be pleased with me. He's never found out about my flings before, but I didn't mean it with that younger man, it was a catastrophic blunder. The way Steven reacted! My God, it freaked me out. Call me contradictory? Hell, you're like a cornstalk in a windstorm too. Oh, I cannot figure men at all. Like Nick.' A tear leaked out of Mary Jane's blue eyes. 'I'm no better than you are, Sophie, and I've had enough miserable affairs to know what I'm talking about!'

The café had gone quiet. A couple at the next table glanced at them.

'Hush,' hissed Sophie. 'You're completely incoherent.'

'But that doesn't mean I'm too old now to play around!'

'Of course you're not. I mean, of course you . . .' What the hell was Mary Jane saying? What did she want Sophie to say?

The chef had come out to peer over the counter.

'It should be my choice, Sophie! Whether I do, or not! And who I do it with!' Pearly tears raced each other down either side of her nose. 'But shouldn't a husband want you to himself?'

Sophie forced a bright smile at the abstracts on the walls.

'Men,' said Mary Jane.

The men concentrated on their coffee cups, but a rueful warm female voice rose near the window. 'They're human beings too,' it said, 'so what chance have they got?'

'They're gorgeous in white shirts,' another woman called. 'The corporate image gets me, every time.'

Some men blushed.

'They're delicate beings,' said a tall woman with a husky purr. 'Their secret life is all marshmallow beneath those double-breasted suits.'

The men looked sheepish and pleased.

'Mysterious, vulnerable creatures,' sighed the chef, and smoothed his moustache as he vanished back to the kitchen.

Mysterious? Good grief, tell Sophie something new. But vulnerable? It didn't sound like Russell much. Nor Matthew. Now she came to think of it, it didn't sound like her much either, any more.

Sophie ordered fresh coffee and a blueberry muffin, and considered. The house. Months of work to be done before anyone was likely to make a profit on the place. The strips of wallpaper by the locked door dangled like the fronds of an anemone lying in wait to capture little fishes. New drifts of spider webs had appeared like insubstantial seaweed blurring the corners, darkening the air. Outside, the roof needed the lichen cleaned off, chimneys straightened, the guttering cleared of grass and leaves.

Apart from Bluebeard's flat, the main bedroom and the smeary promise of the stained-glass window, the house was so neglected it would be kinder to raze it to the ground. What a welcome home for Russell.

Tempting, tempting, Sophie.

No. Blowing up the outside toilet was insufficient rehearsal for letting a bomb off down the person access point. But, each man should be a law unto himself: so saith the anarchists, and every boy-child likewise — look at Hugh.

Therefore, should every girl-child, every woman, unto herself be law.

Thank you, I'll think about that, Sophie said to the tomb of the unknown anarchist. If there wasn't one, there darn well ought to be.

The children and Mary Jane gathered in the kitchen. The pairs of eyes regarded Sophie, the clock, the stove.

She grabbed a packet of mince from the fridge, sliced a fat onion to set a bolognaise sauce going for pasta, squashed three cloves of garlic with the side of the Sabatier knife, and asked Mary Jane to make a salad. Then she dropped to her knees and yanked open the cupboard under the sink. Cake tins, muffin pans, the steam pudding basin and its lid with metal wings. She hauled out the gem irons. They were ancient heavy things, but not too rusty.

'Mum,' said Hugh. The first thing he'd said since he came in from school. She'd been waiting for it. You never had to wait long, with Hugh. She scrambled up and he leaned against her. 'Mum. I am ashamed. Mr Watson told me I'm a cattle thief, and rustlers are the lowest of the low.'

'Yes, you are a low-life, and you ought to be ashamed,' Sophie said. 'Make up your own stories. You're not getting any more of mine.' She ducked safe inside her own head where no one could bother her.

And safe inside that safe, safe place? You've never known a child called Sophie?

Todd's eyebrows wriggling, first best grin. 'Turn the knob, Soph, high as it will go. Now slide the gem irons in to get 'em hot, and we'll get on with the mixing.'

Drop the butter in the pot: *sizzle*! And *hiss*! It's yelling *ouch, ouch, spit*! Add sugar, *crunch* when you spill it on the floor.

'And honey — yeah, use your finger, Mum's not home to see. D'you want to beat the egg in?'

Smudge wiggling her eyebrows too, astonished that he asked. The beater with its curvy blades and little painted handle. *Clatter, whirr.* The air all warm from the oven, so cosy you could rest on it, it wrapped you up. Another painted handle on the sifter, and the blades over and over like a tiny rattly lawnmower. The falling rain of flour, baking powder, pinch of salt, mixed like magic when she turned the little stripey handle. Todd's laugh when it spills on the bench.

'Dad sad? Dad in the workshop?'

'Sssh.'

And tipping the milk in, careful, but you slop some, pearly puddles. Now out of the oven come the gem irons. Drop knobs of butter in their little beds, the butter spits, jumps, turns brown quick as a blister.

Todd and Sophie racing to spoon the batter now. 'Mind your paws, Soph, don't burn y'self.' *Clang*! the oven door as he shoves the gem irons back.

The golden spicy smell from the oven and inside, if you peek, gems rising up like pillows for a teeny tiny child. And the sloppy floury bench, the dripping beater, crunched egg shell, and giggling because Mum would never know how mucky they could be, and what did they care, because she was out having fun.

But once Mum did find them and she yelled like anything and cried, and it didn't look like she'd had a good time at all. And Todd grabbed her and whisked her round the kitchen in a dance all bouncing but his hands so big and careful like she was precious as a treasure, and Mum cried harder, deep sobs from her tummy, and bunched his shirt front in her hands, head tight against his chest, and Todd was kind and stroked her tears away but his eyes were blinking too. Stone blinking, eh, those crows.

'What are you doing, Mum?' asked Hugh. 'Mum!' He nudged

her. 'What is that old thing? I used it in the sandpit. It was a garage for my midget cars.'

'I thought you were being ashamed,' said Sophie, and her voice wasn't too much like tissue paper. 'You've turned into a normal boy again.'

'It's easier than being ashamed.' Hugh picked his nose and Sophie slapped him. 'Anyhow, it's horrible when you ignore me.'

'These are gem irons,' said Sophie. 'I'm baking gems to take to Uncle Todd. He can eat them or choke on them, they'll be a day old, but gems he is going to have.'

A knock at the back door. Mary Jane looked up from the cucumber she had chopped into chunks. Another knock. A series of questions, variations on a theme of let me in, the All-High's hopping mad and if you won't speak to him I'm first in the line of fire. Come on, be reasonable.

Reasonable? Choose your words.

At last a key fumbled at the lock. Silence. Another knock. Sophie felt like a jelly-clown at a party: softening, about to be demolished.

'The key won't work!' Damon, aghast.

'Try ascension,' she called back, loud so her voice wouldn't shake. 'Or translocation. But I doubt they'll work any better than your key. You're not getting back inside this house while I'm still here.'

The door rattled furiously, and the artificial sunflowers wobbled. Sophie reached to save them, changed her mind and batted the jar to the floor. Damon didn't knock again. The windows shook, but that was the wind on the prowl.

Another e-mail would soon be on its way to Russell. Though he couldn't collect it mid-air between Gambia and Cape Town. Or Cape Town and Sydney, if he'd got that far.

Sophie felt as if she were mid-air too, a falling Madonna having second thoughts on the long plummet earthwards.

'Have you ever seen Dad mad?' Lisa, sounding cautious.

Of course not. Russell knew it wasn't charming to be angry.

Please, God, let Sophie bounce.

The rest home looked very restful, a long smooth lawn and neatly trimmed shrubs, and plenty of parking near the front door. Sticking up in the flower beds were a few green needles, too late to be daffodils, but regimental, so they must have been planned by someone.

Todd. It was nuts to rush off to see him now. He didn't know anyone called Sophie.

Hey, Sophie, keep the unknown anarchist in mind.

Would she recognise Todd? In her memory he was tall, but he mightn't be now. People shrank. She didn't even know how old he was: seventy-five, nearer eighty, probably.

Mother would be incensed when she found out.

The horrid little worms that meant Sophie was about to cry began to writhe, so she shoved Mother off into a mental back closet and slammed the door, gathered her handbag and the little box of baking out of the car, and found the front desk.

'I'm not sure about this,' said the boss person with a very straight boss-person mouth, a direct gaze and a round badge on her lapel which in jokey green letters said *Matriarch*.

The badge gave Sophie a smidgen of hope. She clutched the plastic container to her side and made her eyes say please. 'I should have phoned first. But I thought you'd just say I couldn't visit him at all.'

The boss person frowned as if she couldn't work something out, even though it was as simple as two plus two. 'Well, your mother does phone every week, if you're who you say you are,' she said at last. 'I'll come with you. If he's at all upset, you'll have to leave.'

'Sure,' said Sophie. 'If I get upset, I'll leave right away as well.'

The boss person's frown deepened, which meant that the jolly green badge might not be funny after all. 'Come along, then.'

'I'm scared.' Sophie stood still.

'He won't bite,' said the boss person. 'He's got a thing about his dentures. We'll find him in the sunroom.'

Against the far wall, a tiny old man wearing a tam o'shanter snored erratically on a cane sofa. The boss person walked over to another old man in a wheelchair, waited till he looked at her, then adjusted the rug over his knees.

He was bald, except for bushy eyebrows sticking out every which way. Deep lines bracketed his nose and mouth, wrinkles chicken-wired across his sunken cheeks. Shoulders that once were broad and held back solidly, leaned forward, narrow and stooped. The woman spoke to him softly and nodded towards Sophie.

Head down, he glared like an angry chimpanzee. 'She is not.'

'Who am I, then?' Sophie asked.

'Sophie was a dear wee thing,' the bald man said.

'You didn't ever know a child called Sophie,' she said.

The boss person crossed her arms, but didn't look as if she was going to yell for the rest home bouncers to deal with Sophie quite yet.

He pulled his head further in towards his shoulders, pushing them up at the same time. Concertina-man.

'Uncle Todd was a sweetie,' Sophie said. 'He took away the scary picture of that ancient ancestor woman.'

The old man's head came up. 'What woman?'

'The trapped one, with the mouth like a tin of pins.'

He leaned further forward in the wheelchair, peering at her with faded blue eyes.

'How tall are you?' he said, a kind of growl, reluctant.

He must be senile. Or just plain bonkers. 'I'm five foot four, and a little bit extra when I stretch. I have grown six inches since I last saw you. If you are Uncle Todd.'

'Uncle.' His grim old mouth turned down at the ends. Mr Misery Guts. 'No one wants me for an uncle.'

'I didn't ever think you were my real uncle.' Sophie glanced at the boss person for clues, but she was watching Todd. 'Mother and Dad both called you Uncle Todd when they talked to me.'

'Mother.' He sounded more than a misery guts: Old Uncle Agony. 'Not always much of a mother to that kid.' He huddled back. His knuckly, age-freckled hands drew the tartan rug to his chest.

'I'd better leave,' Sophie said to the boss person.

The woman shucked her shoulders. 'This is one of his good days. Stay if you want to.' She marched briskly from the room.

Todd glared steadily at Sophie. She tightened her own lips a little, and backed up till she felt a sofa behind her. She settled down and folded her arms. Silence. Sophie played the stitch-mouth game. Todd gave in first: he always used to. He wiggled an eyebrow at the little box she had on her knee.

'Gems,' said Sophie.

Crusty old codger, head down, glaring again. 'They don't give me gems here.'

'First best gems,' she said.

He shifted slightly on his cushion. 'Ginger.'

'Some plain, some ginger.'

'Sophie wasn't too good on gems.' His fingers twitched on the rug. 'Let's see what you've come up with.'

She opened the container and held it out. The little oblong cakes, already buttered, lay on a white paper napkin with a tiny sprig of baby's breath she'd begged from a greengrocer for decoration.

'What's that white stuff?' he growled.

'Gypsophila. You don't eat it. It's just for looking pretty.'

He shuffled his dentures; there was a faint click and clack. She kept holding the box out.

'Sophie never was a pretty child,' he mumbled at last. 'Long grey socks and roman sandals. *Tcha*! Mind you, Kathleen couldn't have cared less. Out gadding.' Something trembled in his eyes.

'Sometimes there were meetings. School committee. Evening classes. City council.'

'Gadding.' His lower jaw shifted back and forth. 'But I'm not a one to blame her. She had to have a bit of fun.'

Contradictory old coot. Sophie gave up and put the box down beside her on the cushion.

'Hey, hey!' Todd waggled a hand at her. 'Give a chap a fair go.'

She stood to put the whole container in his lap. He chose a ginger gem, sniffed, and took a bite. 'Mmmph. Better than Sophie's.'

She opened her mouth to tell him not to be stupid, she was Sophie, but he shook his head and a hand came up again, shaking, quieting, telling her to hold her patience. The twinkle was there. Uncle Todd was there. She wished she hadn't come.

'It didn't pay to argue with Kathleen,' he said. 'Soft as a kitten that one looked, but my word she grew claws. I promised I never would tell Sophie all about it. But Jack and me, we got on fine. All you can do is your best for your mates.'

'Right,' said Sophie.

Todd squinted. 'I'd never have said little Soph would turn out pretty. A chap can smell these things.' One of his eyes still twinkled at her, and the other dropped into a watery fat wink. 'Plain as a sausage, that child.'

Here came the worm, that old awful feeling of being on the edge of something and not wanting to look down and see exactly what. She cleared her throat.

'A man might like a cup of tea, since he's got a gem,' she said.

'A woman might too,' said Todd. He nodded at a round bell-push set near the door. 'They'll bring one, if you give it a jab.'

She gave it a jab. A round-faced aide brought a pot of tea on a tray, tucked Todd's blanket over his knees again and, in a tip of her head, asked if he was all right with this unexpected visitor, and did he mind the other old man, still asleep in the corner? Todd nodded back. The aide moved off.

His big spotty hand reached out. It took Sophie a moment to realise what he wanted. She took hold of it, so large and dry in her little paw, and he gripped with his long rough-textured fingers. Surprising how strong. The worm said: *Run, Soph, run.* But she waited. Todd's hand held hers while he had a sip of tea and put the cup down, and rubbed his free hand over his egg bald head, pressed the fingers to the line between his eyes. Her hand still felt warm, still shaped to his, when he let go.

'You were a first best mate,' she said. 'Jack was lucky he had a mate like you.'

His hand came down to the rug where it rested like a big curled leaf. 'Good bloke. Didn't give himself a proper chance, that was the trouble.' He shook his head.

'Painting those sheds,' said Sophie. 'Wherever we went — sorry, wherever Sophie went, her Dad would always paint things, work on things.'

Todd's mouth flicked at one side. 'Calmed him down, he reckoned. It did too, now and then. Slow and easy, and he could concentrate on one thing at a time.' His faded eyes looked away into nothing.

'Yes?' said Sophie.

He gave a jagged laugh. 'Could have been a chief accountant no trouble, but it would have been the pressure, you see. I knew.' His hand flexed and fell again into its loose crumple on the rug. 'Well, we all knew. It wasn't something you could talk about.' Todd's mouth pressed soft and turned down, moving a little as he thought. Thin man lips, which used to be so full of grins and smiles, the quirk at the side, the air of swagger, of being there to keep you safe. 'You couldn't tell a woman, but the wives all knew enough, I reckon. Some had it worse than others, not that anyone said. You couldn't say.' His mouth moved again, the slightest tremble.

'Were you Dad's mate in the war, before the time he saved you? I never knew for sure.'

This time he didn't seem to notice she'd forgotten the game, that she said who she was with no pretending. He didn't answer, was on some track of his own, gathering up the strings of memory, following connections that only he could see: the lines on his forehead deepened. 'Some of the blokes at Maadi, when you saw them, even if nothing showed you knew they'd had a rougher time than you. You just did what you could. The ladies, the little wives of the diplomats, and the nurses, at the dances and lunches . . . ' His eyes were awash but the tears didn't fall. 'It was like rain after years without a drop. A sweet soft face: just to look at it could heal you. I reckoned, if only Jack could get a girl, he'd have to come right. But Kathleen was so young, y'see, and those brains of hers . . . ' Todd stared across the room, unfocused except on something he remembered.

Sophie watched his eyes. 'You did what you could for years,' she said. 'That's more than a good mate, I'd say.'

He shook his head, a twist of pain between his eyebrows. 'Broke your heart to see the waste of it. First Jack, then Kathleen too. Ah, what a mistake. No, no one blamed her, he'd be a wrong one who'd do that.'

Sophie was completely lost. 'You must have been pretty young, when you signed up,' she said for lack of anything else.

He snapped off a look of astonishment. 'No, no. I was a man already, twenty-one.' He drew himself up in the wheelchair. 'But you couldn't get by without your mates.'

Behind the old blue eyes, the memories moved on. What should she say? What did she want to know? What did she want to stay hidden?

'You and Jack came home together,' she said. 'And then you met Kathleen. She was just out of school?'

It looked as if he were going to say more but it was only a sigh, a short out-puff of breath.

'We lived in seven places, till I went to boarding school.' She watched him closely but he didn't glance at her. 'We moved a lot. And you came too.'

Something stubborn showed in the line of his mouth.

'Kathleen made you promise not to say,' said Sophie. 'Not say what?' Silence. Dogged. Stubborn. 'Todd was a godsend to little Soph. Just like Todd's angel was to him. "Get your backside moving, mate."'

A flicker in his eyes now: he'd heard all right.

'Mum — well, she left you to it really,' Sophie said. 'And Dad was —' What? What was he like? The quietness, the closed-off mystery, the way so often he couldn't eat. But other times, all smiles and calm, so handsome, dark hair, brown eyes, the narrow face, curve of his jaw, little scar. The lovely man-bounce of his knees, the way he held his shoulders easy whenever he was calm. How it broke her heart, her little girl growing-up heart, to see the change come over him and never know what caused it.

'Don't say a word against Jack.' Todd glared, savage though his voice was low.

'Well, what?' she asked. 'What is the problem? God, anyone would think . . .' She stopped. Matthew had said . . . 'Is that why he and Mum didn't get on, though they pretended to? I know he was wounded badly but — were you and he not interested in women?' That was the way they'd said things then: it had toppled from her before she'd even thought it clearly.

Todd pressed a hand to his chest, shook his head, and words shot out of him. 'It wasn't anything like that. You had to mind your mates. He was my mate.' His old mouth worked. 'He never said. I had to hear it from another chap, what happened, and it was all on my account.' His colour had whitened. Sophie felt her heart would break again; she felt the worm inside. 'Poor blighter. They reckon now we bottled up too much, our generation, but what else could you do? Not even the doctors talked much to a bloke. Poor Kathleen. To have to watch her realise; the way she drooped. Ah, well. Had every right to go out gadding if she didn't get much chop at home.'

He sat up, brushed both hands over his ears as if he still had hair, and suddenly showed a grin like sunshine. 'Mind you, we had our moments, Katie-Kate and me.' His eyebrow wiggled. So did his dentures. A bubble of laughter escaped her.

'But you never got married. Why not?' God, could she say it? 'Should — you have married Mum, instead of Dad?'

'No, no, girl, you don't see.' Todd smiled, but his eyes had a sheen of tears again. 'Jack was best left on his own, as long as he had me around. You had to keep control of things, you see. You had to keep control however you could. I thought Kathleen seemed right for him, and I reckoned that I'd be away. The look of her was just too much for me, I tell you. Oh, that smile of hers could send your heart to heaven. But then she didn't look a happy bride. So there you were. Ah well, I did my share of gadding too. A bloke's got to let his hair down now and then.' He peered at Sophie with a shade of sad amusement.

'You did love Jack.'

He drew back in his wheelchair. 'Good heavens, no. Deep feeling, that's another matter, but good heavens, you didn't have to make a meal of it.'

Sophie's hands spread helplessly in front of her.

'Oh, girl, you don't know much about men, do you? We jogged along. And Katie-Kate and me, we had our might-have-beens.'

He was telling her everything and nothing. Words floated around but didn't settle and make sense.

Todd sighed and looked at her. 'Then little Sophie arrived, didn't she? Five — six years after they were married. A little surprise if ever there was one. Well, how could I leave then? Ah, Jack. And Katie-Kate. I had to be on tap for both of them.'

He stared out the window. The muscles of his face shifted, a little bunch near his jaw, the flick near his eyes, a tiny frown. Pieces of a jigsaw moved in Sophie's mind, nearly fitted, moved apart again. Smooth dark-haired Dad — was maybe not her dad. Shaggy Todd was not her father either.

Oh Katie-Kate, what did you have to do? The dream gone sour. You're on your own, kid. Yep.

He shook his head and the little laugh floated from him. 'I can't complain. Kathleen still visits, now and then. She calmed down not long after Jack died, although we never — ' His hands folded back into the rug. His old mouth pressed into a line. He wasn't going to say another word. Old stitch-mouth.

Sophie stood up and looked at him: a few feathery white hairs on the nape of his neck, the tiny wrinkles where his ears met his head. The slope of his shoulders, under the knitted jersey he had on.

'You came from a big family,' she said. She didn't know why that was important, but it had something to do with the way Todd had mothered her, and fathered her, given her a peaceful flowing childhood, kept her from seeing the rocks in the stream.

There was a tear now, just waiting at the corner of Todd's eye. She wasn't sure whether to kiss him goodbye, whether she wanted to or not, whether she'd come back again or not.

He still didn't move. She let her hand rise and brush his shoulder, just a touch, before she walked out of the room.

She found the boss person at the main door, and said thank you. As she reached the parking area an avalanche of tiredness fell over her. She leaned on the driver's door and closed her eyes. A slink of sunshine touched her lashes and she remembered long lines of little boys and little girls all holding hands, no ground for them to stand on, hanging in the air like lines of washing, waiting till it was safe to go inside. She remembered playing with the Ranch Family under the grapefruit tree. The Mom and Dad were always smiling and the Ranch children always had someone in a gingham shirt to play with.

And her handsome quiet Dad moved round the garden, and now and then he'd look at Smudge. And sometimes he looked sad and sometimes he would smile, and he never blamed her once for being there.

The house creaked in the thin wind sneaking up the hill. The stained-glass window seemed to shift in its setting, a trick of the fading daylight. Shadows on the staircase shifted too as Sophie stood at the foot of the stairwell, thinking. Lisa hovered near her. The wind roared, quietened and roared again.

Hugh, trudging out of the dining room, mouth open in a *what's for dinner* plaint, jumped at a far-off thud from behind the locked door.

The sound didn't come again, but she knew exactly what it was: a little thing, a tiny one, the final straw that sent a wise worm scooting past its point of no return before the camel collapsed on it.

'We're going up to pack.' Her voice was a bubble of fright and determination.

'But why, Mum?' whined Hugh. 'Dad's coming home. Where are we going?'

'Just pack,' said Sophie. The wind grew louder, tireless.

'I will never understand my mother,' mumbled Hugh.

'Shut up,' Lisa said. 'You don't have to understand. You just have to do what she says.'

Sophie took his shoulders, turned him round and sent him up the stairs. 'Where's Rory?' Lisa shrugged. 'Have you seen Mary Jane?'

Lisa jerked her fuzzy skull towards the dining room. Sophie popped her head around the door.

Mary Jane, standing at the dining table, closed a large book with a slam. The atlas. 'He — um, he would have had to overnight in Dakar.' She braced herself as if she had to hurdle something. 'But he could get here tonight.'

The wind leapt at the windows and the whole house shook.

'If this gets worse, no one will be landing at the airport till tomorrow,' Sophie said. 'Lisa, sweetheart, go and pack.'

Lisa dashed for the stairs.

'I've decided,' cried Mary Jane. 'I'd better go as well!'

The house shook with the wind once more, and with a series of knocks at front and back doors. The telephone went, too. Sophie called Lisa to get the front door, Mary Jane to take the back, while she darted for the phone herself.

'Sophie!' said a male voice she recognised. A flash of Matthew, gravelly deep, a hint of Russell's energy and drive; but this, thank God, was neither.

'Steven?' She glanced round, but Mary Jane was ushering Excuse Me and a bundle of clothes through the dining room. The wind hurled itself around the house then fell into a crouch as if it waited, growling low, to pounce.

'We have to talk.' Steven sounded as if he'd been crying. 'It's ridiculous to keep things smothered.'

'Pardon?' The windows clattered in the wind. The back door blew off the latch: Mary Jane can't have snibbed it. Sophie put a hand over her other ear so she could listen to him properly. 'You mean about Mary Jane?'

'Sophie, what can I say?'

She didn't like to hear him so upset. Steven was a Labrador of a man, soft sides and a wriggly attitude, drooping pouches under worshipful brown eyes.

'Don't worry, I'm sure it will be all right.' She tried to see through the dining room into the hall to let Mary Jane know who was on the phone. 'Look, I really can't talk now, but I think she'll be back with you soon.'

'She's spoken to you?' Steven gave a sequence of half-words and woofing noises. 'She has! Ah! Sophie! Did she tell you the effect on me? A ruddy miracle! Can you see my point of view?'

All Sophie wanted was her suitcase. Besides, what on earth can you say to a man you know is impotent?

'Steven, we're men and women, of course we have problems with, well, with this and that. She's coming to terms with things, I'm sure she is.'

'You've seen her?' Steven shouted, *eureka*! in his voice as well as shock, as if he'd slammed into a high stone wall.

He was safely five hundred kilometres away, so there was no harm in letting him know that Mary Jane was here. 'She's been here all the time,' said Sophie. 'I've been telling her to phone you.'

'Staying with you. She's staying there.' The words echoed with respect, with awe. 'Sophie, I realised it was a milestone for me. But Sophie, you're a saint.'

'Well, it's time she moved on now,' said Sophie. 'Look, there's someone at the front door, and I have to . . . '

The back door flung wider. Damon marched in without knocking. Two white-overalled men followed. A gust of wind made the house almost roll on its foundations.

'Knock!' said Sophie. 'Don't you come in here before you knock!'

'What?' Steven asked. 'Of course I'll knock.'

'Not you, you're miles away. It's . . .'

'The Choi-Berunda Institute leases the premises,' Damon cried with an archangelic point at Sophie, an element of Lord Kitchener about his finger too. 'I've got to protect the interests of the trust. You've no right to change the locks.'

'Miles away? No,' Steven panted in the receiver. 'I'm at the airport. It's a nightmare here, queues and stranded travellers, all flights have just been grounded, there's a gale warning out. I'll try and grab a taxi.' The line went dead.

She didn't want more house guests, but it would be up to Russell to deal with them. She could be gone before Steven arrived, as long as Rory was back home in time.

The white-overalled men began to unscrew her new locks on the back door and Damon was intent on maintaining his archangelic stance, though Sophie could recall seeing an angel hand on hip only in a sixteenth-century Turkish miniature.

Pursuit of the enemy? When they're just standing there, and smugger than a publican? *Ah, what the flaming hell!* the vixen thought.

A pinch of anarchy, a tablespoon of insurrection, this would only take a moment. She dialled her own locksmiths.

'You're joking!' said the sticky-toffee voice she recognised. 'No worries, love, we'll be there in a half hour. Less.'

In the manner of busy men, the locksmiths hadn't noticed what she said or did. Nor had Damon.

Oh, George II, Seventeen Forty-something, Soph shall not forbear the chase, but she shall do it her way. It's a mutiny of one. A solo revolution. Lo! the tumult! Thick clouds turbid in the sky, with secret angels of her own getting ready to shout bravo.

A pulse beat in her head but she couldn't slow down for a migraine, and this was not the time for another Gothic faint. She found the gin, took one sip straight from the bottle, promised herself more later when she'd packed, and left Damon and the locksmiths to it.

She wanted to see that Hugh was ready, throw something into Rory's case if he still wasn't home, haul her own down from the top of the wardrobe. But she found the front door wide open too, with fierce wind bowling down the hallway. Mother was there, holding the chamber pot and examining the dried-out Boston fern.

'If you must have this in the front hall, Sophie, at least you could water the thing.'

'Have the potty if you want it, Mum.' Sophie put her hand on the newel post, about to run upstairs. 'Put it with the picture you stole. Why did you, by the way?'

'I wasn't going to have that fatuous expression on display.' Mother clutched the chamber pot a little tighter. 'Sophie, I would like to have a word.'

'Later, Mum. I'm getting out of here.'

'Good,' said Mother. 'You've decided. I knew you'd do the right thing . . .' Her voice tailed off, just a little.

Lisa charged down the stairs in a flood of tears. 'I'm sick of it, Mum, sick to death!' she sobbed. 'They just keep disappearing! Bloody boys!'

'Has anyone seen Rory yet?' asked Sophie.

'I'm not talking about Rory!' Lisa screamed.

A crash at the top of the stairs, and Mary Jane appeared with her suitcase on wheels.

'Don't bring that any further,' Sophie called. 'That was Steven on the phone. He's going to be here soon.'

'I must get out! I must!' Mary Jane slithered and bumped her case down as if she were in an obstacle race. 'Oh, what am I to do?' She plumped on the bottom step and wailed into her hands.

'A word, Sophie. Just a quiet one.'

'Bloody boys! Damn, damn the male sex!'

Sophie tried to get upstairs again. But get past Lisa, Mother, Mary Jane?

A white-overalled locksmith marched through the dining room and began to unscrew the front door locks. He turned the hall light on, but it was dim and flickered in the gusts of wind.

Hugh's voice shrilled from the top of the stairs. 'Can I use your bathroom, Mum? I don't want to go in with the computer nerd. I think he had a shower at last. He's vomiting in the toilet.'

'Have you packed your things?' cried Sophie.

'Yes!' from Hugh.

'I bloody can't!' yelled Lisa. 'I can't find any knickers!' She crumpled into a heap of fury next to Mary Jane.

'But where are we going?' screamed Hugh.

And over the porch now thumped Rory, strangely dressed, jet black on one side, bright purple and raspberry on the other. He shouldered past the locksmith and, red-faced, grinned at Sophie.

'Had a rehearsal,' he said. 'I'm doing Macbeth. And Lady. Together.'

'*You* pinched my knickers!' Lisa screamed.

'Lisa!' Mother said.

'Rory, Lisa, I want you to pack,' Sophie demanded.

Rory dumped his backpack and jumped so the raspberry side faced Sophie. The cover of *Vogue* had nothing on this. 'Make thick my blood!' he cried in pure falsetto.

Hugh shrieked with laughter through the banisters.

'Will you children go and pack!' shouted Sophie.

Rory vaulted over Lisa and Mary Jane on to the stairs. Conga, snake locks dripping, clutched his usual bundle on his way down, face a dreadful shade of yellow-grey and a sweet smell of soap coming from him.

Now Rory's jet-black side faced Sophie, the strutting and primp of invincible man. 'Blood will have blood!' he roared.

''Scuse me,' said Excuse Me, but Rory flung both arms up, shook his fists and jolted Conga's elbow.

Conga staggered. His bundle scattered. A damp towel, torn jeans, sweatshirt, grubby undershirt. Conga dived to gather his things. As he scooped them, dropped them, scooped again, out of the tumble fell one, two, three clean pairs of lacy nothings, blue, and yellow, and pink.

'What's that! What's going on?' said Mother.

'Lisa's knickers!' shrieked Hugh.

'*Ungh*?' Rory quartered the staircase with an efficient big-brotherly stare.

'My knickers?' Lisa's face flamed beetroot red.

With a bellow of outrage, Rory hurled himself at Conga.

'Kill, kill, kill!' Lisa scrambled up to kick him too. Hugh cheered from a safe distance. The locksmith twisted round to watch, but didn't stop working.

'Oof!' said Conga. Rory and Lisa still belting him, he rolled down to the hallway. They tripped over Mary Jane and her suitcase, wrestled to their feet and fell over Rory's backpack. Rory shunted Conga down towards the study door where they stumbled over Sophie's little box and tipped it up. Hugh dived after them like an excited puppy. Sophie tried to bustle him back upstairs, but he squirmed out of her grip and jumped about with Lisa.

'Kill!' he squealed. 'Kill, kill!'

'What were you doing with my sister's knickers!' Rory thundered.

'They were so clea . . .' wheezed Conga before Hugh launched and put his little hands around the Viking's neck. In a flourish of purple and black, Rory ripped the heat gun from its packet and Lisa began plugging it in to the hall point.

'Drop that!' Sophie'd sounded just like Mother.

Rory let the tool clatter down. Lisa kicked Conga once more and turned from him with a shudder of disgust. The computer nerd huddled in the corner, arms tight around his head. The tattered wallpaper rustled and flapped.

'Hugh!'

He hopped to attention. 'Yes, Mum!'

'Pick up that box, put it by the front door now. It's coming with us.'

He shoved Sophie's little box a fraction with his foot, then aimed another kick at Conga.

'Sophie!' Mother seemed close to a hiss of temper. 'I just want a quiet word. I hear that you visited Todd.'

Sparks erupted inside Sophie. 'I'll do what I damn well like! Just as you did. I have every right. Now will you let me go and pack!'

Mother's face went blank for a moment.

'It's all right, Mum,' Sophie said more quietly, though the purr in her voice, the Baba Yaga flare, burned on. 'You didn't seem to want your daughter much when I was little. I didn't blame you. I always said the wrong thing, somehow. I realise now, I was your scarlet albatross. The weight round your neck. The sign that you'd been sinful. Good God, Mum, it just doesn't matter now. You were

Butt out,' said Matthew. 'I'm taking care of Sophie.'

Butt out!' Sophie yelled back.

meone bashed at the door. Without its lock it opened easily outside, but Mary Jane forced it shut again. 'Go away!' she ed. 'Go away!'

hat right has she!' Mother jammed the chamber pot and fern thew's belly so he had to clutch it, stalked over and pushed ane aside. The door flew open.

en stood there, flanked by locksmiths.

n I come in?' he asked. 'I don't want to keep my taxi waiting g.'

rid of it.' Sophie came down a step. 'There's heaps of room here, Steven.' Especially since your wife's here too, and getting out.

ve a lovely smile and ran back to pay the driver. Big house, stay, relatives and teachers around. All ordinary, and sane. e'd put a double bed in the guest room. A night together bed could do wonders for a shaky marriage. If you were ybe. Hell, when she'd got herself and the kids out of here, and Steven could have their reconciliation in the main on the dais.

turned around, and there was Mary Jane seated on the next to her. Friends were just people to trip over. Sophie hed Mary Jane yet, but a peculiar wail seeped from her. ght you were going back to him,' said Sophie. 'He's this way, that means a lot.'

whooped and hollered. Rain plummeted outside. Steven ter the hall as headlights circled in the driveway, gravel iously and ended with a terrible metallic grinding. A as tight against the first. The drivers hopped out. Collars ainst the wind and rain, they duplicated the gestures w had been performed by locksmiths on the porch. inst the weather, a tall dark figure from the second taxi own the side of the house.

all victims, if you ask me. It's all right, Mum. Okay?'

Mother sank on the stair beside Mary Jane, arms still around the chamber pot.

Tyres crunched in the driveway. A van drew up, two blue-overalled locksmiths emerged, ran up to the door and began arguing with the white ones in the porch. A car drew up behind the van. It couldn't be Steven so soon, and it wasn't a taxi. A man got out, obscured behind the four locksmiths and Damon, who'd materialised between them, his arms gesticulating like an angel doing semaphore. It had begun to rain.

Hurry, Sophie commanded silently, suitcase. Climb over these two, and go and pack your suitcase now. She put a hand on Mother's shoulder, but couldn't squeeze past without treading on Mary Jane's fingers.

A ferocious gust buffeted the house: the men on the porch ducked until it lessened. Nick climbed the steps, wove through the locksmiths, stopped on the threshold and knocked. Mary Jane's hands shot up to fluff her hair.

'Hello, Mr Watson!' cried Hugh from the end of the corridor. He still hadn't shifted the box. The children (Rory with raspberry side out) seemed to be guarding Conga to make sure he didn't move.

'Have you got a moment?' Nick asked Sophie.

'No,' she said.

But Nick stepped in, shook rain off and smiled at Mother. 'Dr Briddleton, great to see you again.' Mother grabbed the chamber pot tight and stood up with a lecture theatre glare.

Nick drew an envelope from inside his leather jacket. 'Ms Pugslie returns. I — ah — ' He shot a look at Mother, like a nervous teenager about to ask for a date. 'Hugh won.'

'I said no. And Hugh didn't win. I did.' Sophie snatched the envelope and tore it in half. The pieces blew down the end of the corridor towards her little box.

'It took ages to write that out,' Hugh grumbled.

With another sideways smile at Mother, Nick handed Sophie a business card. The PR manager of a large breakfast food company. 'I confessed, on Hugh's behalf. They want to know if you can really cook, if you've had much experience with kids, if you have any experience with communication . . .'

'I don't believe in fairy godmothers any more,' said Sophie. And fairy god-deputies? No chance. She dropped the card, which spun to join the larger scraps of Pugslie.

Mother stood square next to Sophie, with a fearful, quelling stare at Nick above the fern and chamber pot. 'Don't bother making eyes at her, she's far too bright for you.'

A second car pulled up outside: the stained glass blazed momentarily in its headlights. This one was a taxi. The wind blew through the doorway so hard that a rain flurry reached down the hall.

Sophie turned for the stairs. 'Come on, kids. Pack.'

As the taxi headlights curved back down the drive they lit Damon's golden curls wild in the wind, and a dark figure lurched up the steps.

'Sophie!' Deep male voice from the doorway. The gravel voice, though the chocolate seemed to have disappeared: this was raw Matthew, desperate. 'Darling, I don't care who knows it. I love you. I need you. I won't retire if you don't want me to. Order me round, I deserve it. I've treated you abominably. Marry me.'

Arms out, Matthew barrelled at her across the hallway.

'Get off my mother!' Hugh charged down the corridor, shunted past his grandmother and threw himself at Matthew's stomach. Matthew scooped the battling boy easily into one armpit and held him there. Nick did a side-back shuffle.

'Him!' said Mother.

Oh God, the balding head, that panda look, the black and white moustache. Even though she wanted to laugh, to scream, her toes had bunched up, her stomach tried to melt. That was the trouble with Matthew, he was so goddamn sexy. That was the trouble with

Sophie's stomach: those easily excited ovaries.

'I have to get my case!' she cried.

'You're coming with me!' Matthew dropp[ed] his hands to the heavens in thanks.

'Ouch,' said Hugh.

'No!' cried Sophie.

Matthew snatched her arm. 'I've been i[n] lawyer. Sweetheart, I know about the t[...] monumental screw-up. Although I'm not t[...] I'll make it up to you. You've got no one t[...]

He sounded lost and terrified. Jenny ha[d] No takers for the Swedish kitchen: pity, Sophie nearly fell against him.

'You should have seen the mutton-[...] Chinatown.' Mother's voice sizzled with[...] heard him call her. Sophie, you can do b[...] have a bone of logic in you somewhere[...]

'Rory! Hit this old man, he's after [...] 'Mr Watson, that nerd pinches knicke[rs...]

'Can someone recommend a cou[...]

Sophie began to run upstairs aga[...] her way, trying to cling to her, ask[...] woeful shortage here. The barney o[...] locksmiths wrestling, making und[...] Damon, flailing as if he conducted[...]

She got her foot on the secon[d...] her, the sobs you have when you[...] that you can't understand at all.[...]

Tyres crunched on the grave[l...] The locksmiths stopped wrangli[ng...] his arms like an angel directing[...]

Mary Jane screamed, lunge[d...] One blue and one white locks[...]

'Should I call the police?'

Sophie had to get out before Steven learned how Russell had betrayed her. She wouldn't be able to bear his wounded eyes. Once again she put her foot on the second stair. But Steven hadn't seemed to notice Mary Jane was right there sobbing fit to tear her lungs out. Droopy eyes excited and adoring, he grabbed Sophie by the elbow and pulled her back into the hallway.

'Sophie, you're a saint, a total saint. You know what ordinary people would say about it. But it worked wonders on me. What else can I say but thanks to you and Russell?'

'Pardon?' Sophie asked.

'I was upset at first, I wouldn't be normal otherwise. But I couldn't be offended too long by a guy like that. When I thought about it, fantastic! It made a man of me again. Thank you, Sophie, thank you!'

Steven flung his arms round her, then dropped on his knees in front of Mary Jane; his beige raincoat billowed like the floppy sides of a Rex or Benji. 'I'm sure I'll be as good in bed as Russell now,' he cried to Mary Jane.

Lo! The silence was unnatural. The children, Mother, Nick, Matthew, Damon, the locksmiths all stared at Sophie, Mary Jane, and back at Sophie.

Tick tock. Little gears clicked into place.

'Dad fucked *her*?'

'Rory!' said Mother. 'Good God, it does take all sorts.'

Sophie didn't particularly like this revelation coming in front of the children, nor the sudden fascination shown by Damon and the locksmiths. But her eyes began to blur with tears at the absurdity, the way everyone else was jaw-dropped with shock. The Act of God, her own tidal wave of laughter, swamped her against the wall. She gasped for breath.

Strange silence covered the hallway like a cloak.

Steven shook his head: a Labrador with water in his ears. 'You didn't know,' he whispered into the hush. Though it wasn't altogether silent: wind sighed in and out of the corridor like a great animal breathing just before it sprang; the rain fell as if the silver sea was overflowing, and outside taxi drivers wrangled and yelled, slammed car doors, opened them to shout again. But it was relatively quiet in the hallway. Apart from Sophie's hiccups.

A thump resounded through the house. Everyone jumped. Another thump. Outlandish scrabbling noises, metallic, claw-like, growing louder.

Rory and Lisa edged away from the locked door, Hugh ran and pressed against Sophie. Conga scrambled away too on hands and knees, and bumped into Sophie's tipped-up box.

'Hugh!' She pointed. He scurried back and picked it up at last.

The door creaked slightly open. There was a cracking and ripping of the soundproof barrier being torn down from the other side, and a foul miasma oozed into the hallway: it reminded Sophie of Russell's sleeping bags when he came home from foreign parts.

Hugh cheeped with fright, dashed to drop the box by the front door and disappeared into the dining room. Sophie didn't care what monster would appear: her gasps had turned to sobs, quiet but deep, like babies when they've cried for hours.

The door creaked further open. A drenched shape, half-hidden, stood there, tall, broad-shouldered, in a big black billowing coat.

'Where's Sophie!' Russell's voice boomed from the dripping figure. 'What the hell is going on!'

Suddenly Damon was in front of her, concealing her, an angel welcoming the Advent, a rugby crowd of one. 'The boss! Gidday!'

'Dad?' A weak chorus from Lisa and Rory.

'Presumptuous brute.' That low exclamation was Mother. Good on you, Mum.

Russell shook water off his oilskin and pushed the door wide: Sophie stayed screened behind the angel. 'I had to overnight in bloody Sydney,' he said more quietly, though not much. 'Where's Sophie? Steven! And . . .'

'Hello, Russell,' sobbed Mary Jane.

Sophie had never seen Russell recoil before, not even when she'd

family matter, that's all.' Russell's arms made encompassing,
ous gestures. 'Sorry you've come out on such a dirty night.'
ven, who had risen again (again), cried 'Thanks!' (again) and
his arms round Russell in a bear hug. They collapsed. Russell
ed, the officers grabbed them both and all four slipped, like a
on the rain-wet floor.
w then,' a policeman said (they're meant to).
lm down,' Matthew thundered. 'I am a lawyer.'
wants to marry Mum,' Hugh shouted to Russell. 'He looks
ke a grandad to me.' He grabbed Nick's cuff. 'My grandad
mpled to death by an ostrich. Emu.'
eat-grandad, you little dork,' said Lisa.
erie silence fell again. Rory's raspberry-coloured arm pulled
s bath towel from between the banisters. He walked over
ded it to the bloody-nosed taxi driver.
he muttered. 'Nice lad.'
ell smiled and shrugged at the crowd. His black oilskin
and crackled. He turned to Sophie: 'Darling.' She ducked
ds and found she was against the banisters by the foot of the
haven't been fair, love, I know it. Another chance, love.

ing,' said Matthew.
etheart,' Russell countered.
ge of warmth began to pulse in her once more. Russell,
ouldered, thick red hair, the firm intelligent jaw. And
behind him, firm intelligent forehead, broad-bellied, long
ighs.
ouldn't it be easier to drift, and smile, and sigh?
s a terrific house,' Russell said. 'We can sell it for a fortune.
t great kids . . .' he glanced at Lisa who cast her eyes
y at Hugh. 'Sweetheart, I'm desperate to spend some time
Soph, I've got tremendous plans for us, you'll see.'
e eased round the newel post and backwards, up a couple

told him she was leaving him the first time. He'd laughed, and tried to hug her. When she'd thrown a wooden spoon at him, he'd laughed again, grabbed his pack and told her he'd be in touch as soon as he found a phone in Suhbaatar (which is in the middle of page sixty-three, right on the fiftieth parallel). Then he caught her unawares and gave her a searching kiss which left her limp with rage and passion against the kitchen bench.

Now, Russell's bright green eyes held chagrin as they flicked from Mary Jane to Steven. They held a trace of doubt as they flicked to Matthew. They blinked, as they flicked to Nick.

'Hi,' said Nick. 'I hear you're a man of many parts. Pleased to meet you, I'm Hugh's tea . . .'

He hurtled to the wall as Steven powered through. Sophie jumped further back and peered from behind Matthew. If there was going to be a fight she didn't want to be in the way, but she certainly wanted to see. Mary Jane sped after Steven to drag his arm down.

'I only want to shake his hand!' cried Steven.

'You're disgusting!' Lisa screamed.

'Loathsome,' pronounced Mother.

Mary Jane plunged into another storm of tears.

'Whoa!' Russell cried. 'Is Sophie here? Let's calm down! Are we having a party? Lisa? Good God, what's happened to your head? Rory, what the hell is that you're wearing? Who'd like a drink? Filthy night to be without a dram or two. Take your coats off, make yourselves at home.'

The charm, on full. Sophie couldn't bear to watch. And sure enough, Russell was offering rounds of whisky (duty free) and trying to avoid Steven while Steven tried to shake with him, and Mary Jane, arms open, sprang from side to side like a netballer, trying to keep her resurrected husband off.

Russell nodded at Matthew (still holding the chamber pot, but with the fern in one hand and squinting at the maker's mark on the bottom), and stepped energetically towards Sophie. 'There you are! God, darling, how I've missed you!' He ducked another of Steven's out-thrusts and tried to sweep her into his arms.

Sophie dodged behind Mother. Mother gripped her hand and gave an encouraging squeeze.

'Sir!' cried Damon. 'Dr Redlove, good news! You've got the funding for the Kirlian photographs, from Millennial Golden Link in Yokohama!'

Conga choked, and tried to sit up. 'Fungi. Emotional life of. Proof of. We can do it.' He fell back again as Lisa kicked him.

'Bloody men!' she yelled. 'Ant farms? Civil war in? Like hell. Tell him, Rory!'

'*Ungh*!' Rory gave a mammoth grin.

'God, Dad, you're so stupid!' Lisa cried. 'When you and the other scientists were out of the garage, Rory and I used to put fresh ants in.'

'Cool,' said Hugh.

'His first award,' said Mother. 'Skewed data. What a come-down.'

Conga tried to sit up and failed again. Damon seemed punctured, like an airship. The eerie silence. Tick tock.

Sophie found she'd slumped into the alcove, her shoulder near Todd's photo. Russell's reputation, based on the naughtiness of a four- and six-year-old. And Kirlian photographs now. To prove that fungi have an emotional life. Good grief. The golden idol was not only a cheat but a hollow man, stuffed with straw.

She sank right down to the floor, churned up with sobs and laughter. And reader, lo! get this: she'd married him.

'Darling.' Russell had paled, but he was smiling now. 'Take no notice of the kids. Sweetheart, what kind of welcome's this? How do you like this place? Isn't it amazing? Perfect for us, right? Not a lot of decorating yet, but you've bought a heat gun, great. What did you think of the bedroom? Luxury, the perfect love nest, eh!' He chuckled, the warm and cosy laugh: *Come sit by the fire and purr.* 'Can you folk entertain yourselves for a bit? There'll be gin in the pantry, make yourselves at home.'

The charm and energy: they'd hexed her. Despite everything her

hips longed to move towards him, her eyes t
out, to feel herself sink into the comfort, stro
did move, and touched a little metal tube aga
The dancing eye: it must have rolled out of
and tucked it into her jeans side pocket.

'Come on, Soph,' urged Russell. 'A qui
what you've done upstairs.'

Her hips straightened. 'More to the poi
particular floor was it that you and Mary Ja

Russell's smile grew forced, the energe
eyes twinkled harder.

'It was an accident,' whined Mary Jane.

With a shout, Steven lunged at Russell'
screamed. Russell jerked his shoulders and so
in Steven's throat. Steven sank, coughing,

'Russell!' Damon cried. 'You're behind
I've held the bank off. The Kirlian funding
and . . .'

He was pushed aside by locksmiths, blu
want done about the locks, mate?'

'There's a call-out charge. Fifty bucks
overalls.

'Fifty-five here,' said a blue one.

A taxi driver staggered to the door
hair and blood from his nose. Hugh rush
took one look at the man, shrieked and
Hieronymous Bosch's *Last Judgement,*
expressions of torture and woe: the wo
Outside, a siren screamed. A flashing
showed slanting spears of rain and cast
stained glass.

'Wow!' cried Hugh. 'I dialled
worked! Oh, hello, Dad.'

Two policemen arrived on the do

Russell followed Sophie up one stair. 'Sweetheart. You and me, Soph.'

She reached over the balustrade, took the chamber pot from Matthew and handed him back the fern.

'He didn't ever tear up the separation order,' Matthew said. 'Ask him if he's staying here tonight.' She took two more steps. 'Ignore him, Soph, he's after your share of the marital property.'

She was nearly at the landing, aware of the ring of faces in the front hall, eyes fixed on her as she raised the chamber pot.

'What share? What property?' she asked. 'You're the lawyer who screwed up my finances. How much do you owe, Russell, and who to? What's the Choi-Berunda Institute, Russell?'

'Sophie!' His charm, full flood. The smile, the deep green eyes. 'Sweetheart, this isn't like you.'

'High bloody time it was, then,' Sophie said.

She hurled the chamber pot at the rose-coloured window.

Mother's cry, 'Crown Derby!', was smothered by a clash of glass. The chamber pot bounced back, landed beside Sophie, rolled down to the hall and fell like magic into three separate pieces. The rose-coloured window trembled and broke. One tinted segment at a time toppled, tumbled, slid on to the porch roof; some clattered into the hall.

The wind sprang at the broken opening. How odd it was, how silent the hall could be when outside — and in — the wind spun furiously, licked her face, pawed at her hair.

How odd to be stared at by policemen, locksmiths, two sidekicks and two taxi drivers, a slightly sycophantic younger man, a cheating friend and her cheated-on husband, an inefficient divorce lawyer doubling as your older lover. Your kids. Your mother. Your cheating husband too.

The secret life of men.

Hey, guys are human. What chance have they got? It must be very like the secret life of women: dark there, private, little bags and boxes you've forgotten, those tiny hurts, sad memories that gather up and gradually crush down on you. But also bits and bobs that make you smile. How hard to find a soul you trust to share them with, someone you dare to bring inside your secret room.

Sophie would have liked to complete the scene by firing up the heat gun. That tattered wallpaper begged to be aflame in the licking, urgent wind. But she'd never get away with it: Hugh had called the police, and there was a lawyer present.

Mother's lips twitched. Good old Baba Yaga, she was on Sophie's side.

She'd burnt the bridges back to safety now. She'd crossed her river just like Caesar did, and it took him long enough, too. She'd fought by bringing the enemy out into the open, for all the world to see.

A pinch of anarchy, that's all. A *soupcon* of subversion.

Revenge is a dish best eaten whole.

'But what will you do?' moaned Mary Jane.

'I'll think about that tomorrow.' Sophie clung to the banisters in the manner of a famous romantic heroine. In the manner of a famous romantic hero she added, 'Tonight, I do not give a damn. Because I'm out of here.'

The wind pounced through the front door and broken window. The lashes of air smelt fresh and beckoning.

Yes, trust the future, Soph, it's all you've got.

Just feel the wind, kid, smell the spring in it, the fun in it, the leap. The wind's got wings, kid, see them? The wind's a big black animal with shining pelt and eager eyes, with huge wild-feathered wings.

It wants to go exploring. It wants you, Soph. It dares you.

So go on, kid. Try, Soph. Try now.

You are a bobby dazzler.

E-MAIL US FOR A COPY OF
BARBARA'S GINGERBREAD RECIPE

gingerbread@godwit.co.nz

THE WARRIOR QUEEN
Barbara Else

'*The Warrior Queen* is laden with good qualities. Convincing characters, confident dialogue, and colourful textural devices make this an enjoyable novel.'
The New Zealand Herald

'*The Warrior Queen* is a splendid debut: sharp and funny, but also complex enough to be satisfying, and eminently readable. I hope Barbara Else is well on the way to finishing her next book.'
The Listener

'I read it avidly to find out what happened and enjoyed it for its humour, for the fast-paced, clever plotting, lovingly detailed backgrounds, and for the strength of the relationships between Kate and her female friends.'
The Dominion

'Sweet and devious revenge is plotted. The book is lightly and cleverly written.'
Next